CALL THE ROSTER
OF THE HARD CORPS...

WILLIAM O'NEAL — the baddest and the best. This one-time Green Beret captain picks the wars and calls the shots.

JAMES WENTWORTH III — Proud Oklahoman, well-rounded killer, master of the East's deadliest fighting arts.

JOE FANELLI — Street-corner wiseguy turned demolitions expert, he's far more explosive than his beloved TNT.

STEVE CAINE — silent lone wolf, who works behind enemy lines with blade, crossbow, and strangler's cord.

JOHN McSHAYNE — top sergeant, master mechanic, and keeper of the incredible Hard Corps arsenal.

THE HARD CORPS

THE HARD CORPS

CHUCK BAINBRIDGE

A JOVE BOOK

THE HARD CORPS

A Jove Book / published by arrangement with
the author

PRINTING HISTORY
Jove edition / December 1986

ISBN: 0-515-08841-2

Jove Books are published by The Berkley Publishing Group,
200 Madison Avenue, New York, N.Y. 10016.
The words "A JOVE BOOK" and the "J" with sunburst
are trademarks belonging to Jove Publications, Inc.

PRINTED IN THE UNITED STATES OF AMERICA

To the 8,744,000 American men and women who served in the Vietnam Conflict.

CHAPTER 1

WILLIAM O'NEAL POINTED the government issue Colt pistol in the face of Luis Moya, and the young Mexican terrorist stared back at the black muzzle of the nine-inch silencer attached to the threaded barrel of the big .45 caliber pistol. Though he was trying to act tough, Moya's lip trembled slightly and his face was dead white. Otherwise his tough guy image held up pretty well.

O'Neal wasn't impressed. He admired toughness —physical, psychological, or spiritual—even in his enemies. But Moya belonged to a crackpot terrorist outfit that called itself the People's Army for the Liberation of Mexico, whose idea of "fighting for liberation" included shooting police officers in the back, blowing up restaurants with American tourists inside and occasionally kidnapping a U.S. citizen to try to suck ransom money out of the "gringo's" family.

Moya sure didn't deserve kid glove treatment, and

1

since that had never been a specialty of the Hard Corps anyway, O'Neal didn't feel like wasting any reserves of compassion on this human maggot. He thrust the muzzle of the pistol into the terrorist's mouth. The Mexican fanatic's eyes widened with fear—it's pretty hard to act tough when you're sucking on a .45 automatic.

"I understand you speak English, punk," O'Neal snarled. "That's good, because my Spanish isn't exactly fluent. We've got some questions for you, Moya. You're gonna answer them or I'll blow your fuckin' brains out."

"Why do him any favors?" Mr. James Wentworth III inquired as he leaned over O'Neal's shoulder. "If Moya's too stupid to talk to us, we can make an example of him for the next PALM scumbag we get our hands on."

Wentworth was bluffing. The Hard Corps had been in Mexico City for four days, and Moya was the only PALM scumbag they had been able to find. Time was running out fast, and they couldn't hope to find another People's Army terrorist before the bastards killed Hector and Shelly Arguello.

The Arguellos were young newlyweds from New Mexico. Hector was a second generation Mexican-American who had brought his new bride to Mexico City to visit some of his relatives on a trip that was supposed to be an extended honeymoon. It had turned into a nightmare when the People's Army grabbed the couple at gunpoint and demanded one million dollars from Hector's father, Ricardo, for their release.

Ricardo Arguello was a self-made millionaire. A true American success story, he had risen from the barrios to become president of a nationwide chain of clothing stores. Arguello had worked his ass off to make a good

2

life for himself and his family. He had the kind of toughness O'Neal admired and respected. Nobody handed anything to Arguello on a silver platter. The guy had worked for what he earned, and by God, he deserved it.

Arguello didn't like the idea of rewarding a bunch of terrorists for kidnapping his son and daughter-in-law, but he might have paid the ransom if the People's Army didn't already have a reputation for returning hostages in pine boxes. He tried all the usual sources for help. The U.S. State Department sympathized, the U.S. embassy agonized, and the Mexican government apologized. None of them had done a damn thing about the PALM terrorists in the past and this time didn't promise to be any different.

The situation demanded drastic action. Arguello decided to hire a team of professional soldiers to rescue Hector and Shelly. He needed the best in the business, and the best, most highly trained, and experienced mercenary team available was the Hard Corps.

The Hard Corps was made up of four Vietnam veterans, former members of the United States Army Special Forces—the Green Berets. They had worked as a team for more than a decade, first in the jungles of Southeast Asia, then as soldiers of fortune. They had earned a reputation for being the best in the business, and the long list of their successful missions proved it.

The best is always expensive, but that didn't bother Arguello. He decided he'd rather pay the million bucks to the Hard Corps than PALM, which was the amount offered to the mercenary team when O'Neal met with Arguello. One million in cash if they could rescue Hector and Shelly and return them safely to the United States.

• • •

O'Neal pulled the pistol out of Moya's mouth and wiped the saliva from the silencer, using the punk's shirt. He sure as hell didn't want to use his own. Moya was securely bound, ankles tied to chair legs and his hands cuffed behind the backrest. He could do nothing but stare up at the Hard Corps commander.

This did nothing to sooth Moya's nerves. O'Neal was a big guy, with lots of muscle, and a rough voice that sounded like he gargled with bourbon and scouring powder. Deep lines were etched in O'Neal's face from exposure to all types of weather and the even harsher realities of life. His eyes were as hard and cold as two blue marbles. O'Neal was not the sort of guy who puts up with much bullshit—and he didn't intend to make an exception in Moya's case.

"Talk to us, Moya," O'Neal growled. "We're getting impatient."

"Fuck you," Moya spat back, glaring up at O'Neal.

"Well, that's a relief," Wentworth remarked as he jammed the brass head of a swagger stick under the terrorist's head. "You do speak English. Don't you, son?"

James Wentworth III spoke softly, a hint of an Oklahoma drawl in his voice. Wentworth had been born to an upper class family which believed in two great American truths—Oklahoma crude and fightin' for your country.

Wentworth men had gone to West Point ever since it became the U.S. military academy in 1802. James had followed the family tradition. That was probably why he could carry a swagger stick without feeling like an idiot. The guy was eccentric, maybe a little crazy, but his IQ bordered on genius, and he had stainless steel balls in combat.

At thirty-seven, Wentworth was a year younger than

4

O'Neal, although most people would have guessed he was older than the team leader. Wentworth was a bit paunchy at the middle and his hairline had receded, leaving a bald spot at the top of his skull. Wentworth didn't look much like a Hollywood soldier of fortune, but he was second-in-command of the Hard Corps, as tough and deadly as any of the others on the team.

"So, now that you've proved you can say profanities fluently," Wentworth told Moya. "Tell us where PALM is holding Hector and Shelly Arguello."

Luis Moya replied by spitting in Wentworth's face. The merc sighed and calmly took a handkerchief from his pocket. He wiped the saliva from his face and shook his head.

"That was pretty stupid, son," Wentworth said softly, as he suddenly whipped his swagger stick across the terrorist's face.

Moya cried out as the hard wood struck the bridge of his nose, breaking cartilage. Blood oozed from Moya's nostrils and tears clouded his vision.

"I'd advise you not to do anything like that again," O'Neal told Moya. "None of us are exactly Peace Corps material and we'd probably be in a VA mental ward if the army shrinks had known us a little better. You don't mean shit to us, so don't push your luck, asshole."

"I am not afraid to die," Moya announced, his voice distorted by blood in his nose. "I won't tell you Anglo fuckers nothin'!"

"Maybe your girl knows something," Joe Fanelli remarked. "You might have a high pain threshold, Moya. How much do you think she can take?"

Fanelli asked the question in a casual manner, a smile playing at his lips. The wiry, tough little Italian stood near Juanita Reyes. The emaciated young hooker was cowering on her cot, holding a tattered blanket against her small breasts. Fanelli held a silenced Colt pistol in one fist and a NATO military push button knife in the other. He pressed the button and a four-inch steel blade snapped into view.

"¡No, señor!" the girl begged, staring at the knife in horror. "Por favor . . ."

"¡Cállate!" Fanelli snapped. "Unless you want your tongue in a pickle jar."

Of course, Fanelli was bluffing. He had no intention of harming the woman. Juanita was a whore and a junkie, but Fanelli didn't care about that. Some of his favorite people were prostitutes, and Fanelli understood how people get messed up with drugs. He'd seen a lot of that as a kid on the streets of New Jersey. Poverty and despair can make getting high very attractive.

So could Vietnam. A lot of guys in the trenches of Southeast Asia had passed the hash pipe around. Some did it too often or got into harder drugs. Others, like Fanelli, sought escape through booze. But Fanelli's problem with alcohol hadn't really gotten out of control until he came back to the States. Hell, he'd probably have wound up on Skid Row or in a psycho ward if O'Neal hadn't found him, kicked him in the ass, and given him a reason to live. The reason was the same in America as it had been in Vietnam . . . the Hard Corps.

Juanita Reyes' only real crime, in Fanelli's opinion, was in associating with a terrorist. She was probably a mental cripple by the time she'd met Moya. None of the Hard Corps wanted to harm her, but she didn't know this. Neither did Moya. Fanelli was a good actor and a born con artist. He appeared to be willing and able to use the knife on Juanita.

"The bitch doesn't matter," Moya declared. "I don't care what happens to the little slut. Go ahead and cut

6

her up. I won't tell you shit!"

"You know something, Moya?" O'Neal remarked as he lowered the aim of his .45 pistol. "You're a real asshole."

He squeezed the trigger. The pistol rasped through its nine inch sound-suppressor. A 185 grain semi-jacketed, hollow-point bullet crashed into Moya's left instep. Bone and cartilage exploded. Moya screamed in agony as blood streamed from what remained of his left foot.

Juanita screamed and bolted from the cot. She nearly ran into the blade of Fanelli's knife. The Italian tough guy moved the knife to avoid stabbing the panicked woman. He shoved a forearm into Juanita's chest and pushed her back to the cot.

"Shit, lady," Fanelli rasped. "Calm down before you hurt yourself."

Moya whimpered as he tried to keep his shattered foot from touching the floor. The bonds at his ankle made this almost impossible. O'Neal grabbed the terrorist's hair and pulled his head back. The Hard Corps commander stared into Moya's face. His eyes were as hard as blue steel.

"Okay, scumbag," O'Neal announced. "We're through being nice. You want to do this the hard way? Either you tell us where to find Hector and Shelly or we'll take you apart, piece by piece."

"We've got all night to work on you," Wentworth added. "You've still got another foot. Then we can start on your knees or elbows or maybe your hands."

"Let me have him," Steve Caine cut in, drawing a survival knife from a sheath on his hip.

Caine was tall and slender, with jet black hair and an unkempt beard. His voice seldom revealed whether he was angry or upset, serious or joking. Caine's eyes dis-

7

played even less emotion than his voice. Some people said Caine had a dead man's eyes.

He approached Moya, the knife held ready. Caine had been sweet on survival knives since he first got his hands on one. He had carried it ever since. The heavy six-inch blade was razor sharp, with a sawtooth back. The hollow handle contained matches, sewing needles, fishhooks, sinkers, and line, as well as a wire saw that could also serve as a garrote.

"Do you guys remember the time we hit that Viet Cong patrol near Qui Nheh?" Caine suddenly asked his teammates. "One of the gooks was still alive, so I peeled all the skin off his fingers."

"Oh, yeah," O'Neal said with a nod. The incident had never happened, but the Hard Corps's commander played along with Caine's lie.

"Then I pulled those raw fingers like I was milking a cow," Caine continued, holding the knife closer to Moya's face. "I haven't had that much fun for a long time. And, after that, we'll have some more fun . . ."

"Jesus! Moya cried. "Get this *hombre loco* away from me!"

"Start talking, punk," O'Neal replied gruffly.

"They're being held in a farmhouse near Cerritos," Moya gushed. "There are a dozen comrades there with them."

"We'd better put a tourniquet on your ankle so you don't bleed to death," O'Neal announced. "You're going for a little ride with us, Moya."

"Really nice of you to offer to be our guide," Wentworth added, as he tapped the terrorist on a shoulder with his swagger stick. "If you're a real good boy, we might even let you live."

"Aw, shucks," Caine said with disappointed sigh, as he returned his knife to its sheath.

● ● ●

Joe Fanelli drove the battered old Ford pickup along the dirt road. The headlights were off, but Fanelli had no trouble seeing the road, thanks to a pair of TH70 Nitefinder goggles. The special projecting lenses of the night vision glasses transformed pitch black into mere dusk. James Wentworth sat on the passenger side, scanning the countryside with a pair of infrared binoculars.

William O'Neal and Steve Caine were in the back of the truck with Luis Moya. A wooden frame and canvas tarp concealed the three men and the two large duffle bags which lay next to O'Neal. The stock of a rifle jutted from the mouth of one bag. Moya glanced at it hungrily, wishing he could get his hands on the weapon and kill all four gringos. However, with his hands cuffed behind his back, one foot crippled, both ankles wired together, and Caine's .45 Colt aimed at his chest, there was little chance this wish would become reality.

"There's a farmhouse," Wentworth announced, loud enough for all to hear. "It's about two kilometers east. Fits the description Mister Sunshine gave us."

"That's it," Moya confirmed.

"It better be," O'Neal warned. He turned to Caine. "Stuff a gag in his mouth and make sure those cuffs are double locked."

Fanelli stopped the truck by the side of the road. All four Hard Corps mercs emerged silently from the vehicle, and O'Neal handed the duffle bags to Wentworth and Fanelli.

"Moya told me the setup at the farm," the commander explained. "There are three sentries on duty. Two at the front, one at the rear. There's a small barn at the back with two or more PALM scum in there, so watch out. The rest of the bastards should be in the house. Of course, you never know when somebody'll

9

step outside to take a leak. No indoor plumbing. Hector and Shelly are being held in the kitchen at the rear of the house. Moya says there's at least one terrorist in there with them. Supposedly, there are no curtains on the windows and you should be able to see everybody in the kitchen unless somebody is squatting directly under the window—or PALM has improved their shitty security."

"Maybe we'll be lucky and they'll all be as dumb as Moya," Fanelli remarked as he pulled Uzi submachine guns from one duffle bag. "Gee, I feel just like Santa Claus."

"Ho, ho," Caine said dryly. "Using Uzis inside the house might not be a good idea. Full auto weapons spray all over. Might waste the hostages."

"There's always a risk to hostages regardless of what we do," O'Neal stated. "But you've got a point. Safer to use our .45's inside the house. Don't use the Uzis unless you have to."

O'Neal didn't have to explain that Uzis fire 9mm parabellum rounds, a high velocity bullet with penetration force nearly equal to that of a .357 Magnum. The .45 caliber slug lacks penetration, but the size of the slug makes it ideal for bringing down a man-size target.

"What about the barn?" Fanelli inquired, slipping the strap of an Uzi onto his shoulder.

"When we're sure the hostages aren't inside the house," O'Neal said with a shrug, "take it out any way you want. Blow the fucker up if you like."

"Oh, I like," Fanelli assured him. He was the unit demolitions expert and he liked his job.

"So Joe gets the back," Wentworth replied, taking a rifle from the other duffle bag. "And I'll handle the sniper job. I am the best choice for the task."

"That's debatable," Caine muttered. He and Wentworth were the best marksmen in the unit, but they argued constantly over who was number one. Their verbal conflicts were always subdued due to Caine's lack of emotional response and Wentworth's intellectual self-control.

"Jim's got the rifle," O'Neal said. This was no time for competitive games. "I want you to help with sentry removal, Steve. Okay?"

Caine nodded as he removed a small but sturdy bamboo bow and a quiver of arrows from a duffle bag.

"Okay," O'Neal announced. "Everybody knows what to do. Let's get close enough to make sure of our targets. If Moya lied to us, he's gonna wish his parents had believed in abortion."

"*I* wish they had," Wentworth commented, as he checked the Starlite nightscope to the .300 Winchester Magnum rifle.

The Hard Corps approached the farmhouse, moving in a wide horseshoe pattern. The mercenaries kept low and made the most of natural camouflage, melting into the tall grass and dense shadows. They moved silently, creeping with the padded tread of a prowling cat.

O'Neal and Caine drew closer to the front of the house, as Wentworth and Fanelli covered the rear. Sentries were posted at the building as Moya had said, two at the front and one at the rear. All three terrorists were armed with 9mm Mendoza submachine guns.

Caine slithered through the grass like a serpent and stopped seven yards from the farmhouse. He assumed a cross-legged position and kept his head and shoulders low, as he drew the first arrow from its quiver. The arrowhead and part of the shaft was smeared with a black substance. It was curare, a poison derived from the bark of *genus stychons* plants, in a manner taught to Caine during the years he spent with the Katu tribes in 'Nam.

O'Neal crawled toward the front of the house, his Uzi cradled in his arms. The Hard Corps commander peered between blades of grass at the target site. A sentry sat on the front steps. The tip of a cigarette glowed at the guy's mouth. Good, O'Neal thought. PALM wasn't expecting trouble. O'Neal hoped all the terrorists would be as careless. Of course, if Murphy's Law applies to life in general, it goes double in combat.

Fanelli crept to the barn and cautiously shuffled to the corner. He peeked around the edge and saw the one guard at the rear of the farmhouse. The guy seemed nervous. Terrorists are almost all high-strung, paranoid and at least half crazy. Fanelli wondered if many of them had stomach ulcers.

Whatever had the terrorist uptight, the bastard was on his toes. He might be quivering in his boots, high on cocaine, or just alert and jumpy. The sentry appeared ready to trigger his Mendoza chatterbox if anybody whispered "boo."

Wentworth assumed a prone stance, the butt of the Winchester braced against his shoulder. He dug his toes into the ground and gazed through the Starlite scope mounted on the rifle. The Starlite was better than infrared scopes because it increased the light density of reflections on objects invisible to the naked eye. If a marksman fired a weapon with an infrared scope, the glare of the muzzle flash could cause temporary blindness. This didn't happen with the Starlite, thanks to special optic fibers in the lens.

He shifted the rifle slightly to gaze into the kitchen window. Everything looks green and yellow through a Starlite scope, but he still recognized Hector and Shelly

Arguello. He had seen photos of the newlyweds supplied by Ricardo Arguello. Wentworth was relieved to see them alive.

Naturally, they had suffered some physical abuse. Terrorists only treat hostages well if they plan to parade them in front of a television camera. Hector's face was badly bruised, with one eye swollen shut. Shelly sat next to her husband, clutching the remnants of a dress to her breasts. A dark mark on her cheek suggested someone had used a fist on her.

The bastards had raped her, Wentworth realized. He wasn't surprised, but it still made him angry. But he'd learned to control his emotions in combat. The anger wouldn't make him careless, just more determined to make PALM pay in blood for what they'd done to Shelly Arguello.

Wentworth turned his attention, and his weapon, to the terrorist maggot in the room with Hector and Shelly. The PALM goon appeared to be about twenty, with curly hair and thick eyebrows. He sat on a wicker chair, facing the Arguellos with a revolver in his fist.

James Wentworth III fixed the scope on the terrorist's face. The cross hairs centered on the bastard's forehead, Wentworth eased the safety to "fire" position. He waited.

Steve Caine glanced at the luminous dial of his watch. Three minutes had passed since they closed in on the farm. Everyone should be in position. The show was about to begin. He notched the arrow to the bowstring and pulled it back. The merc aimed carefully and released the arrow.

The missile sliced through air and slammed into the chest of a terrorist sentry stationed at the front of the house. The arrow struck left of the sternum and pierced the guy's heart. The sentry opened his mouth to cry out, but the curare rapidly took effect. Paralysis froze his muscles. The terrorist wilted to the ground and died without uttering a sound.

O'Neal assumed a kneeling stance, his Colt .45 in a two-hand Weaver grip. The startled terrorist at the front door saw the Hard Corps commander an instant before he felt the first bullet smash into his breastbone. The silenced pistol rasped again. The second slug punched through the hollow of the guy's throat. His thyroid cartilage burst, and the bullet kept traveling upward. Cervical vertebrae popped apart as it plowed an exit wound at the neck. The terrorist half-turned and fell dead.

Fanelli considered attaching a foot-long Sconics Noise Suppressor to the threaded barrel of his Uzi submachine gun. He shook his head. The Uzi is one of the best military small arms ever made. Many consider it to be the best submachine gun ever invented. But the Uzi isn't the best weapon to use with a silencer. Accuracy is reduced, and a 9mm parabellum is a high-velocity slug which "cracks" loudly when it breaks the sound barrier.

The only way to neutralize this effect is to use subsonic ammunition with a lower grain and powder level than usual combat loads. The Hard Corps's Uzis were loaded with regular 115 grain NATO solid ball ammo and 120 grain hollow points. The ammo was "Dutch-loaded" in the magazines, with ball and HP rounds alternating. This was a very effective combat choice which combined powerful penetration and bone-shattering force, but it was a lousy selection of ammo to use with a silencer.

"Miguel! Cómo está?" a voice called out. It was

close enough to Fanelli's position to put a knot in his Adam's apple.

Fanelli heard the creak of hinges. Someone had opened the barn door and stepped outside. He carefully peered around the corner. Two terrorists walked from the barn toward the hyperactive sentry at the rear of the house. Fanelli hoped the rest of the Corps were ready for a little noise, because he was about to make a lot of it.

Joe Fanelli stepped from cover and opened fire. Uzi slugs hammered the three terrorists mercilessly. One man's spine snapped in two from the first salvo. Another PALM flunky whirled and got two 9mm rounds in the face. Bullets split a cheekbone and burst through the bridge of his nose. The parabellums sizzled through his brain and blasted a gory exit at the back of his skull.

The third terrorist returned fire with his Mendoza subgun. Fanelli ducked behind the barn as enemy bullets splintered wood. The Italian merc didn't have time to play peek-and-shoot with the PALM gunman. He removed an M-26 hand grenade from his belt, and pulled the pin.

Fanelli poked the Uzi around the corner and triggered a quick burst of 9mm rounds to keep his opponents off balance. Then he lobbed a grenade. The M-26 hit the dirt and rolled a few feet before it exploded.

"So long, asshole," Fanelli muttered, as he glanced around the corner. A severed leg twitched in the dust. It was the only part of the enemy gunman which hadn't been shredded by the blast.

A sudden noise above drew Fanelli's attention to the door of the hayloft overhead. The twin muzzles of a double-barrel shotgun stared down at him. The mercenary raised his Uzi and fired his last three rounds at the gunner. Sparks flew when bullets struck metal and the shotgun flew from the terrorist's grasp.

The PALM ambusher might not have won any IQ awards, but he was no coward. The lunatic dove from the loft and crashed into Fanelli before the merc could draw his .45 Colt. Both men tumbled to the ground.

Fanelli planted a boot in the terrorist's chest and kicked him away, but the Mexican goon rolled quickly and jumped to his feet. Fanelli rose just as his opponent charged. There wasn't time to draw a weapon, although the terrorist was three inches taller than Fanelli and outweighed him by at least twenty pounds. He was also about ten years younger than the thirty-four-year-old mercenary.

Fanelli dodged a wild right cross, then jabbed with his left. The terrorist's head recoiled from the punch. Fanelli jabbed again and hooked a left to the bastard's temple. He followed with a right upper-cut that slammed the guy's jaws together hard enough to break teeth.

The terrorist weaved, but did not fall. Fanelli's boot lashed out and caught the PALM creep between the legs. The thug gasped in agony and clawed at his battered manhood. Fanelli slugged him with a hard right and the terrorist fell into dreamland.

"You've never been to Jersey," Fanelli told the unconscious thug as he rubbed a bruised knuckle. "Have you, shithead?"

As soon as James Wentworth III heard the shots, he took action, squeezing the trigger of his Winchester rifle. The recoil of the weapon drove the walnut buttstock forcibly into his shoulder, and the report of the rifle boomed like an announcement of Doomsday.

For the terrorist guarding the Arguellos in the

kitchen, the announcement was accurate. A powerful Magnum round shattered the man's forehead. The bullet smashed his skull, as the back of his head vanished in a grotesque spray of brains, blood, and bone fragments. Hector and Shelly watched with astonishment and horror as the lifeless terrorist slumped to the floor.

Wentworth worked the bolt to the Winchester, ejecting the spent shell casing and feeding a fresh cartridge into the chamber. He jogged toward the house, his attention on the window, although he glanced about, in case the enemy launched an unexpected attack from either end of the house, a window, or the roof.

Hector Arguello turned toward the window and stared at the spiderweb pattern of cracks surrounding a bullethole in the glass pane. Shelly scrambled to the corpse and scooped up the dead man's revolver. Wentworth stayed clear of the window in case the couple started shooting at the first thing that moved.

"Get down, you two!" Wentworth shouted. "And stay down! Let us handle this!"

"You're an American?" Hector's voice cried. "You've come to rescue us?"

"Right both times," Wentworth replied. "Now stay put, keep down, and don't use that gun unless you're sure of the target. I don't want you shooting one of my partners."

Steve Caine dashed to the front door and slammed it open with a kick, standing to the side of the doorway. A shotgun blast erupted from within. Slugs chewed wood from the door frame. Caine held an Uzi in his left fist and a .45 autoloader in his right. He poked the barrel of the Uzi around the corner and fired a quick burst.

He aimed high, more concerned about keeping the terrorists busy than shooting any of them. Caine didn't give a damn about the health and welfare of the PALM slobs, but he didn't want to risk pumping bullets through walls, hitting the hostages in the kitchen. Caine dove through the doorway and onto the floor.

A figure rose up from the shadows with a pump shotgun in his fists. Caine triggered the Colt twice, and because his pistol was not equipped with a silencer, the gun roared and the muzzle flash filled the room with harsh orange light. Caine saw the shotgun man drop his weapon and tumble backward, blood spewing from a bullet wound in the chest.

Another PALM killer pointed a Largo pistol at Caine. A .45 caliber hollow-point projectile smashed into the side of the terrorist's skull and split his head like a ripe melon hit by a battle axe. Brains and blood splattered the wall near the gunman, and another PALM flunky fell lifeless to the floor.

William O'Neal had shot the terrorist from the doorway. The Hard Corps commander prepared to enter, but the door suddenly slammed into O'Neal, striking the Colt pistol from his hand. A figure charged from behind the door and attacked O'Neal, a machete held over his head.

The long blade of the jungle knife swung toward O'Neal's head, but the merc leader dodged the flashing steel as the machete whistled past him. His left fist lashed out and caught the terrorist attacker on the ear. The PALM killer grunted and tried a cross-body machete stroke. O'Neal chopped the sides of both hands into the bastard's forearm. The double blow jarred the ulna nerve, and the terrorist dropped his weapon.

O'Neal didn't let up. He hooked a kick to the man's gut and punched him in the side of the head, and the terrorist staggered. O'Neal rammed a right cross to his opponent's solar plexus, and as the terrorist doubled up,

O'Neal slammed a knee into his face. The blow straightened the PALM creep. Blood trickled from the man's crushed nose.

O'Neal grabbed the terrorist's shirt front with his right hand. He turned sharply and raised the guy's arm, jamming the front of his right elbow into the scum's armpit. He bent his knees and hauled the dazed terrorist onto his back. O'Neal straightened his knees, bent his back and pulled with his left arm as he shoved with his right.

A variation of a judo shoulder-throw, the tactic sent the terrorist over O'Neal's head. The PALM garbage sailed through the doorway, tumbled down the steps and sprawled unconscious in the dirt.

"I think that was the last one," Caine remarked as he carefully approached the kitchen door.

O'Neal held up a hand to urge Caine to wait. He knew Wentworth should have taken out the guard or guards inside the kitchen, but one of them might be alive. Even if the last terrorist was out of action, Hector or Shelly might have grabbed a gun from a dead PALM goon. Now would be a hell of a time to their heads shot off . . . especially by the people they had come to rescue.

The merc leader unslung his Uzi, in case the former was true. He moved to the one side of the doorway and Caine moved to the other. *God*, O'Neal thought. *One million bucks. Please, let them be alive . . .*

"Hector? Shelly?" he called out in a loud voice. "Are you two okay?"

"We're fine!" Hector Arguello's voice cried out. "Who are you? Are all those sons of bitches dead?"

"We're friends of your father," O'Neal replied. "And they're all dead or out of commission. We'll give the *Federales* an anonymous phone call and they can come collect this garbage—living and dead. But that can wait. Now we've gotta get you home."

"Oh, Christ yes!" Hector agreed as he opened the kitchen door. Shelly clung to his arm. She looked like she was holding up better than her husband. "Get us outta here . . ."

"That's what we're here for," O'Neal assured him. "That's our job."

CHAPTER 2

TWO HOURS INTO his watch, Paul Haggerty was already cold and wet. Small patches of his field jacket were still dusty where the light rain had not rendered the coating of dust into a grimy clay paste. He surveyed the game trails and wider paths left by dirt bike riders during the day. These were strewn haphazardly over the rolling, rugged topography of Dead Man's Canyon, which ran a couple of miles eastward from the Tijuana Slough, a fraction of a mile north of the San Ysidro border crossing into Mexico.

The valley was a principle crossing point of the *pollos,* or illegal aliens, most often Mexicans, although some came from strife-torn Central American countries. Their attitudes ranged from enthusiastic to outright desperate. The illegal emigrants had paid exorbitant fees to the *coyotes* who smuggled illegals across the border. This granted them the privilege of running the dangerous, often fatal gauntlet of Dead Man's Canyon.

Crossing the border immediately north of Tijuana was generally the easiest part of the journey, since ragged holes were daily torn in the six foot high chain link fence which runs the length of the border. The steel barrier was designed to prevent a wholesale flood of illegals, but it did more than leak in many places—it gushed. Thousands of illegals each and every night, and more on holidays, when only skeleton crews of the Border Patrol were anticipated.

The flow of illegals showed that the United States Border Patrol was severely undermanned. On a good day, they might intercept ten percent of the total number of outsiders. These unlucky emigrants were returned by bus to random points in and around Tijuana.

Most promptly turned around and began, anew, their quest for the Holy Grail in the United States. *La Migra*, as the Border Patrol was called by the *pollos* and *coyotes,* had been reduced to little more than moving bodies.

Paul Haggerty was a member of the San Diego Police Department Border Crime Task Force. The Task Force had been initiated to deal with the constant influx of victims of assault and rape, unfortunates who ran afoul of the opportunistic criminals who crossed the border with the *pollos* to take anything of value which the *coyotes* had not already extorted from them already. But the Border Crime Task Force was instituted not so much to protect the aliens as to discourage their victimizers from plying their trade on the U.S. side of the border.

A short time after the inauguration of the program, the SDPD administration ordered a temporary halt in operations. The duty was deemed too hazardous. The *bandidos* in question were not an extinct species, but alive and dangerous. There is nothing amusing about modern Mexican outlaws, who had put several SDPD officers in the hospital. It was only a matter of time before cops would be killed under these conditions.

A typical encounter with bandits would begin shortly after dark, as small groups of illegals began their trek across the pitch-black canyon. They would suddenly be accosted by groups of Hispanic men dressed much like themselves. The bandits pulled guns and demanded all their belongings. After being relieved of their valuables, the young women were culled from their groups, pulled off the pathways, and raped.

In order to lure the *bandidos* into incriminating encounters, the special operations group of the Task Force had to refrain from patrolling with weapons ready. Hence, they often found themselves face to face with bandits who had the drop on them. Some men in the police group, such as Paul Haggerty, were Vietnam veterans. Their personality profiles showed them to be more than adventurous. Some said they grew steadily crazier as successive nightly patrols thrust them into one life-threatening situation after another.

Some officers experienced, first hand, the often touted theory of handgun enthusiasts that if you have to, you can actually draw and fire a weapon faster than a man holding a gun on you can react. It was a hair-raising and far from positive experience, and it quickly took its toll on the mental well-being of the Task Force.

Haggerty's initial assignment that night was to man a listening post at the rim of the canyon until it was time to begin the foot patrol. His team leader, Ralph Mendez, consulted his wrist watch and sighed.

"Get ready to hit the bush and dangle the bait," he announced.

Mendez touched Haggerty's shoulder.

"We'll be linking up with a man from the command post shortly, and beginning our patrol up the valley," he added. "Maybe we'll get lucky and have a nice quiet shift tonight. Eh, *amigo?*"

"So long as boredom doesn't become a habit," Haggerty replied with a grin, but he secretly shared his team leader's hope for a peaceful watch that night.

Fate had decided quite the opposite. The small group of officers would be subjected to far greater danger than they had been prepared for by any of their previous brutal experience at the border.

It is a little known and less publicized fact that the San Ysidro border crossing has been used by Soviet intelligence agencies to infiltrate non-Russian agents into the U.S.A. since the Stalin era—when the KGB was still called the NKVD.

Standing amongst the numerous small groups of *pollos,* waiting for twilight to mature into darkness, were four men with long, shiny black hair. Three of the four bore features of an Asian cast. The fourth man was a *coyote,* a professional guide who had hired out his services many times to the *pollos* who desired to cross the valley of death to the promised land beyond. His line of work seldom brought him into contact with the Oriental refugee subculture. The *coyote* suspected they were Southeast Asians, but he could not distinguish a Vietnamese from a Filipino. As long as the price was right, the *coyote* did not care if they were from Saigon or Mars.

"*Chung ta di ngay bay gi, thua co?*" one Asian whispered to another, asking if they would go immediately.

"*Thua khong!*" answered the other man, telling his comrade "*no.*" He added a few harshly whispered words in Vietnamese.

All three Asians carried large, newly purchased sports bags, slung over their shoulders. Except for the newness of their clothing and the unusually bright colors of their shirts, they were difficult to distinguish from other illegals in the dim light.

"We leave soon," the *coyote* said softly.

Ban Ban, the leader of the Asian trio, barked instructions to the others in Vietnamese. The other *pollos* began to depart, and the Vietnamese prepared to follow, but the *coyote* restrained them with a hand gesture, waiting for the first wave of foot traffic to put some distance between them.

Ban Ban trailed his men, allowing the *coyote* to take the lead. The guide did not hear the metallic scrape of the MAC-10 machinepistol as it was removed from the polyester bag. Ban Ban did not expect trouble, but killing was his business. It came as naturally to him as breathing did to other men.

"This is BARF Unit One," Mendez spoke into his radio. "We are beginning our foot patrol."

He signed off with the unit coordinator. BARF was an acronym for their unit designation, the Border Area Robbery Force. Members of the unit thought the name especially appropriate, since they often referred to the targets of their patrols as scumbags, puke-brains and other colorful names.

Dressed in multiple layers of Salvation Army cast-off clothing, the three policemen ambled down the path, looking for a group of *pollos* to merge with. They were "dangling the bait" for the border bandits. The work reminded Haggerty of his days in Vietnam when he was in small patrol units of United States Marines, trying to lure out Vietcong from their hiding places. True to the principles of guerrilla warfare, the Cong were reluctant to engage any force larger than themselves.

"At least in 'Nam we were allowed to carry our M-16's at ready," he muttered sourly.

"Hey, Mendez," Dan Powell, the third cop, remarked. "If you don't cut down on the beans and beer before patrols, your smell is gonna drive off bandits . . . and probably any bears in the area."

"Hey, mon," Mendez chuckled. "It's natural camouflage. The *pollos* wouldn't trust us without it."

They soon encountered a group of about ten illegals. The *pollos* hesitated at first, then welcomed the trio to their group, glad for the increased numbers.

Ban Ban wasn't sure what first alerted him to the strangeness of these newcomers. Perhaps it was their posture, or the military step that left the dust beneath their feet largely undisturbed. He compared it to the hesitant shuffle of the farmers around them. Or it could have been their well-fed stockiness, which set them apart from people of hard times. Ban Ban's level of alertness increased.

Haggerty's first feelings of uneasiness began when he noticed the way the long shiny black hair fell away from the faces of three members of the *pollos*. He could not see their faces clearly in the dark, but something about them seemed familiar. The cop found their large sports bags provocative. Haggerty even noticed the faint scraping sound of the criss-cross stitching at the inner thighs of the trio's jeans. It suggested that the clothes had been recently purchased. New clothing was unusual attire for *pollos* sneaking across the canyon.

Suddenly, four figures appeared in the path of the illegals. They were dressed in much the same manner as the emigrés. All four men had worn boots, battered hats and tattered jackets. But their manner was arrogant as they swaggered toward the group.

"*Eh-ey, pollos!*" a tall man called out as he aimed a flashlight at the emigrants. "*Dénme su dinero! Por favor, eh?*"

The bandit's voice was sarcastic as he demanded money. The guy turned the light toward his own face. The glare created a satanic mask, highlighting his bushy eyebrows and widow's peak. The *bandido* obviously believed in living the role. He even had a drooping black mustache and a shiny copper tooth in the center of his mouth. Maybe he hoped to get enough money from the pollos to buy a gold one.

The three undercover policemen moved as one, whipping out their hanguns from concealed holsters at the small of their backs. The Hispanic canyon pirates were fortunate that they did not point weapons at the cops, who would have been inclined to shoot first and declare themselves later.

"*Policía!*" Mendez shouted, both hands wrapped around the butt of his .357 Magnum. "You are under arrest! Don't move!"

"*Cristo,*" the *coyote* rasped under his breath. He turned to warn the Asians to play it cool. The guide glanced about for Ban Ban, but he was already too late.

The former operative of the Viet Cong and ex-member of the fraternity known as the "Saigon Cowboys" —the Southeast Asian version of the "Hell's Angels"— had been prepared to let the *coyote* take the initiative in all areas but this. Ban Ban knew his group would not fare well in even a cursory examination by the armed American security forces who stood before him, their weapons pointed at the four newcomers.

The *bandidos* raised their hands in surrender as Ban Ban trained his Ingram machinepistol on the three cops.

He triggered the short-barreled full-auto weapon. A rippling cadence of death split the night.

Paul Haggerty was certain he was imagining ghosts, flashing back to 'Nam. He heard someone shout something in Vietnamese and turned to see a fierce Asian face illuminated by the muzzle flash of an automatic weapon.

"N-No . . ." he stuttered involuntarily. Three 9mm rounds slammed into his torso, puncturing his lungs and snapping his spine.

It can't be . . . Haggerty thought. A moment later he was dead.

Mendez and Powell reacted immediately to the unexpected gunfire. So did the four *bandidos*, who quickly reached for pistols in their belts. Mendez fired his Magnum and blasted a .357 slug right through the mouth of the bandit leader. The outlaw's teeth—including the copper one—exploded as the high-velocity projectile drilled a path of destruction which severed the junction where the spinal cord meets the brain.

Officer Dan Powell swung his revolver toward Ban Ban, but three 9mm shots caught him in the chest before he could trigger his Magnum. Bullets cut the cop's heart to bits, and the impact hurled his dying body to the ground.

Ralph Mendez concentrated on the *bandidos*, aiming and firing his .357 with remarkable speed and accuracy. He managed to pump Magnum messengers into two more outlaws before the last bandit cut him down by firing three .38-Special slugs into the cop's upper torso. The lone canyon thug was no more fortunate than his slain brethren. Ban Ban sprayed the bandit with his MAC-10. Cops and robbers died together.

The *pollos* bolted, running in different directions and

rapidly melting into the night. One of the Asians shouted, *"Didi! Didi!"* Yet, Ban Ban did not run. He walked calmly to the supine lawmen and examined them with an efficient, professional eye.

"We have to get out of here," the *coyote* urged in English, aware the Asians understood the language. "The police will be all over this place . . ."

Ban Ban glared at him, then realized that the *coyote* was right. He stood erect above Haggerty's corpse, putting away his knife and his grisly trophy. The Asian left the other bodies intact and strode toward his two comrades.

"Hurry!" the guide insisted.

The *coyote* and his three clients headed for the pickup point approximately two kilometers away. There was no time for being discreet. Within twenty minutes, the guide intended to be far from the site of the gunbattle and shed of the three crazy, warlike Orientals. He comforted himself with the knowledge that the deaths of the three policemen would result in little more than a welcome rest. Regardless of the official reaction, he would be back to business as usual within a week.

The Border Crime Task Force unit commander took news of the attack from the watch captain with little comment. They were both aware of the mountain of paperwork, hours of meetings and painful moments that would surely follow the incident. The existence of the Task Force was still tentative and fragile, and the murders of three officers wasn't going to improve its position worth a shit.

Even more disturbing, the commander could not imagine how he was going to explain to Judy Haggerty about the mutilation of her husband's corpse. That information was tucked away into the modus operandi file in his memory. He probably wouldn't be one of the officers assigned to track down the killers. That was the province of the intelligence and homicide divisions. But, he was damned sure going to pass the information on to his own personal contacts in those departments. He was an old fashioned cop, and had little faith in computerized information-sharing bullshit.

Besides, he concluded, as he leafed through his bedside telephone book for Haggerty's home number, his own interest in this case was far too intense to leave the matter at the official level. He was going to personally nail the bastards responsible for the deaths of his men, or at least be able to say he'd made the effort.

Trang Nih paced the confines of the condominium's ample living room. The quarters seemed painfully small and crowded with fifteen men crammed into it.

"I'm glad to see almost everyone made it to our meeting tonight," he began, addressing the others. "Psar Phumi did his work well."

But where is Psar Phumi? he thought anxiously.

Trang Nih was tall for a Vietnamese, his presence exerting a commanding influence over the men he had called together. A trace of gray at his temples added a distinguished quality to the sharp features of his angular face, which reflected hawk-like concentration.

It was a face well-known to the intelligence network of the Communist government of the Democratic Republic of Vietnam. Trang Nih was regarded as the their Number One enemy, the most influential and best organized freedom fighter in Southeast Asia, with followers throughout Vietnam, Laos and Cambodia. The anti-Communist forces regarded Trang Nih as their greatest hope for liberation. But to the Communists,

Trang Nih was the most wanted man in Southeast Asia. Even the Soviet KGB had a file on him.

They had tried to assassinate him at his headquarters in Thailand, but the Hanoi triggermen had missed their target. Thanks to Qui Nhung, Trang Nih's most trusted lieutenant, they didn't get a second chance. Qui had cut down the gunmen before they could fire another shot. Trang Nih and his people had left Bangkok immediately and set up a new headquarters near the Burmese border.

Qui Nhung was seated on a folding chair in the San Diego condo where Trang's team had gathered for their meeting. A Laotian, shorter and younger than Trang Nih, Qui Nhung was in excellent physical condition, after years of training in the martial arts. He was intelligent, highly competent and extremely loyal to Trang Nih and the cause to which both men had dedicated their lives.

"Transportation is confirmed for the next leg of the trip, through California and Oregon to Washington," Qui Nhung reported. "Our contact with the American intelligence liaison assures us he'll refrain from informing the mercenaries of our arrival until the last moment."

"Good," Trang Nih said. "Nothing is more important than maintaining our security at this time."

"The three rented automobiles are outside, ready for the journey," Qui Nhung continued. "I have purchased three walkie-talkies to communicate from car to car to avoid getting separated."

Trang Nih wagged his head from side to side with a smile.

"Leave it to the Americans," he commented with a smile. "Well, the M-16 seems to function quite well despite being mounted on a stock fabricated by an American toy manufacturer."

"It is my hope," Qui Nhung ventured. "That this American mercenary group will be of equal use to us. I have read many disturbing articles about fanatical, poorly trained paramilitary groups in this country . . ."

"The Hard Corps comes highly recommended," Trang Nih said quickly, hoping to ease the concerns of everyone in the room. "They are accustomed to fighting successfully against overwhelming odds. There is much that they can teach us."

"I hope these claims are not exaggerated," Qui Nhung stated as he glanced at his wristwatch. "I will call in the perimeter guards and have them bring the cars to the street entrance."

As he moved toward the front door, the double roar of twin shotgun blasts erupted from outside. The doorknob disappeared in a shower of splinters. Qui Nhung immediately threw himself to the floor and reached inside his jacket for the 9mm pistol holstered under his arm.

The first gunman kicked open the door and braced himself on bent knees, a Remington 12 gauge shotgun in his fists. His partner followed close behind, an identical weapon braced in his hands by a broomstick-grip attached to the lower front stock, below the sawed-off barrel. Both men were Caucasians, oddly dressed in long rain coats, gloves, and wool knit hats.

As shotguns roared, there was nowhere for the Southeast Asians to dive for cover. But they were well-acquainted with the strategy of shock attack, and even as two of their number fell, chests crushed by buckshot, with streaming guts oozing from torn bellies, the others jumped to counterattack.

Pistols appeared in their hands in a sudden flash of metallic blue, Qui Nhung the first to trigger his S&W M-59 autoloader. Other weapons snarled a microsecond later. Like a group of killer whales in a feeding frenzy, the Asians returned fire furiously, with no apparent thought for their own safety. Each knew from personal experience that seeking cover under such circumstances would only hasten death. They stood their ground and pumped rounds into the two attackers.

The acrid smell of burnt pistol powder filled the room. The Caucasian gunmen suffered numerous bullet wounds. One of them had been killed instantly by two rounds that blasted open his skull like an eggshell. Incredibly, the other gunman was still alive. He lay in the doorway, Remington blaster inches from his fingers, blood seeping from holes in his chest.

Qui Nhung scrambled up from the floor, M-59 aimed at the wounded man. He kicked the shotgun beyond the killer's reach, and glancing down at the invader, realized the man's temporary survival was not as incredible as it seemed.

More than one projectile had penetrated the gunman's protective vest. The pink froth that bubbled from his trembling lips suggested the guy had been hit in the lungs. He coughed violently and deep crimson ran from his mouth.

"Jesus Christ," he cursed weakly. "Th . . . This was s-suppose to be a . . . a tur-key s-shoot . . ."

"You got it, turkey," Qui Nhung replied. He had learned English from American GIs and was familar with most slang expressions. "You must also realize there is nothing anyone can do for you now. So why not tell us who sent you?"

"F-Fuck you," the man moaned, his eyes glazed with pain. "Not do-doin' you no f-favors, gook . . ."

"Then we'll make your final moments on earth even more painful," the Laotian said, aiming his pistol at the wounded man's crotch. "How about it, turkey?"

"No!" the triggerman rasped. "I . . . I'll talk. An-another gook hi-hired us. C-Captain some-thin' . . ."

The man's body twitched weakly and lay still, his eyes staring up at Qui Nhung with mute accusation. The Laotian felt a familar knot of fear in his belly. The other men in the room could easily relate to this feeling.

"Captain Vinh," Trang Nih voiced their fear in a soft whisper.

"Didi mau lin!" Qui Nhung shouted. "Run quickly!"

The Laotian grabbed Trang Nih's arm and hauled him across the threshold outside. The others dashed for the door. They knew about Captain Vinh's reputation. He would never have sent just two hired thugs to hit a whole roomful of opponents. There had to be a back-up team for the shotgunners.

The assumption proved to be deadly accurate, as a spinning projectile suddenly shattered the front window. The missile exploded within the condo, and only six men managed to clear the door before the room burst into flames. The lucky escapees tumbled away from the building. Inside, only burning wreckage and death remained.

Veterans of many wartime missions, the freedom fighters recovered quickly from the shock and sought targets for return fire. The backup hit team hastily dove into a van which was already pulling away from the scene, but the last of the enemy team was slow getting into the vehicle. Qui Nhung fired his S&W auto at the bastard and nailed him with a 9mm round. The man cried out as he dropped the short-barreled launcher that had caused the devastation in the condo. However, he wasn't hurt that badly, for he managed to climb into the van as it accelerated from the battleground.

Trang Nih moved to follow two of his men who re-entered the building to search for survivors. The odds weren't good, but they could not abandon their people without making certain none were alive and trapped beneath the burning rubble.

"Toy rat an han," one of them told Trang Nih, as he emerged from the building, coughing from the smoke. "They're finished, Trang Nih. No one could live through that."

"The cars are ready," Qui Nhung announced. "We must go."

"Thua co," Trang Nih agreed. "Yes, let us get away quickly. Then we must reestablish communications with our contact. Our mission is more important, more desperate than ever."

Three cars pulled up to the sidewalk, and Trang Nih and Qui Nhung climbed into a Chevrolet Caprice. The others piled into the other two cars, and the drivers bolted from the area and sought a feeder road to Highway 5, headed north.

CHAPTER 3

AT FIVE IN the morning, the rising sun illuminated the peak of the rocky crag which towered a thousand feet above the lake and the settlement below. The area was a buffer zone between the Pacific Coast and Cascade Range forests. Sitka spruce, western hemlock and Douglas fir trees gave way as the mountain rose, to lodgepole and Ponderosa pine. Mule deer and a few elk shared the area with black bears and an occasional mountain lion, as well as the omnipresent coyote, racoon, and bobcat.

William O'Neal was winding down from his five-mile morning inspection run. His route criss-crossed the one mile square area of the compound, situated at the southwest corner of the holding, near the Pacific Coastal mountain range in the state of Washington.

Following the head waters of the stream feeding the lake, he paced himself to the final exercise station one hundred yards ahead. O'Neal's wristwatch was a model designed for runners. It displayed a digital estimate of his pulse. The display figure changed constantly, but hovered around sixty-four per minute.

"A little slow for a man my age," he muttered and wind-sprinted the final distance to maintain the maximum training effect from the exercise.

As a professional mercenary and team leader of the Hard Corps, O'Neal did not regard the Iron Man concept as a dinosaur notion, something he could allow to slip gracefully away with age. Although the idea of fucking off was not without attraction. At thirty-eight, he found he had to work harder at staying in shape between assignments.

Running through the forest, O'Neal recalled how fortunate they had been to acquire the compound. It had formerly belonged to a local marijuana rancher who had been forced into a protected witness program, squeezed between his former cronies and an aggressive federal prosecutor. The land had come up for sale at a very low price and the Hard Corps readily moved in.

The area was ideal. It even included several buildings and a few other creature comforts—although most of the marijuana plants had been removed by the DEA. Since they were financially flush (thanks to their most recent mission) they had considered converting one of the larger structures into a barracks, but that wouldn't be necessary until their outfit expanded beyond its present four men complement, if, indeed they ever had to expand.

Each member of the Hard Corps had been assigned one of the individual cottages constructed for the former residents. They were comfortable dwellings, similar to ski chalets.

O'Neal neared the cottage assigned to Steven Caine. Even the other members of the Hard Corps considered Caine to be a rather odd character. Quiet, withdrawn, and mysterous, Caine was devoted to exotic weaponry, modern or ancient, well known or obscure. O'Neal seldom visited Caine's quarters, but there wasn't really much to see anyway. The guy kept the place in spartan condition. Caine probably didn't care, because he didn't spend much time there.

Caine had not been in his cottage since the morning of the previous day. Such behavior was not unusual for the most reticent Corps member. Although they had been in the compound for six months, the men of the Hard Corps were still familiarizing themselves with the five hundred acre facility. Caine, however, seemed determined to memorize every inch of the territory.

Of course, Caine was always testing himself and keeping his survival skills at peak condition. He liked to live off the land in a manner most would find primitive. This affinity was probably due to the time he spent with the Katu tribes after the fall of Saigon.

But Caine's special talents were varied. What O'Neal saw fit to inspect at a dead run, Caine wanted to examine more closely. He looked beyond the point of view of conventional military strategy, and always considered topography for weapons emplacement and cover from fire. Caine studied his surroundings, with special consideration for natural environment. In fact, O'Neal was growing curious about the progress of Caine's newest project: hand drawn color sketches of the compound's animals, plants, and minerals of military or medicinal value.

Now, how many other guys would volunteer for a job like that?

The next quarters O'Neal passed belonged to Joe Fanelli. In contrast to Caine's stark austerity, Fanelli's quarters boasted many of the newest electronic toys. He was a recovering alcoholic and didn't believe in depriving himself of non-liquid diversions. The walls of Fanelli's cottage were decorated with posters, nude pinups and bumper stickers with odd, frequently obscene slogans. Fanelli probably had one of the largest collections of porno videotapes in the state of Washington.

O'Neal noticed Fanelli's windows were closed, a sure sign the fresh air freak was absent. He was probably at the mess hall, since it was about meal time.

He jogged past the walled patio ajoining Wentworth's cottage, which testified to the Hard Corps second in command being an unabashed Japanist. O'Neal wondered if Wentworth ever got confused. Half Old South gentleman, half would-be samurai, he seemed a paradox, unless one examined the two cultures carefully and learned they had much in common.

O'Neal continued past his own quarters, situated next to the "head shed," the communications center of the compound. It housed computer equipment, transatlantic radios, and other gear essential to the operation of the base. And operations were going to get bigger in the future.

It was going to be another busy day, O'Neal thought, heading for the mess hall. Wentworth was scheduled to meet with him later to discuss the logistical status of the compound: inventories of TA-50 field gear, armaments, air and ground transport, power and fuel, and supplies for the mess.

Such information for an army of four men shouldn't be reported by a second in command. But, although limited to a four man nucleus, the Hard Corps didn't suffer from narrowness of vision. They didn't think small, and their assignments would become bigger and bigger, which meant they'd have to use more people and more supplies in the future.

The last mission had been ideally suited for the Hard Corps's four-man team. It had been completely successful—and very profitable. A million bucks could keep the compound stocked with supplies and equipment for a long time. Of course, the facility was already self-sufficient. The hydroelectric power generators built into a small dam had been constructed by the previous owners. The Hard Corps had also set up windmill generators and solar panels to provide other sources of electricity. Finally, they had a number of diesel generators if all else failed.

Underground tanks contained thousands of gallons of fuel for the generators as well as for vehicles, aircraft, and chainsaws. Their motorpool inventory included motorcycles, jeeps, trucks, and two helicopters. The Bell UH-1D they had was a troop transport with a three-hundred-mile range. Their other machine, a Huey Cobra, was a swift fighting gunship, and both choppers were equipped with biosensors and arms. O'Neal was a licensed helicopter pilot and was also qualified to fly several types of planes. Fanelli had been taking flying lessons for more than a year and could handle the choppers if necessary.

The Hard Corps had not neglected security for the compound. An alarm system was built into the heavy steel chain-link fence that surrounded the five hundred acres of private property. Surveillance cameras and microphones were installed in the forest. No one could break through without alerting the Hard Corps Command Center. Advancing invaders would be observed from any direction thanks to television monitors and radio receivers. The observation tower at the helicopter base had a radar unit that could also be integrated into this effort.

The line of sunlight on the rocky face above O'Neal dropped lower as the sun rose. He was grateful that the last leg of his path to the mess hall lay in chilly darkness. He slowed to a walk and drank in the delicious, cold, fresh air. He wanted to cool off before entering the heated building. He checked the pulse meter on his wrist, and allowed his breath and heartbeat to ease back to something closer to normal.

He entered the mess hall. John McShayne peered out from his gleaming kitchen. The chunky, white-haired grizzled veteran was an Army "lifer." He'd spent thirty years in the armed forces and still couldn't get enough of the military. Although twenty years O'Neal's senior, McShayne was still a rugged individual descended of hard-working Scots and Norwegians. The type of guy who reaches forty-nine and never seems to age another day.

McShayne was the "support group" for the Hard Corps. He acted as first sergeant, chief mechanic, supply NCO, bookkeeper, accountant, and mess sergeant, all rolled into one. He was the Hard Corps's mother hen —in the sense that a St. Bernard can adopt a flock of baby chicks.

"Morning, Top," O'Neal announced, as he headed for the serving line. He referred to McShayne by the universal nickname for a first or "top" sergeant.

"Hope it'll get better, sir," McShayne growled in reply, as he shoveled chipped beef on toast. This was the famous GI gourmet delight, affectionately known as "shit on a shingle."

"Something wrong?" O'Neal inquired, aware that

grumbling and bitching was part of McShayne's nature during the best of times.

"I just think it's about time one of the enlisted personnel around here helped with KP duty," the senior sergeant replied. "One of 'em goes off on a three day pass and the other decides to play Grizzly Adams in the goddamn woods. Bears probably got him by now."

"The bears?" O'Neal repressed a smile. "Well, I think Caine can avoid getting eaten by the bears around here."

"Who cares?" McShayne shrugged as he uttered a bullshit lie if ever there was one. "Fanelli's back and I'm gonna put him to work today."

"You could have gotten Jim or myself to help with some dishes," O'Neal offered.

"Have an officer work in *my* kitchen?" McShayne glared at O'Neal. "With all due respect, no fuckin' way, Captain."

"It's your mess, Top," O'Neal assured him, taking his breakfast tray from the line.

He located Fanelli, who was seated with Wentworth at a table in a corner of the mess hall. O'Neal headed for it and placed his tray on the table. Fanelli looked up with bleary eyes as he nursed a steaming cup of hot coffee. Wentworth was dipping a stainless steel tea strainer into a handleless porcelein cup.

"Top wants to see you," O'Neal told Fanelli.

"C'mon, Captain," Fanelli replied. "Wait until I get my eyeballs in and my engine started."

"He needs his morning transfusion before he can greet you properly," Wentworth mused.

Joe Fanelli had returned the previous evening from his pass to the closest whistle stop with a house of ill repute.

"I see you got your ears lowered," commented

O'Neal, referring to Fanelli's freshly cropped military haircut.

"And his horns trimmed," Wentworth added. "By the way, did you read that article about how AIDS is increasing among heterosexuals?"

"Spare me the scare tactics," Fanelli said, sipping his coffee. "Besides, it's a little late now."

"Does that mean we have to hear about your conquests and bedroom acrobatics?" Wentworth asked wearily.

"Yeah," Fanelli answered, perking up. "I'll give you all the heroic details later."

"I'll expect a full report on my desk by eleven," O'Neal declared with mock severity.

"I can wait until the movie comes out," Wentworth said dryly.

"Hell," Fanelli said with a shrug. "A guy can get a bad case of cabin fever up here—without occasional exposure to female charms."

Actually, O'Neal took a professional interest in anything in the lives of his men which could affect their performance in the field. Besides, they were all friends —probably the only friends any of them really had. But Fanelli was the only one who went to whorehouses. O'Neal judged this to be consistent with Fanelli's experience and lifestyle. The Hard Corps commander felt safe assuming his man would avoid trouble . . . pretty safe anyway.

The only other member of the group who ever indulged with prostitutes was McShayne. But he tended to get a hotel room in town, buy a bottle, then call a favorite girl for the evening. McShayne had once told Fanelli, "When you get older, you don't win too many footraces, but you enjoy a long walk a helluva lot more."

Neither O'Neal nor Wentworth deprived themselves of female companionship, but their tastes involved more traditional relationships. Not lasting relationships, of course, but they didn't buy hookers either.

Steve Caine, however, seemed almost celibate. He had been through two tragic marriages, and did not experience the same needs as his fellow team members.

Fanelli sipped his coffee as he leafed through a newspaper he'd picked up in town, but hadn't read while he was busy seeing to his personal passions. One item caught his eye, and he decided to share it with the others.

"This sounds like old home week," Fanelli announced. "Says here there was a big gangland killing in San Diego. Ten people killed, mostly Southeast Asian refugees and two white guys."

"Was it at a fast food restaurant?" Wentworth inquired. "I hear those can be dangerous in Southern California."

"A condo," Fanelli explained. "The cops found an M-79 grenade launcher there and a witness said he saw a couple guys with sawed-off shotguns, and a lot of fellas with pistols."

"Interesting," O'Neal admitted. "How old is that paper?"

"Three or four days," Fanelli said.

"Shit," McShayne growled. "The cops probably solved it by now. Drugs for sure. I ever tell you guys how the Chinese Triad has been moving into Mafia territory when it comes to drugs in this country?"

"I think so, Top," O'Neal replied. "Right after breakfast, we've got to go over the morning report. Check out intel for possible new missions."

"You know, Top's right about the Triad," Wentworth said. "They have been growing very rapidly and gaining international power as a crime network. So has the Japanese Yakuza . . ."

"Ain't none of them gonna out-do the Mafia," Fanelli said, almost defensively.

"Jim," O'Neal began. "Don't forget the logistics report this afternoon."

"It's not much different from the last one," Wentworth said with a shrug. "But you'll have it."

"Good," O'Neal replied as he finished his S.O.S. "And Joe, you can help Top in the mess hall after we finish with the morning report and research of intel."

"Didn't Caine come back from communing with Mother Nature yet?" Fanelli asked.

"You see him here?" McShayne growled.

"That doesn't mean anything when you're talking about Steve Caine," Fanelli reminded him. "When you were taking your run, Captain, did you see Caine out there?"

"No," O'Neal said with a shrug. "Maybe the bears got him after all."

"Are you finished with your breakfast yet, sir?" McShayne asked gruffly. "If we're gonna get to those morning reports, I'd like to do it and get on to my other work."

"Right," the unit commander agreed.

O'Neal and McShayne left the mess hall. They walked past a large television satellite dish and a microwave transceiver antenna, equipment which never failed to remind O'Neal of props in a 1950 science fiction movie. They stopped at a square building, slightly smaller than the mess hall. Horizonal slits near the roof line resembled gun ports more than security windows. Actually, they could serve as both.

McShayne selected a key from the chain on his belt and unlocked the oversized padlock from the hasp on the door. O'Neal smiled thinly.

"You don't want any bears to get into the radio shack do you, Top?" O'Neal remarked.

"Will you stop with the bears, Captain?" McShayne answered. "I'm not worried about bears. I just figure anything that'll stop a bear will stop a man. That's why I put sturdy locks on doors and that's why I carry this baby."

McShayne patted the Smith & Wesson .44 Magnum revolver on his hip. The four mercenaries also carried pistols, Colt .45 automatics. O'Neal remembered when McShayne had rejected the idea of carrying a .45 and selected the more powerful Magnum because he said he wanted something that would stop a "goddamn bear" if he ever found one of those "hairy bastards" in the food supply.

Actually, McShayne had once found a female bear and two cubs in the garbage before the fence was completed. He only fired a shot in the air to frighten them away. The Top Kick had vowed that next time he'd kill 'em. Uh-huh, sure.

When they entered the head shed, red and green lights flashed from diodes, blinking on the modem by the desk mounted printer. The flashing green-red tubes looked like leftovers from a Christmas tree in the dimly lit room. McShayne flipped the switch for the overhead lights.

The Hard Corps commander and his Top Sergeant inspected the intelligence updates for the previous twenty-four hours. They were plugged into a number of intel sources, including unclassified sources open to the general public—and quite a few that weren't.

A group of plantation owners in Sri Lanka had offered to hire the Hard Corps to protect them from bandits. Sounded like yet another version of *The Seven Samurai*, but O'Neal didn't trust the story. He suspected it was either a front by the Sri Lanka government to recruit mercenaries to fight the Tamil separatists or vice versa. The Hard Corps didn't want to get involved in that turmoil either way—especially if their would-be employers wanted to play bullshit games.

Another offer was supposed to be from a group of anti-Communist freedom fighters in Angola. The job sounded intriguing, but McShayne checked his disks for other recent data about activity in Angola. Information appeared on the viewscreen. McShayne grunted.

"Donally's merc team was contacted by this bunch last month," Top stated. "They headed to Angola and the Marxists arrested them as soon as they arrived."

"I remember now," O'Neal added. "Donally and his men were executed and the Angolan government claimed they were CIA spies sent by the United States to plot against their country."

"Yeah," McShayne said. "It's a trap. The bastards are trying to lure Americans into going to Angola to fight Commies, but they're playing right into the hands of the Red shits running the country."

"Sounds like the KGB came up with the scheme," O'Neal added. "Angola's crawling with thousands of Soviet and Cuban 'advisors'. Well, the hell with that."

O'Neal and McShayne also checked out a couple of offers for work in Central America, but the details weren't complete enough to decide one way or the other. Maybe when more information came in, but not now.

"I don't see anything here from Old Saintly," O'Neal remarked.

"Old Saintly" was Joshua St. Laurent, a CIA case officer stationed in Canada. He was generally concerned with spying on the Soviet Embassy in Ottawa—and on the Canadian government itself. St. Laurent was also the Hard Corps's unofficial "federal connection." The U.S. Government, or at least St. Laurent and some of his superiors in "the Company," were aware of the Hard Corps's activities, but chose to look the other way as long as the mercs continued to act in the best interest of the United States.

St. Laurent kept tabs on the Hard Corps. He frequently requested information from them, aware that the mercs had intelligence sources of their own which the CIA and National Security Agency couldn't hope to get cooperation from. He occasionally gave the mercenaries inside government information, cut through red tape, and warned them when they were stepping on Uncle Sam's toes.

The Hard Corps and St. Laurent weren't friends, but they had established a cooperative working relationship, based on mutual interests. One advantage for the mercs through this association was they didn't have to pay any income tax. This proved to be a double-edged sword because it also meant the CIA could coerce them into taking on a mission, or they'd face a visit from the Internal Revenue Service.

"Here it is," McShayne announced as he began to read from the continuous sheets of paper that dropped from the printer. "Saintly says there are currently no less than four contracts on Kaddafi. He is 'strongly advising' us not to accept any offers to liquidate the Libyan bastard."

"Does he think we're amateurs or just plain stupid?" O'Neal muttered with disgust. "You'd think he'd know that we'd never even consider an assignment like that."

"Leave it to the CIA," McShayne grunted. "They don't know the difference between a professional and a hired assassin."

There were also a few inquires from prospective students looking for a school for mercenaries. These were made from indirect sources which were looking for a merc school in general, not the Hard Corps in particular. O'Neal never accepted any of these would-be student mercs. He knew that one learns to be a soldier by pulling a hitch in an official branch of the armed forces. Those who wanted to do it privately had to look somewhere else. The Hard Corps commander didn't have time to teach beginners the fundamentals of soldiering and combat. He also didn't want "60 Minutes" to show up at the compound, poking around for a story.

If the Hard Corps needed to recruit personnel for an assignment, they could pick experienced veterans through international merc connections which they had already established. Most of the men they selected were fellow Vietnam vets who had settled in foreign countries, like Mexico, Thailand, the Middle East, or Europe.

Hence, the Hard Corps expected and received few visitors.

O'Neal met with Wentworth to discuss logistics, although the former Green Beret lieutenant had been right when he said there were few changes since the last report. It was a boring way to spend the afternoon, but the two men examined the material for hours. Then O'Neal took the data to McShayne to use the computers to estimate the probability of future needs and expenses.

"I was just about to contact you, Captain," McShayne declared when O'Neal entered the head shed. "I was monitoring the FAA channel when a message came through. We're receiving a distress call from a civilian helicopter. They claim they're having engine trouble and request permission to land."

"Here?" O'Neal asked.

"You got it, sir," McShayne confirmed.

CHAPTER 4

"ENGINE TROUBLE?" O'Neal muttered into the mike. He didn't buy the story. Too damn convenient that the chopper just happened to reach the Compound. Did they plan to try to sell the Hard Corps the Brooklyn Bridge while they were in the area?

There was a remote chance the pilot was telling the truth. Coincidences do happen. O'Neal didn't want the chopper to crash in the Compound. Besides, he didn't want the lives of innocent people on his conscience, and O'Neal realized that if a civilian 'copter crashed, he'd never be able to convince Old Saintly that the Hard Corps hadn't shot the sucker down. The mercs had a symbiotic relationship with Uncle Sam. They could exist without it, of course, but having an "in" with the feds was advantageous—for now at least. O'Neal would never really trust any government bureaucrat. It was sort of like owning a pet crocodile. The beast will sure discourage people from skinnydipping on your property, but you have to watch your fingers when you feed it.

If government bureaucracy isn't a croc, what is?

O'Neal was pretty sure the helicopter's "engine trouble" was another crock. Logic told him it was probably bullshit, and instinct told him likewise. O'Neal, like most seasoned combat veterans, put a lot of stock in his survival instincts. If he really considered the subject objectively, O'Neal would probably have recalled numerous occasions when this "sixth sense" gave him a false alarm. O'Neal did not think about this very often. He was perfectly content to just believe in his instincts —like a fundamentalist Christian who doesn't question anything in the Bible.

But O'Neal's instincts weren't flashing red alert signals to gut and spinal cord. The "engine trouble" crap was almost certainly an excuse to try to get permission from the Hard Corps to land at the compound. That did not necessarily mean the newcomers were a threat.

Friend or foe, or stranger in distress, O'Neal decided the only answer was to give the chopper permission to land.

"Okay," McShayne said with a broad shrug. "But I hope you've considered that the chopper could be loaded with machine gun totin' hoods . . ."

"Or terrorists, enemy spies, hired killers, so on and so forth," O'Neal assured him. "Just tell them they can land at the helipad and then make sure your M-14 is loaded."

"Now you're talking like you still got a little sense left," the grizzled senior NCO growled as he reached for the radio microphone.

"I'm going to tell the others to get ready for company," O'Neal commented, taking his Colt .45 from the holster on his hip. He worked the slide to chamber the first round, and switched on the safety.

"Remind them I still expect help cleaning up the mess hall," McShayne stated.

"I'll tell them," O'Neal promised, returning his pistol to leather.

Wentworth and Fanelli appeared at the orderly room before O'Neal could call them. Both men were already armed with M-16 rifles and .45 sidearms. O'Neal smiled.

"You guys must have noticed the 'copter," the Hard Corps commander remarked.

"Couldn't miss it," Fanelli replied, a cigarette dangling from the corner of his mouth. "You can hear the son of a bitch over the compound. Those rotor blades ain't quiet. Step outside. You'll hear 'em, Captain."

"Any idea who they are?" Wentworth asked, adjusting the shoulder strap to his M-16.

"Claim they have engine trouble," O'Neal answered, leading the others to the exit. "Probably crap, but it just might be the truth, so don't start shooting until you're sure there's a good reason for it."

"Oh, they're bullshittin'," Fanelli assured the team leader. "I could be wrong, but I could swear that chopper sounds like a Bell UH-1D. Ten to one it's some jackoffs from DEA poking their snouts into our business."

"Maybe," Wentworth commented. "In which case it'll be just another annoyance—but it could be something more serious. That's the joy of being a mercenary. You get enemies you never knew about and nobody is going to help you deal with them."

"Figure we need help?" Fanelli inquired with a grin.

"If they fly over us and fire rockets from a gunship,"

Wentworth sighed. "Then I wouldn't object to some help."

The three mercs emerged from the head shed. The shadow of the approaching helicopter stretched across the ground in front of them. Fanelli had been right on the money with both guesses. The rotor blades' small tornado and one glance at the aircraft confirmed it was indeed a Bell UH-1D. The chopper had been painted white with red trim, but it was the same sort of whirlybird as the Bell chopper in the Hard Corps's "air force."

O'Neal and Fanelli were both chopper pilots, so the sight of the great bug-like metallic shape was actually a relief. Their trained eye immediately noticed the 'copter jockey was handling his craft with admirable skill. The pilot kept his chopper on a steady path toward the heli-pad. He obviously had good control of the helicopter. At least there wasn't much of a chance that the "flying chainsaw" was going to swing off-course and nosedive into one of the compound buildings.

Wentworth did not have to be an expert on choppers to notice the new craft did not carry mounted missiles or machine guns. Naturally, the Bell could be loaded with enemy gunmen, but the men of the Hard Corps were used to that sort of confrontation, and they preferred that to dodging rockets launched from an airborne opponent.

"How do you want to handle this, Bill?" Wentworth inquired.

"When the bird lands, I'll go forward and meet them alone," O'Neal answered. "You guys handle backup. Okay?"

"You ought to let me go instead," Wentworth offered. "You're team commander . . ."

"Right," O'Neal confirmed. "So I go like I said. Top will supply extra firepower if we need it."

"What about Caine?" Fanelli inquired. "He's still out in the woods somewhere. Probably armed only with that damn survival knife."

"He's certainly noticed the helicopter by now," O'Neal replied. "Caine will probably head for the 'copter pad and stay hidden in order to observe the new arrivals before taking any action . . . if it's required."

"At least he could have taken a walkie-talkie with him when he decided to play *Man in the Wilderness*," Wentworth said sourly. "I wish Caine was a bit more of a team player. How can we coordinate if he's always running off by himself without giving us any way to communicate with him?"

"Don't worry," O'Neal urged as he marched toward the helipad. "Caine coordinates with us whenever we need him, but he also does some of his best work on his own. You fellas get settled in somewhere so you can cover my ass."

Wentworth and Fanelli separated, heading for different positions to supply backup fire if needed. O'Neal continued to walk to the pad. The visitors' Bell chopper began to descend. Dust swirled up from the ground as the slashing rotor blades created a violent air current. The undercarriage wheels touched down, and the tail settled into place. The chopper had landed.

O'Neal swallowed and took three deep breaths to calm himself. Facing an unknown, possibly hostile element he was tense. O'Neal was an experienced combat professional, but that didn't make him immune to fear.

The blades of the chopper spun more slowly as the craft settled onto the pad. A sliding door opened on the carriage and seven men climbed from the Bell 'copter.

All seven were Asians. They wore casual clothing, slacks, sneakers, and baseball caps. Their windbreakers concealed the pistols they carried, but O'Neal's trained eye noticed the suspicious bulges under armpits. However, none of the Asians attempted to draw weapons. O'Neal's .45 also remained in its holster.

"Hello," a tall man announced as he approached O'Neal. "Perhaps I should introduce myself. I am Trang Nih."

"Trang Nih?" the mercenary raised his eyebrows.

"You've heard of me?" the Asian asked with a smile.

"Oh, yeah," O'Neal confirmed. "You're probably Number One on the hit-parade of the Hanoi government. I heard the Communists were offering a reward of one hundred thousand *dong* for you. Dead or alive."

"Last I heard it was one hundred fifty thousand *dong*," Trang Nih replied. "Sounds like a great deal of money, but in American currency it's only about fifteen thousand dollars."

"In 'Nam that's a small fortune," O'Neal commented. "Especially since their economy is in the toilet. I heard you were in Thailand."

"I was," Trang Nih said with a nod. "Of course, Thailand isn't far from Vietnam. It borders on Laos and Cambodia. Hanoi's government bounty hunters were hot on our trail. On two occasions, they found us."

"But we killed them," a well-muscled Asian added, joining O'Neal and Trang Nih.

"Oh," Trang Nih began. "This is Qui Nhung, my right hand. He's saved my life more than once. A very good man."

"Toy rat han hanh duce gap ong," O'Neal greeted as he shook the Laotian's hand.

"I'm pleased to meet you too," Qui Nhung assured him. "We all speak English, if you'd be more comfortable speaking your own language."

"My Vietnamese is a little rusty," O'Neal confessed.

"Hello, sir." A short Asian with a moon face smiled up at O'Neal. "I am Psar Phumi, Trang Nih's liaison officer with the Cambodian Resistance Forces here in the United States. May I ask your name, sir?"

"Before we get too chummy," O'Neal answered. "I'd like to know why you guys are here and how you found us."

"Of course, Captain O'Neal," Trang Nih nodded. "You are Captain O'Neal, correct? You certainly fit the description."

"You guessed it," O'Neal confirmed. "Now, who gave you the description?"

"A man named St. Laurent," the Vietnamese replied with a thin smile. "I believe you refer to him as 'Old Saintly.' "

"That figures," O'Neal muttered. "Be nice if the son of a bitch would check with me first before sending people here."

The Hard Corps commander raised a hand and signaled to Wentworth and Fanelli to come forward. They advanced with M-16 rifles held high, barrels pointed at the sky. The pair had noticed that O'Neal had been conversing peaceably with the visitors, so they did not menace the group with their weapons.

But one Vietnamese bodyguard in Trang Nih's group was startled by the sight of two men approaching with assault rifles. His hand dove into his jacket for a pistol. The man nearly drew the weapon when he felt a sharp object under his right side.

"Thua khong," a voice warned. It continued in

fluent Vietnamese. "Raise your hands or I'll run you through like a pig on a spit."

The bodyguard slowly raised his arms. He glanced at a shape via the corner of his eye. A bearded face glared back at him. Steve Caine held an improvised spear in his fists, with his survival knife tied to the end of a tree limb roughly five feet long. The steel tip was poised at the man's heart.

"We got a problem back there?" O'Neal inquired.

Trang Nih and his group turned to see Caine with the disgruntled bodyguard. The other Asians were as surprised as the guy with Caine's spear braced at his ribs. They were all combat veterans with highly developed senses tuned for detecting danger. Yet they had not seen, heard, or felt Caine's presence until O'Neal's remark drew their attention to the two men at the rear of the group.

The helicoptor pilot emerged from his craft. A tall, lanky black man dressed in blue jeans and a T-shirt, he was about to speak when he noticed Caine and the Asian bodyguard, whose arms seemed frozen overhead.

"Jesus," the pilot gasped. "Where the hell did he come from?"

"I think we were all wondering the same thing," Trang Nih admitted.

"Caine is the strong, silent type," O'Neal said with a shrug. "What you doing with that guy, Steve?"

"Just gonna kill him if he draws a gun," Caine explained mildly. "That's what he was about to do."

"I'm sorry," Trang Nih told O'Neal. "Chinh overreacted when he saw your men approach with weapons held ready."

"You tell Chinh to keep his gun in its holster," O'Neal instructed. "Tell him in Vietnamese or Lao or whatever his native language is—just make sure he understands. If he pulls a gun on us again, we'll kill him.''

Trang Nih relayed the message to his bodyguard in crisp and rapid Vietnamese. Chinh nodded in reply. Caine moved the spear from the guy's side and allowed him to lower his arms.

''I was told that your men are good,'' Trang Nih commented. ''That appears to be an understatement.''

''We try to keep mistakes at a minimum,'' Wentworth replied. He turned to O'Neal. ''Who are these fellows, Bill?''

''He claims to be Trang Nih with some friends,'' the Hard Corps commander answered.

''*Claims* to be?'' the Vietnamese inquired. ''What does that mean, Captain?''

''Trang Nih is a legend,'' O'Neal explained. ''His name is well known throughout Southeast Asia. Some regard him as a potential George Washington of Vietnam. But I've never heard of Trang Nih coming to the United States. As far as I know, he hasn't left Indochina for more than ten years.''

''I've been in this country for the last six months,'' Trang Nih stated.

''No offense,'' O'Neal assured him. ''But I have only your word on that. We haven't received any intelligence data to support that. Hell, I've never even seen a photograph of Trang Nih.''

''Unfortunately,'' Trang Nih sighed. ''They have one in my file in Hanoi.''

''But we told you about Mr. St. Laurent,'' Psar Phumi stated. ''Doesn't that prove who we are?''

''It proves you convinced Old Saintly,'' Fanelli replied. ''He's not infallible. The guy puts his pants on like anybody else. One hoof at a time.''

''This is a bit frustrating,'' Trang Nih sighed. ''How

am I supposed to prove who I am?''

"You can probably do that by telling us why you're here," O'Neal suggested.

The group of visitors followed the Hard Corps to the mess hall. John McShayne stomped out of the head shed and approached them. He had left his M-14 in the orderly room, although he still carried the big .44 Magnum revolver on his hip. The old soldier muttered something under his breath as he unclipped a key ring from his belt.

"Hold on," he growled. "I'll have to unlock the door."

"What did you lock it for?" Fanelli asked. "You scared the bears were gonna sneak in and rip you off, Top?"

"No bears had better try to steal our food," McShayne replied gruffly. "But the reason I locked it was to keep you from makin' a bigger mess than we got already."

"What the hell, Top," Fanelli grinned. "It is the *mess* hall, right?"

"You know, I'm almost thirty years older than you, Fanelli," McShayne stated. "And that was an old joke when I was a kid."

He unlocked the door and the Hard Corps and their visitors followed him inside. McShayne headed for the kitchen. O'Neal told the others to shove some tables together to make a single extended one so everyone could sit around it.

"What do you guys want?" McShayne called from the kitchen. "Just somethin' to drink?"

"Just brew up some coffee for us and some tea for Trang Nih and his friends," O'Neal answered.

"Trang Nih?" McShayne leaned over the server's line and stared at the newcomers. "I'll be damned. I've

62

heard a lot about you, mister. The Communists think you're a real pain in the butt. Keep up the good work."

"Thank you," Trang Nih laughed. "I intend to. That's why I'm here. I hope to get you gentlemen to help us."

"People usually contact us because they have a problem," Wentworth commented, as he leaned his M-16 against the table. "As I recall, your problem is the Communist government in Vietnam. That's a little bit more than the four of us can handle."

"I'm not asking you to take on Hanoi all by yourselves," Trang Nih assured him. "But we hope to see the reign of Communism in Southeast Asia toppled. We plan to drive them out of Vietnam, Laos and Cambodia. I understand there's a lot of wide open spaces in Mongolia. Let them go there."

"Then you guys plan to help us?" Fanelli asked, eyes wide with mock surprise. "Gee, eleven of us against one of the largest armies in the world. You sure that'll be a fair fight? Us ganging up on them."

"Iran had the third largest army in the world when the Shah fell," Trang Nih reminded him.

"True," Wentworth agreed thoughtfully, resting his chin on his thumbs. "But the Shah was an extremely unpopular leader in his own country. His secret police used Gestapo tactics, like those guys in Haiti, the *tontons macoutes*. In fact, Duvalier had a lot in common with the Shah of Iran. Both had dumped on their people for decades and both revolved around a single strongman. The same isn't true in Vietnam."

"Yeah," O'Neal added, firing his Zippo to light a cigarette. "And neither one had the Soviet Union for a Dutch Uncle. Moscow has a lot of practice at holding onto the satellite nations it gets its claws into. Hungary, Poland and Czechoslavakia found that out when they tried to rebel. If Hanoi gets worried about domestic unrest, you can bet your ass they'll call Uncle Ivan for help.''

"But the Soviets have overextended themselves,'' Trang Nih declared. "They've been conducting campaigns in Central America and Africa—along with their Cuban allies. They've also been busy with a war in Afghanistan. International Communism is having some problems these days. There is growing resistance to it in eight different countries—including Vietnam.''

"Sorry, Trang Nih,'' O'Neal said, shaking his head. "I'm afraid I'm not convinced Vietnam is ripe for revolution. You freedom fighters have a lot of guts and I certainly don't want to dash any dreams of liberation, but your goals are long range, not immediate.''

"Of course,'' the freedom fighter agreed. "But if present trends continue in Vietnam, if the Communists continue to ruin the economy, fail to improve living conditions for the people—they are much worse than they were under twenty years ago—and commit inexcusable atrocities such as the genocide of more than three million Cambodians—then we'll be able to lead a successful revolt against them.''

"From within or from outside the country?'' Steve Caine asked, his eyes fixed on Trang Nih's face as if trying to read his expression.

"Both,'' Trang Nih confirmed. "There are hundreds of thousands of Vietnamese, Loatian, and Cambodian refugees in the United States and Western Europe and other countries. We've been recruiting personnel for some time. And we'll continue to do so. They are patriots who want to return to their country and overthrow the tyrants to establish a representative government similar to the United States.''

"Sounds nice,'' Fanelli commented. "But you might

recall that a lot of folks fought a war which lasted twenty years trying to keep the Communists from seizing power in Vietnam. Almost nine million Americans went to Southeast Asia—fighting or supporting others in their fight. More than two hundred and eleven thousand were casualties. What makes you think it'll work any better this time?"

"Hey, America never declared war in Vietnam," Wentworth reminded Fanelli. "If Washington had let us take the gloves off, we would have won. That 'police action' nonsense was absurd."

"All the Americans and all of my people who died in the war," Trang Nih shook his head sadly. "Wouldn't you like to see that their sacrifices were not in vain?"

"The war's been over for more than a decade, Trang Nih," O'Neal declared. "We were all casualties one way or the other."

"You can say that again, man," the black chopper pilot remarked. "I was in the Marine Corps over in 'Nam. Where I learned to fly a whirlybird. Shot down three times. How many chopper pilots you know are still alive after bein' shot down three fuckin' times?"

"Didn't catch your name," Fanelli said with a smile.

"Didn't throw it," the black guy replied. "But the name's Franklin T. Willis. Anyway, like I was sayin' about being casualties, I got shot down all those times. Got me two purple hearts and some other uniform trimmings and finally I got to the World. That's when I really found out I was a casualty."

"Are you part of Trang Nih's outfit?" Wentworth asked.

"Me?" Willis laughed. "Hell no. I just work for a little outfit here in Washington. Fly supplies out to folks in the wilderness. And, every once in a while, I do a little work for our mutual friend in the CIA. St. Laurent pays me under the table and I fly somebody or something from one place to another for the Company. I get the money, I don't ask questions—and I keep my mouth shut.''

"Well, Trang Nih,'' O'Neal began drawing the last puff from his cigarette before crushing it in an ashtray. "You know what we do for a living, right?''

"You're professional mercenaries,'' the freedom fighter said with a nod. "But we know you're more than that. The Hard Corps was something of a legend in Vietnam. I heard NVA officers had nightmares about you gentlemen. Maybe they still do.''

"That makes us even,'' O'Neal said with a shrug. "We still have nightmares about the NVA. Look, Trang Nih, regardless of how good we may or may not be, four mercenaries aren't going to make a helluva lot of difference.''

"Naturally,'' the Vietnamese confirmed. "If we were talking about flying to Southeast Asia tonight and trying to launch a revolution. As I said before, we're recruiting thousands of refugees and we plan to recruit others as well. Vietnam veterans and professional mercenaries will be at the head of the list. Since you're the best, you're at the very top.''

McShayne placed two tea pots and a pot of coffee on the table. He pulled up a chair and sat ass-backwards, folding his arms on the backrest and leaning his jaw on a brawny forearm. Fanelli hauled over a rack of cups and everyone helped themselves to the hot drinks.

"You know,'' the senior NCO began. "If you guys are planning a mission that's maybe five years from now, you're kinda jumpin' the gun trying to recruit people now. What's the rush?''

"The rush is because we need qualified people to keep recruiting new personnel,'' Trang Nih answered. "And, most important of all, to train those recruits so we can fight the NVA and win.''

''They're not the North Vietnamese Army anymore,'' Wentworth commented. ''North and South Vietnam are now the Socialist Republic of Vietnam.''

''They will always be the NVA to me,'' Trang Nih replied. ''And what we need are the men who were most efficient at fighting the NVA and the Viet Cong. We need the Hard Corps. You are the perfect instructors to teach our revolutionaries how to fight and win in Vietnam. Hopefully, you'll also be able to command at least a division of special forces personnel when the revolution actually takes place.''

''Intriguing,'' O'Neal admitted. ''But you must realize we have other commitments. I don't know how often we could train your personnel.''

''If it is a question of money,'' Qui Nhung began. ''You'll be paid what we can afford, and, after the revolution, you'll receive a very large bonus from the treasury.''

''Money isn't really the problem,'' O'Neal assured him. ''You see, any of us could have stayed in the army and worked as instructors. None of us wanted to do that. We're combat soldiers and field commanders. Not teachers.''

''Maybe we can do it between missions,'' Caine suggested.

''I guess we can consider . . .'' Wentworth began.

The mercenary's remark was interrupted by an unexpected explosion outside the mess hall. The four members of the Hard Corps immediately jumped from their seats. Fanelli and Wentworth grabbed their M-16's. The seven Asians, McShayne, and Willis followed their example.

''Looks like it came from the 'copter pad,'' Fanelli

announced, gazing out a window at the column of smoke that rose in the distance.

"Oh, shit!" Willis hissed through clenched teeth. "You mean my goddamn chopper blew up?"

"We'll know that when we get a better look," O'Neal answered. "Steve, go get your rifle. Top, check the monitors. See if security's been violated."

"Right," McShayne answered. "Left my M-16 in the orderly room anyway."

"The rest of you come with me," the Hard Corps commander instructed. "And keep your eyes open . . . just in case."

CHAPTER 5

FRANKLIN WILLIS' FEARS proved accurate. His Bell helicopter had been torn apart. Chunks of metal and flaming debris were scattered across the airstrip. Joe Fanelli dashed to a hanger and grabbed a pair of fire extinguishers. He hurried from the hangar and thrust one extinguisher into the hands of the closest Asian bodyguard. Willis balled his fists in hopeless rage and uttered a string of profanities.

"What happened?" Psar Phumi asked in a confused voice.

"Looks like someone put a bomb on board," Qui Nhung answered, drawing his 9mm Smith & Wesson autoloader from shoulder leather.

"Put that thing away," O'Neal told him. "Wait until you've got somebody to shoot at."

Fanelli and the Asian he'd selected for the task hastily put out the fires burning amid the wreckage. Wentworth checked the hangar to make certain no one was hiding inside, waiting to ambush them while they were distracted by the flaming debris. He found no one.

"Let the wreckage cool for a few minutes," Fanelli ordered the others. "Don't touch *anything* until I get a chance to look for more explosives and detonating devices."

"Do you think there will be anything left?" Psar Phumi asked, staring at the charred ruins.

"You'd be surprised," Fanelli answered. "Explosions tend to blast force outward. Frequently, the wiring, casing, even paper wrappings will still be recognizable after an explosion."

"I am familiar with demolitions," Qui Nhung stated. "Perhaps I could help . . ."

"No thanks," Fanelli answered. "Just stay away from the wreckage. I'm going to check our 'copters to make sure nobody planted anything in them."

"I can still help . . ." Qui Nhung began. He suddenly frowned. "Just a minute. You think one of *us* planted the bomb, do you?"

"That's a strong possibility," Wentworth said in a hard voice. His stern gaze shifted from Qui Nhung to the other Asians.

"Why would anyone do such a thing?" Psar Phumi asked. The Cambodian turned to Trang Nih for an answer.

"Good question," O'Neal said with a nod. "You have any answers for us, Trang Nih?"

"I have enemies," Trang Nih confessed. "Don't you?"

"Lots of them," O'Neal confirmed. "But your chopper was the one that blew up. If Joe doesn't find any bombs planted in our 'copters, that'll be pretty good evidence that you guys were the target."

"And one of your own people is responsible," Wentworth added.

"Not their goddamn chopper," Willis complained bitterly. "That eggbeater was my responsibility. Sure we had insurance on the sucker, but my ass is gonna be hangin' out in the wind when my boss finds out what happened."

"Tell Saintly you need a new job," O'Neal told him. "He'll get you set up somewhere else. Might even try to get you to join the CIA."

"Sure," Willis muttered. "Well, what are we gonna do now? Hang around here until you guys decide to fly us outta here?"

"Something like that," O'Neal replied. "Let's go back to the mess. I want to check with my first sergeant about our security."

"In other words," Qui Nhung began. "You want us away from the helicopter pad."

"I want you guys where I can keep an eye on you," the Hard Corps commander admitted. "At least until we've got some answers."

O'Neal and Wentworth walked behind the others as they escorted them back to the mess hall. James Wentworth III sighed and shook his head. An orderly, highly disciplined man, he did not appreciate unexpected mysteries.

"Any idea what the hell's going on?" he whispered to O'Neal.

"I'm not sure," the commander said softly. "But my instincts tell me our guests know more than they're telling us so far. After we get these guys in the building, I want you to head back to the airstrip and stay with Fanelli in case he needs help. Caine can help me watch over the visitors."

"Right," Wentworth agreed with a nod.

"You can go now if you want," a familiar voice whispered behind the two men.

"Jesus," O'Neal hissed through clenched teeth, startled by Caine's sudden appearance. "You think you're a fuckin' Apache or something?"

"Something," Caine said with a shrug. "I got my rifle and headed for the choppers, but you were all heading back to the barracks area so I just tagged along . . ."

"Keep sneaking around like that and one of these days one of us is going to shoot you," Wentworth growled.

"Just thought I should keep a low profile until I knew what was going on," Caine explained. "Besides, I don't trust our visitors. Didn't want to announce my presence to them at the airstrip—just in case the saboteur tried something."

"We don't know for certain that one of them is a saboteur," Wentworth replied.

"You think that 'copter exploded from spontaneous combustion?" Caine asked dryly. "Somebody sabotaged that bird and we all know it."

"We're ninety-five percent sure," O'Neal said. "The big question I want answered is: Why?"

"How about: Who?" Wentworth added.

"Right now 'why' is more important," O'Neal replied. "If it is sabotage, it means somebody wants to keep our guests from leaving the compound. Which means whatever's going on, we're in the middle it whether we want to be or not."

"Wonderful," Wentworth muttered. "They show up uninvited and deliver a potentially dangerous situation right in our laps."

"Dangerous situations are our profession," Caine reminded him. "We're mercenary soldiers, remember?"

"That means we're supposed to get paid for what we do," Wentworth explained. "I'd better go check on Fanelli."

"Fill him in on what we've been talking about," O'Neal instructed.

"I just hope he finds something to help us figure this mess out," Wentworth remarked, as he headed for the airstrip.

Twenty minutes later, Fanelli and Wentworth joined the others at the mess hall. Wentworth's wish that Fanelli would discover some sort of evidence from the 'copter wreckage had been fulfilled, but the former Special Forces lieutenant could have been happier about the news.

"I found these scattered among the debris," Fanelli reported to the others as he placed a cloth rag on the table.

He unfolded it to display two bits of plastic with numbers stamped on them and a small chunk of metal with wire threads attached. Qui Nhung and a couple others nodded, recognizing the significance of this discovery.

"What you're looking at is part of the dial to a timing mechanism and a portion of a detonator with wire filaments," Fanelli explained, taking a pack of cigarettes from his pocket. "In other words, there was a time-bomb on board. Probably very small, but loaded with a powerful explosive—like C-4."

"Neither of our 'copters had been tampered with," Wentworth added. "So it's official. One of you gentlemen sabotaged that chopper."

"What the fuck for?" Willis wondered aloud. "What's the motive, man? Why blow up my chopper?"

73

"Well, Trang Nih?" O'Neal inquired. "You know any reason somebody would want to keep you and your people here? Maybe there's a meeting you need to attend, or a flight somewhere, and your chopper was sabotaged to delay you."

"No," the Vietnamese freedom fighter assured him. "Nothing like that. I'm afraid someone destroyed our transportation because they want to trap us here in order to close the jaws of a trap—and kill us. Unfortunately, you and all of your men will probably die with us."

"Son of a bitch," McShayne groaned. "Did you know somebody was after you and didn't bother to tell us about it?"

"I hoped we'd thrown him off our trail in California," Trang Nih answered. "Temporarily, of course. He always finds his quarry eventually."

"He?" Caine inquired, noticing Trang Nih seemed to be referring to a particular individual.

"Captain Vinh," the Vietnamese replied grimly.

The wail of a siren erupted within the compound. O'Neal suddenly drew his .45 Colt and aimed it in the general direction of the Asians. The other members of the Hard Corps followed his example, pointing their M-16's at the startled visitors.

"What is the meaning of this?" Trang Nih demanded.

"You get up from your chair and move away from the others," O'Neal instructed. "You too, Willis. The rest of you stay in your seats, take your guns out very slowly and put them on the table."

"I must insist that you explain . . . ." Trang Nih began.

"The siren means somebody penetrated the compound from the outside," McShayne stated as he headed for the door. "With any luck, they should be on the security monitor any second now."

"Go with Top," O'Neal ordered the rest of the Hard Corps. "You take care of the intruders. I'll look after our suspects."

"Suspects?" Qui Nhung glared at O'Neal, but he placed his S&W autoloader on the table.

"You heard right," O'Neal replied. "Somebody give Willis a '16 before you leave."

"Here," Wentworth declared, tossing his rifle to the black chopper pilot. "I've got plenty of rifles. Here's an extra magazine for it."

"Shit," Willis rasped, catching the long-curved 40-round mag. "What do you want me to do with this?"

"For now," O'Neal replied. "You're going to help me with the prisoners. We're gonna put 'em against a wall, spread-eagle, frisk 'em for weapons and lock them in the stockade."

"Fuck you," Willis replied. "I'm not in the Marines anymore."

"You just got drafted, fella," O'Neal said sharply. "I don't have time to argue. Just do what I tell you, Willis. Your ass is on the line along with the rest of us."

"You have no right to do this!" Psar Phumi protested.

"Right and wrong are very vague terms on a battlefield, fella," O'Neal told him. "One of you six is an enemy agent. Maybe more than one of you. Until I know which person or persons is working for the other side, I'm going to have to keep you *all* locked up."

"You will not put me in a cage!" Qui Nhung snapped.

"If you don't go into a cell, I'll have to kill you," O'Neal warned. "Maybe you're innocent—but I'm not going to risk having a spy running around here when our installation is under siege.''

"I am sworn to protect Trang Nih," Qui Nhung insisted.

"We all are sworn to defend him and the cause," Chinh added. The bodyguard glanced down at the .357 Magnum he had placed on the table, obviously considering whether to reach for it or not.

"Don't try it, man," Willis warned, gesturing at Chinh with the barrel of his M-16. "I'll blow you away if I gotta."

"If you men are really interested in protecting Trang Nih," O'Neal declared, "then you'll understand why we have to do this."

"Xin ong lam on," Trang Nih began. "Please. Do as Captain O'Neal tells you."

Wentworth, Fanelli, and Caine had followed McShayne to the head shed. The first sergeant switched off the sirens and checked the monitors. Infrared cameras detected the intruders. Several men dressed in camouflage uniforms were moving through the forest. All carried weapons with silencers attached.

"They're coming from the east," McShayne announced, checking the monitor location. "Looks like there's at least a dozen of 'em. I switched on the receiver for the microphone transmitters in the area. Listen."

McShayne turned up the volume. Only a slight rustle of cloth and faint footsteps were heard over the receiver.

"They move well," Caine said with a nod of approval. He admired skill and respected it, even among enemies. "Whoever Captain Vinh is, he's brought along some well-trained jungle fighters."

"Yeah," Fanelli agreed. "And they're packing plenty of firepower. Christ, look at that arsenal! CAR-15's,

Uzis, MAC-10's. Figure it's all full auto or civilian semiauto models?"

"Better assume everything's full auto," Wentworth stated. "You can bet they got those weapons from black market arms dealers, not from a local gun shop. Probably got the silencers from the same source."

"They're considerate killers," Fanelli snorted. "Don't wanna wake the neighbors."

"They're not the only ones who don't want to attract attention," Wentworth declared. "We don't need any hassles from the cops either. If we start shooting away with automatic weapons, some camper or forest ranger is gonna hear it."

"Nobody seemed to notice when that 'copter blew up," Fanelli said with a shrug. "This place is supposed to be off in the boonies. That's why we took it."

"Somebody could have heard the explosion and thought it was just a mining company or a timber outfit doing some blasting," McShayne remarked. "But the sun's setting now. If anybody hears shots or explosions after dark, they're gonna get curious, fellas."

"That could be to our advantage," Caine smiled.

"Yeah," Wentworth agreed. "Let's get silencers for our guns and bring along our favorite toys that are already silent and lethal. That shouldn't be a problem for you, Steve."

"Of course not," Caine declared, patting the survival knife in a belt sheath on his hip. "I'm never without it."

"We'd better get to work fast or those fuckers are gonna be knocking on the door while we're still talking about them," Fanelli remarked.

"I already said 'let's get the silencers'," Wentworth repeated, rolling his eyes toward the ceiling. "Come on."

"Watch your ass out there," McShayne urged as the

three Hard Corps mercs left the head shed. "Whoever these jokers are they're . . ."

He glanced at the monitors. The east section screen had gone blank. The enemy had spotted the camera and neutralized it.

Twilight was gradually turning into night as Wentworth, Caine, and Fanelli crept through the forest toward the approaching team of invaders. Fanelli and Caine had attached full barrel Sconic noise-suppressors on their M-16 rifles. Wentworth had selected a rifle better-suited for sniping—a Heckler & Koch G3SG/1, with a silencer and a Starlite nightscope mounted on the frame. Caine brought his bamboo bow with a quiver of arrows. Wentworth had left his swagger-stick in his quarters, but carried an even more unusual weapon for a modern American soldier. The *wakazashi*, or samurai short sword, was thrust in his utility belt. Fanelli glanced down at the sword and shook his head.

"You'd better quit watchin' so many Toshiro Mifune flicks," he whispered to Wentworth.

The lieutenant glared at Fanelli and held an index finger to his lips, urging him to be quiet, even though the enemy was still at least four hundred meters from their position. The invaders lurked somewhere among the trees and bushes, blending into the environment like human chameleons.

If they advanced, the well-concealed enemy would almost certainly see them and attack. The odds were at least four against one—in favor of the invaders. The Hard Corps trio waited for the enemy to come to them, but the invaders seemed to be taking their time about it—unless they were creeping through the forest so skillfully the Hard Corps hadn't detected their approach.

"Why don't we draw 'em out with the Recruiter?" Fanelli inquired, his voice barely audible as his lips nearly touched Wentworth's ear.

The lieutenant smiled and nodded in approval. "The Recruiter" was a department store mannequin mounted behind some bushes about two hundred meters from their present position. The dummy was clad in green uniform and matching baseball cap with a silver eagle pinned above the brim. They called the dummy "the Recruiter" because of the broad smile on its plastic features. It reminded them of a bullshit artist army recruiter, the type that grins like an idiot while he tells you a pack of lies about how much fun it'll be to enlist.

There were actually five "Recruiters" set up in the compound forest. Each contained a radio receiver with a powerful loud speaker installed in its hollow torso. The dummy at the east side wore the insignia of a full-bird colonel because Fanelli had pinned the rank on the mannequin's cap. He had explained that this was "in honor of one of my old battalion commanders—a real dummy."

Wentworth took a radio transceiver from his belt and adjusted the frequency for the Recruiter. He pressed the transmit button and spoke softly into the mouthpiece. His voice was picked up by "Colonel Recruiter's" receiver and amplified ten times louder to bellow from the loud speaker.

"You are trespassing on private property!" the voice boomed. "Either leave immediately, or advance and be recognized!"

The enemy immediately responded. Rasping automatic fire from silencer equipped weapons blasted into the bush and smashed "Colonel Recruiter's" plastic chest. The mannequin's head popped from the cracked torso and the broken dummy collapsed.

The sound suppressors also helped conceal the muzzle flash of the invaders' weapons, but the shots still betrayed their positions to the Hard Corps. Wentworth peered through the Starlite scope of his H&K rifle. He located the head and shoulders of an enemy gunman.

Wentworth triggered a single round. The silenced rifle coughed and a 7.62mm NATO slug crashed into the forehead of an invader. The man went down, dead before he heard the shot that killed him.

But the others heard it, and saw the muzzle flash of Wentworth's weapon. They opened fire, but the Hard Corps officer had already rolled from his original position. Enemy bullets tore at bushes and burrowed into the ground, but none came close to James Wentworth III.

He adopted a prone stance, dug his toes into the ground for a firm anchor and sighted onto another enemy trooper via the Starlite scope. He fired his G3SG/1 again, blasting a high velocity round through the side of an opponent's skull. Wentworth did not waste time watching the guy fall. He immediately started to roll to a new position.

A column of bullets ripped into the earth inches from his right elbow before he could complete the move. *Shit,* he thought. They were good, whoever they were. Sons of bitches had already figured out what Wentworth had done before. He nearly rolled right into the line of fire. Another salvo of slugs tore at the ground to his left. Wentworth decided on a different tactic. He low-crawled forward, shifting the position of the sword in his belt, and carrying the H&K across the crooks of his elbows. He kept his head low and his ass down as he slithered for the cover of a thick tree trunk.

High velocity lead hail streaked above him. The enemy was raking the area with at least two dozen rounds, trying to take out the Hard Corps sniper. Wentworth's cap was violently tugged from his head, as a bullet came close to splitting open his skull.

Wentworth hugged the ground. He breathed deeply, through his nose and out his mouth. Air whistled from his tightly clenched teeth. His body was trembling. He concentrated on Samurai *zazen* breathing. Wentworth breathed deep, feeling his diaphragm expand. More bullets slashed all around. Wentworth tried to keep breathing to calm himself. The air smelled as if it had been scorched.

Three invaders were firing at Wentworth with automatic rifles. They were so preoccupied that they failed to notice Joe Fanelli slip across a clearing to a clump of bushes. Suddenly, the tough guy from Jersey leaped up and opened fire with his M-16. The full-barrel silencer reduced the noise of his weapon as he triggered two quick three-round bursts.

A trio of 5.56mm slugs took out one opponent, drilling into his chest to blast apart vital organs. Another man took two bullets in the face. He dropped his weapon, yelped once, and collapsed.

The third opponent returned fire. Fanelli had ducked behind the bush. Slugs punched through the flimsy shelter. Fanelli sprawled on his belly, his nose dug into the dirt. *Maybe this wasn't such a bitchin' idea after all*, he thought sourly. But, he had an idea that might allow him to turn the tables on the enemy gunman.

He pitched his rifle into plain view of the enemy. The invader suddenly held his fire. Fanelli uttered a loud groan, as if he'd been hit. Then he pulled his .45 Colt from a special holster, designed to accommodate the ten inch sound suppressor attached to the extended barrel of the pistol.

Another burst of automatic fire sliced through the

bush. Fanelli heard the whine of bullets among the branches above his head, as the enemy gunman's silenced weapon rasped harshly. Fanelli clenched his teeth and waited. He eased the safety catch of his Colt auto to the fire position. Fanelli gripped the butt with both hands and prayed his idea would work . . .

The shooting stopped. Fanelli peered between the stems of the bush, trying to find the gunman. A shape moved toward the bush. The invader was approaching from the left. He moved slowly, cautiously, believing Fanelli was either dead or wounded—but realizing a wounded man can be as dangerous as a whole one and far more desperate.

Fanelli didn't allow himself to think about what might go wrong. He had planned the action and realized the risks at the time. It was too late to change his mind. He had to play out his hand. Fanelli rolled to the right and thrust his pistol at the gunman. He triggered the Colt, squeezed off three rounds as fast as the mechanism of the semi-auto pistol allowed.

All three bullets struck the invader in the torso. Two big 185 grain semijacketed hollow-point slugs tore into the guy's lower intestine. He doubled up to catch the third bullet in the center of his chest. It shattered his sternum and drove bone shards into the man's heart and lungs. The gunman fell. His body twitched violently, fingers slipping away from the frame of his CAR-15. Fanelli crawled to the fallen figure and pulled the carbine beyond the dying man's reach.

The man's body trembled and lay still. Fanelli examined his opponent to be certain he was dead, and to learn more about the enemy. The guy had been Asian, probably Vietnamese or Laotian. His pockets revealed nothing except a cheap switchblade knife, a small first aid kit, some cigarettes, and two books of matches. He had no identification, good luck piece, or even money of any sort. His wristwatch was a cheap digital, worth about ten dollars.

His ammo pouches revealed two full magazines of 5.56mm ammo. The cartridges were American made—like everything else the guy carried. Fanelli frowned. Whoever was commanding the invaders knew his craft. His soldiers did not carry anything which could link them to any particular group or government. Unless the dead man's fingerprints were on file with the FBI or Interpol, it would be impossible to even confirm his nationality.

Whoever was running the show on the other side, the guy was very professional. He wouldn't be the type to make many mistakes.

Steve Caine peered down from the branches of a large spruce tree. Concealed by the leaves, he blended into the tree like an extra branch. The mercenary had mastered camouflage techniques with the Special Forces and during his years with the Katu. His face and hands were dyed with dark green paint. Leafy twigs were tied to his arms, shoulders, and cap to alter the human shape of his silhouette.

Because Caine was an expert in camouflage, he also knew how to find others who were trying to blend into the environment. A bush moved against the wind. Caine continued to watch. The bush moved again, still defying the wind and slowly approaching. Another bush moved slightly. Crickets and tree frogs stopped singing. Caine smiled with satisfaction. He had located his quarry.

The mercenary had placed his rifle and bow at fork of two branches next to his position. He selected the latter and slowly drew an arrow from his quiver, notching the arrow to the bowstring and waiting for the enemy to appear.

At last, two shapes materialized from the bush. Both men had tied twigs to their clothing in a manner similar to Caine's camouflage. One carried an Uzi submachine gun and the other held a MAC-10. Caine leaned back and raised his bow, drawing the arrow to his cheek. He aimed carefully and released the arrow.

The bowstring snapped forward and the arrow flew from the tree. It streaked like a guided missile and struck the closest gunman in the chest. The point pierced flesh and sank into the left ventricle of the guy's heart. Curare traveled swiftly through his bloodstream. The combination of poison and the deep puncture wound killed him in a matter of seconds.

The other gunman saw his comrade fall and the feathered arrow sticking out of his chest. But he could not see where the arrow had come from. A bow is as quiet as the best silenced firearm, and it does not produce a muzzle flash to betray the archer's location. The invader sung his MAC-10 toward the trees and dropped to one knee.

Caine fired another arrow. The enemy gunman had moved while the arrow was still in flight. Instead of striking the man's chest, the missile hit him in the left shoulder. The invader screamed in pain and anger. He raised his machinepistol and sprayed a salvo of 9mm rounds at the spruce tree. Caine swiftly slithered down from the branches as bullets slashed at the tree limbs.

The mercenary landed behind the trunk while the gunman advanced, still firing his MAC-10. Slugs struck the tree trunk, chipping chunks of bark. The sturdy shelter prevented bullets from reaching Caine, but the merc had left his rifle and bow among the branches. He still carried a .45 in a GI style shoulder holster rig, and his survival knife on his hip, but neither weapon was an even match for a machinepistol. Caine did not have a silencer for the Colt autoloader and he did not want to attract attention with an unmuffled gunshot.

However, he did not wish to be cut down, either. Caine reached for the pistol, but the shooting had stopped. The merc glanced around the edge of the trunk and saw his opponent had fallen to his knees and dropped the MAC-10. The man's eyes were glazed, the arrow still jutting from his shoulder.

The curare had taken effect. The gunman tumbled on his side, muscles rigid from the poisoned arrow. Caine approached, unsnapping the retaining strap to his knife and easing it from the sheath. The wounded, dying man saw Caine and tried to reach for the MAC-10. His muscles refused to respond. He slowly extended a hand toward the Ingram.

Caine stepped forward and shoved a boot into the gunman's chest, kicking him onto his back. The survival knife hopped from Caine's palm and he caught it in an overhand grip. The six inch blade jutted from the bottom of his fist as he dropped to one knee. His powerful arm swung, driving the sharpened steel deep into the invader's heart.

Blood squirted across his wrist and forearm. It felt like heated water. The gunman died quickly, already half-dead before the blade struck. Caine wiped some of the blood off his arm, using the dead man's trousers. He worked the handle of the knife like a stick shift to work the blade loose from lifeless flesh. The saw-tooth back hooked on a rib, but Caine twisted the knife and pulled hard. At last the blade snapped free, crimson dripping from the tip.

Caine calmly wiped the blood from the knife on the

dead man's shirt, slid it into the belt sheath, and returned to the tree to retrieve his bow and rifle. He had won—for now.

James Wentworth III remained at the base of the tree he had chosen for cover. Fanelli had taken out the three gunmen who had had him pinned down, but he stayed put, in case others came to assist their dead comrades. He glanced over his shoulder and checked his rear flank.

Two enemy invaders attacked. They were less than three meters away. One held a machete in a two-fisted grip, while his partner carried a CAR-15 with a bayonet.

Wentworth raised his H&K as the knifeman struck. The heavy blade of the machete struck the rifle barrel, deflecting the aim of Wentworth's weapon, although the gun barrel effectively blocked the blade. Wentworth thrust out a boot and rammed his heel between his opponent's thighs. The man groaned in agony and stumbled backward, clutching his balls with one hand and the machete with the other.

The Hard Corps officer rose as the man with the bayonet lunged. Wentworth blocked the thrust with the barrel of his H&K, but his opponent turned sharply and swung a fast butt stock. Wentworth raised his rifle to block the attack. The CAR-15 butt stock struck hard. The blow ripped the H&K from Wentworth's grasp.

Wentworth jumped back to avoid a diagonal bayonet slash. The invader immediately followed with a thrust aimed at Wentworth's belly. The merc's *wakazashi* hissed from its scabbard as O'Neal drew the sword and delivered a swift cross-body stroke. Steel sang as the sword struck the killer's bayonet.

Before his opponent could recover, Wentworth thrust both arms forward, plunging the tip of his sword into the hollow of the gunman's throat. Sharp steel pierced thin flesh, and punctured the man's windpipe. The killer's Asian features became a mask of horror and pain as he dropped his weapon and blood gushed from his punctured throat. Wentworth clamped a boot on the man's chest and yanked the *wakazashi* from his opponent's flesh.

The man crumbled to the ground, a fountain of scarlet ooze jetting from his torn throat. But the first attacker had recovered from being kicked in the balls enough to launch another assault. He saw the short sword in Wentworth's hands and the machete man smiled, his almond eyes narrowing as he nodded.

He adopted a fighting stance, similar to a kung fu horse stance, his feet a shoulder width apart. The invader held the machete in one hand at chest level, with his other poised like a claw near his hip. Wentworth gripped the hilt of his *wakazashi* in both hands and pointed the blade at his opponent.

The Asian killer attacked, slashing his machete in a rapid series of figure-eight cuts. Wentworth shuffled backward as he parried the jungle knife with deft strokes of his sword. Metal rang against metal as the Vietnamese invader tried again and again to cut or stab his opponent, but Wentworth's defense tactics were too swift and skilled.

Frustrated, the Asian struck out with the machete and launched a kick at Wentworth's groin. The mercenary was ready—he struck the flat of his enemy's blade with the sword and punted a boot to his opponent's shin to check the kick. Wentworth suddenly shoved, thrusting the handguard of his *wakzashi* into the other man's blade. The blow pushed the guy's machete upward.

Swiftly, Wentworth delivered a sideways cut across

his opponent's belly. The man doubled up, screamed, and staggered backward, blood oozing from the long gash at his stomach. Wentworth quickly stepped forward and slashed his sword across the side of his opponent's neck. The cut slit the Asian's jugular, severed the carotid artery, and sliced the thyroid cartilage. Blood poured across the man's shirt as he wilted to the ground and died.

Joe Fanelli had seen Wentworth in trouble, but he couldn't help. Another pair of invaders had spotted Fanelli, and opened fire with silenced Uzi submachine guns.

Bullets ripped into the treetrunk above Fanelli's head as he threw himself to the ground. He quickly crawled behind the base of the tree. Another volley tore clods of earth near his position. Fanelli fired back at them with his M-16. The assault rifle offered greater range than the short barreled Uzis, and Fanelli was more experienced with firing the '16 with a silencer than his opponents were with their weapons. If the Asian gunmen had been armed with Kalashnikov rifles, Fanelli would already be dead.

He nailed one opponent with two 5.56mm rounds. The man screamed and fell, but his comrade continued to fire at Fanelli's position. The Hard Corps merc responded with more M-16 fury. Suddenly, another string of muffled shots streaked into the remaining invader's position. Steve Caine had joined his partners and quickly assisted Fanelli. The pair bombarded the gunman with a deadly crossfire that pumped six or seven slugs into the bastard.

The silence that followed was eerie, with the sounds of combat replaced by grim silence, as if Death himself was there. The Grim Reaper had claimed eleven new recruits, none of them members of the Hard Corps.

"You okay?" Caine whispered as he slipped from the shadows next to Fanelli.

"You almost gave me a fuckin' heart attack," Fanelli started with a jump. "Wish you'd wear a bell around your neck or something."

"That's a brilliant idea for a combat situation," Caine replied dryly. "Looks like we won this round."

"You figure they'll send more?" Fanelli asked.

"Maybe," Caine answered with a shrug. "Or maybe the hit team was all of them. Almost a dozen men, all trained as commandos. It's possible that's all Captain Vinh sent to kill Trang Nih and his group."

"That'd be nice," Fanelli replied. He turned and saw Wentworth had returned his sword to its scabbard. "Looks like the lieutenant's okay."

Wentworth held up a hand, signaling he was all right, and headed toward Fanelli and Caine.

Suddenly, an object streaked across the sky. It spun like a top, plunged to earth, and exploded. Caine and Fanelli ducked low and hoped they'd survive the attack in one piece. Remarkably, the pair were struck by nothing more than a shower of loose dirt.

Then they saw Wentworth.

The Hard Corps second-in-command lay motionless on the ground. A streak of blood extended from his forehead to his chin. Caine examined Wentworth while Fanelli stood guard, his M-16 pointed in the direction the explosive projectile had come from. Caine ran two fingers along the side of Wentworth's neck.

"How bad was he hit?" Fanelli asked, scanning the forest for signs of the enemy.

"He's still alive," Caine replied. "Can't say much else. He's got a head wound and that's always bad. I don't want to move him, Joe. His back or neck could be injured too."

"We can't leave him here," Fanelli stated. "And we can't stay here. Not with those fuckers launching more grenades at us."

"You're right," Caine reluctantly agreed. "Let's get him back to base. I just hope we don't kill him in the process."

"Yeah," Fanelli replied, taking a radio transceiver from his belt. "I'd better let O'Neal know the score."

CHAPTER 6

JOHN MCSHAYNE WAS the first to receive Fanelli's radio signal. O'Neal had just entered the orderly room. The Hard Corps commander was now armed with an M-16 as well as his .45 sidearm. He also carried extra ammunition magazines, a first-aid kit, canteen and a two-way radio. He heard Fanelli's signal on his own transceiver the moment McShayne got the call.

"Is the Captain there, Top?" Fanelli's voice inquired.

"We're both here, Joe," O'Neal assured him. "We heard an explosion. What happened? Over."

"We engaged the enemy and took out a bunch of 'em," Fanelli replied. "I got four, Wentworth probably got three or four and I think Steve took out about the same. The enemy isn't advancing, but there are more of them out there. Guess they decided not to fuck around with us, 'cause one of 'em fired a blooper."

"A blooper?" O'Neal asked with surprise. A "blooper" is a nickname for an M-79 grenade launcher. The weapon resembles a sawed-off shotgun with a huge muzzle, but it fires 40mm grenades. "Are you sure about that? Over."

"Can't swear it," Fanelli replied. "But it was a grenade launcher, and from the looks of the explosion, I figure it was a 40mm shell. The enemy fired blind, so we didn't get a direct hit, but Lieutenant Wentworth is down."

"Dead?" O'Neal asked tensely.

"He's hurt," Fanelli answered. "But he's alive. Steve thinks he might have back or neck injuries, and he's got a head wound. Can't tell how serious it is. He's unconscious and we don't want to move him . . ."

"You've got no choice," O'Neal told him.

"That's what we figure too," Fanelli confirmed. "We've improvised a stretcher with a poncho and a couple solid tree limbs. About to return to home base. Over."

"Make it quick," O'Neal instructed. "The enemy might start shelling at any second. Over."

"Affirmative," Fanelli replied. "By the way, the enemy appear to be Southeast Asians. They aren't carrying any ID, but they're well-armed and well-trained. Pretty good in the bush, Captain. Just like the VC. Over."

"Sounds like old times again," O'Neal commented.

"You got it, Captain," Fanelli stated. "Sure felt like Vietnam all over again. Over."

"Over and out, soldier," O'Neal told him. "Haul ass."

Fanelli ended transmission.

"Jesus Christ," McShayne muttered. "What's goin' on?"

"You know those nightmares we have every so often about being back in 'Nam?" O'Neal replied. "Well, it looks like one of 'em has come true."

William O'Neal had been born in the rough-and-tumble world of southside Chicago on a bleak February night in 1948. His parents were second-generation Irish Americans, the offspring of hardworking folks who'd been raised on tales of how their grandparents had left the old country for a better life in America.

"The Statue of Liberty was the first thing your great-grandparents saw," Bill's father had told him. "They said she seemed to welcome them as she held up her torch of light, justice, and hope. They wept with joy when they saw her."

The O'Neals had a family tradition of traveling to New York to see the Statue of Liberty. Bill's father had called it "the American Mecca." It was a constant reminder of why the O'Neals had come to the United States with their dreams of freedom and hope.

Hope wasn't in plentiful supply in the Chicago slums, though. The neighborhood crime rate was alarming and no one ventured outside after dark unless he or she liked the idea of getting ripped off by street hoods—or unless that person packed a weapon. O'Neal's father did. A Walther P-38 pistol he had taken from a Nazi officer he killed in the World War II. Bill's mother worried about this because Chicago cops arrested anybody without a permit.

"I don't see the cops down here arrestin' hooligans for robbin' honest folks," Bill's father told her. "I see 'em in coffee shops eatin' doughnuts and doin' crowd control when the mayor has his parades and such. I don't see 'em doin' much about criminals. The hell with them and the hell with any law that tells me I can't protect myself and my family. The Constitution gives American citizens the right to keep and bear arms. That overrides any stupid laws the Chicago City Hall comes up with."

Bill's mother would remind her husband that the family would be in a terrible way if he got himself arrested and sent to jail because of that damn gun. The senior O'Neal would simply shrug and tell her not to worry. "This is America," he said. "They don't send people to jail because they want to protect themselves from hoodlums and killers."

His father's attitude had a strong influence on William O'Neal. He learned to love America for what the country stood for, although he frequently disapproved of what the government did. He also believed a man should be willing to fight for what he held dear—family, country, his way of life. Regardless of rules and regulations, self-preservation and protecting what he loved would always have top priority. He also learned to resent authority if it seemed to represent oppression instead of compassion.

In 1965, at the age of seventeen, William O'Neal announced that he had decided to enlist in the United States Army. He wanted to be part of an elite branch of the Special Forces known as the Green Berets. Bill's mother was upset, since American involvement in Vietnam had steadily increased that year. Twenty-three U.S. soldiers had been killed at Qui Nhon in February, when the Vietcong bombed a troop billets. The following month, a battalion of Marines had been sent to Da Nang. In May, the U.S. Army was sending in 173rd Airborne Brigade. The escalation was growing rapidly, and American military personnel were dying in alarming numbers. Mrs. O'Neal did not want her son to be among them.

"What are we doin' gettin' involved in a civil war over in some oriental country?" she had asked, voicing a question millions would ask—over and over again.

"We can't let the Communists grab up everything," Mr. O'Neal answered. "Those bastards are just like the Nazis. We should have taken care of Stalin after we finished off Hitler. Then we wouldn't have this mess."

"You don't want Bill to go to Vietnam, do you?" she demanded, horrified by the idea.

"The boy's a man now," he replied. "If we don't give him permission he'll simply resent us for seven more months and enlist when he turns eighteen. If the war goes on for another two years, they'll probably draft him anyway. Better he enlists and gets into a position that suits him."

"This is your fault, Sean," she snapped. "You never should have told him all those war stories. Now our son is going to go get himself killed . . ."

"It's his decision; he's a grown man," Sean O'Neal told his wife. "And I told him about the war because I knew he'd probably have to fight one too. We've had wars since the beginning of man's history, and we'll probably have 'em right up to the end. I wish it wasn't so, but I don't think it's gonna change. God forgive us all. I don't see *how* it can ever change."

"People could stop fighting," she pleaded. "Just stop fighting and live together in peace."

"That's a nice thought, Mom," young William said. "But there are always the Hitlers, Stalins, and Ho Chi Minhs, who won't let us do that. If we hadn't fought Hitler and stopped him in Europe we'd probably have Nazi stormtroopers in the streets of Chicago."

"You're really determined to do this, aren't you?" she sighed, tears welling in her eyes. "You're just a child. You don't know what you're doing."

"Yes, I do, Mom," William O'Neal insisted.

He would later find out how wrong he was.

William O'Neal got his wish. He enlisted into the army and struggled through Basic Combat Training and AIT (Advanced Individual Training), and went on to become a Green Beret. Growing up in a Chicago slum had made him tough and strong. He took on the challenge of rigorous training and excelled in everything from parachuting in "jump school" to communications and "Psy Ops"—psychological warfare.

O'Neal arrived in Vietnam in March of 1966, as part of the reinforcements rushed to 'Nam after the Communists captured a U.S. Special Forces camp in the A Shau Valley. The young soldier was excited by his first visit to Saigon. The capital of South Vietnam reminded O'Neal of a cross between New York's Chinatown and Tijuana. There were bars and pawnshops everywhere. Most of the Vietnamese traveled by foot or bicycle. A few had mopeds, but cars were rare. Most of the trucks were U.S. Army vehicles.

The new arrivals received an official briefing from a Special Forces captain. He warned them that casualties had been high, but 20,000 troops are being sent in to assist the 215,000 already stationed in 'Nam. The captain warned them about blackmarket dealing with Vietnamese civilians or troops. He told them not to mess around with drugs. The marijuana was supposedly stronger than any dope they smoked in the States, and heroin pushers were everywhere, thanks to the Golden Triangle narcotics syndicates. Finally, he warned them not to tell anything confidential to Vietnamese civilians, because the VC had spies and saboteurs within Saigon. And they were not to say "one fuckin' word" to the United Press International—or anybody else connected with the news media.

As Green Berets, they received a number of briefings about their mission in Vietnam. After three days they were allowed to leave the holding compound, to enjoy some nightlife in Saigon. O'Neal and a couple other 'cruits wandered into a bar and ordered some local beer. A drunken sergeant seated at a nearby table pointed at them and burst out laughing.

"Lookee here," he chuckled. "Brand new Green Berets. Bet you boys figure you're gonna win the fuckin' war all by yourselves, don't you?"

"We didn't come here to lose," a kid named Jenner replied, glaring at the NCO.

"Ooh, you're so big and so bad," the sergeant snickered. "Wait 'til you get in the bush, sonny. Charlie's gonna have you pissin' your pants and cryin' for your mommy."

"Oh, yeah?" Jenner started to rise from his chair.

"Sit down," O'Neal told him. "He just trying to get your goat. Besides, he outranks you. Swing on him and you'll spend your enlistment in stockades."

"What's the matter, kid?" the NCO asked O'Neal. "Don't you like a good fight?"

"Didn't come here to fight each other, Sergeant," O'Neal replied. "How long you been here?"

"Forever, kid," the sergeant's eyes stared at O'Neal, but he seemed to be looking elsewhere. "Fuckin' forever . . ."

"Come on, Pete," the sergeant's companion urged. "Let's get back to the barracks or go get laid or somethin'."

"I gotta take a piss," the NCO muttered as he rose from his chair and staggered across the room.

"Hey, kinda ignore his behavior," the guy's companion, a staff sergeant, told O'Neal's group. "He was at Da Nang three months ago during the big campaign, almost from start to finish."

"Christ," O'Neal rasped. "Heard it lasted almost a month."

"Yeah," the SSG said with a nod. "Poor bastard was with three of his buddies when a grenade hit 'em. Wiped out his pals. He was drenched with their blood and brains. Tried to retreat, but something tangled up his feet and tripped him. It was a gob of his buddies' intestines. He said it felt like slimy rope."

"God," O'Neal whispered. "No wonder he's gettin' fucked up with booze."

"Everybody here gets fucked up one way or the other," the staff sergeant warned. "You'll find out yourselves before you got back to the world."

"The world?" Jenner inquired. "Where are we now? Mars?"

"The world is the United States of America, kid," the SSG told him. "And I'm not so sure Vietnam is part of planet Earth. If it is, we oughta give it to the fuckin' Martians."

"Hey-llo, GI," a woman announced as she moved to O'Neal's table. "You want party? Give you good fuck. Yes?"

"All three of us?" Baker, the third guy in O'Neal's group, inquired. "We're horny young guys who get big American hard-ons. Sure you can handle it?"

She laughed. The woman was young, probably no older than sixteen, but her eyes were flinty and lines of stress in her face revealed that her life had aged her beyond her years. Even her laughter sounded bitter.

"I handle it good," she assured him. "Go get friends. I give you all fuck if you pay good."

"I'll pass," O'Neal stated. "You guys should too."

"Hell with you," Jenner snorted. "I haven't been laid for almost a month. God knows when we'll get another chance."

O'Neal opened his mouth, but decided Jenner wouldn't listen. Damn fool must have forgotten about "black syphilis." O'Neal had heard stories about it ever since Basic. They said black syphilis was a type of incurable venereal disease that was all over Southeast Asia. Penicillin didn't help the victims. The effects were even worse than other forms of VD. Your balls would swell up like grapefruits and your cock would turn black and rot off.

There were stories about special "VD leper colonies" for American servicemen with black syphilis. The military listed them as MIA, but they were really hidden away at some remote, secret spot, where doctors vainly tried to treat the terrible, mysterious disease. The victims soon had to be locked in padded rooms. The VD ate up their brains like rotten cabbage and drove them nuts before they finally died.

"You guys do what you want," O'Neal told him. "But I'm not gonna play Russian Roulette with my dick."

Forty-three hours later, O'Neal was cursing himself for his decision in the bar as he and thirteen other soldiers were being transported to a base near Hau Bon. The vehicle was part of a small convoy of four trucks which was attacked by a Vietcong ambush.

The lead vehicle was taken out by three hand-grenades. The VC hurled the explosives from the cover of roadside trees. The truck exploded in a mini-nova of flame and flying metal shards. Everyone in the first vehicle was killed by the blast.

The other three trucks came to an abrupt halt. Troops scrambled from the rigs as the enemy opened fire with AK-47 assault and Type 56 rifles—a Chinese version of the Soviet AK. A hailstorm of 7.62mm slugs ripped into the Americans. O'Neal and Jenner jumped from the back of their vehicle together, and dropped to the ground. Jenner's body trembled violently, his feet kicking at the ground as he lay on his back. The guy was acting as if he was nuts.

"Shit, man . . ." O'Neal began as he turned to face Jenner.

He was about to tell the other man to stop kicking dirt on him, but he saw the reason for Jenner's convulsions. The short shaft of a crossbow shaft jutted from Jenner's throat. Blood sprayed from the deep wound as the soldier's body thrashed wildly for a second or two, and then lay still.

O'Neal's stomach knotted. His mouth was bone-dry, and a cold shiver slithered up his spine. The young soldier tried to repress his fear, his mind racing for a decision about what action to take.

To remain by the truck would be suicide. The enemy would chew them to bits with full-auto slugs or blast them to pieces with grenades. That left only one alternative. He would have to head right for the enemy. It could mean racing straight into death, but it was still better than lying on his belly, waiting for the enemy to pick him off.

That's when O'Neal thought about the whore in the bar. He was eighteen and still a virgin. The opportunity to change that had presented itself and he had refused to take advantage. Worrying about veneral disease seemed pretty damn stupid as he crouched beneath a stream of sizzling bullets. In the blink of an eye, he could be dead.

O'Neal didn't want to die a virgin. He wasn't a goddamn priest. He wasn't even a practicing Catholic—despite what it said on his dogtag. If a chaplain showed up to give him last rites, O'Neal would have told him to shut the fuck up and get him a woman before he died. Song lyrics about how a boy became a man after he got laid nagged at him. He wanted to cry. These VC fuckers wanted to kill him before he reached manhood . . .

"No!" O'Neal shrieked as he hurled an M-26 fragmentation grenade into the bush.

He hadn't even realized he'd taken the grenade from his belt. He didn't remember pulling the pin. Yet, the grenade exploded among the green pine trees and elephant grass. Voices cried out in agony. O'Neal leaped to his feet and charged into the bush, M-16 held ready.

Two VC lay dead from the grenade blast. Another had been severely wounded by shrapnel from the fragger. Two more figures in black pajamas had ducked when they heard the explosion, although neither had been injured when the M-26 went off. They raised their heads and stared into the muzzle of O'Neal's rifle.

"Fuckin' bastards!" the Green Beret snarled as he triggered the '16.

A line of 5.56mm slugs caught one Cong across the middle of his face. His cheekbones caved in, and his nose vanished in a spray of crimson flesh. The other Charlie managed only to raise his T-56 blaster before O'Neal shot him through the forehead. His skull blossomed into a hideous halo of blood and spattered brains.

The VC who had been wounded by the grenade tried to crawl to his assault rifle, but O'Neal leaped forward and stomped on the man's head, driving both heels into the side of his skull. Bone cracked. An eyeball popped from a socket and hung across the bridge of the Charlie's nose. O'Neal barely glanced at the man's corpse, as he continued to stalk the enemy.

Two other GI's had chosen the same plan of action as O'Neal. They had charged into the bush, but unlike O'Neal, they failed to clear a path by lobbing in a grenade. The pair ran right into the path of a volley of Vietcong bullets. The Americans fell. Charlie raked the soldiers with another burst of T-56 rounds.

"Son of a bitch!" O'Neal hissed as he came upon the scene. He raised his M-16 and blasted the VC with six rounds in the chest.

Charlie fell and O'Neal hurried to the bodies of the two Americans. He knelt beside the first soldier and stared down at the man's face—or what was left of it. His features had been crushed by the enemy's bullets. Brains and blood oozed from his shattered skull.

O'Neal immediately moved to the next man. The GI uttered an ugly rasping sound as he lay on his back. His fingers clawed earth and his face was contorted in agony. Purple and pink intestines bulged from his bullet-torn abdomen. He gazed up at O'Neal, eyes pleading for help. His mouth opened, but his lips merely trembled when he tried to speak.

"Just relax." O'Neal managed a smile. "Must hurt like a bitch, but you're not hurt as bad as you think you are. You're gonna be fine. Just lie still and let me . . ."

An Asian face appeared from behind a tree trunk. The Cong raised a MAT-49 submachine gun. The chattergun was a French weapon. Ho Chi Minh's followers had seized hundreds of MAT-49s during more than a decade of war with French occupation forces in Indochina. The Communists usually modified their MAT subguns to handle Soviet 7.62mm cartridges, instead of 9mm parabellums.

O'Neal fired his M-16, burning away the last few rounds from the magazine. The Viet Cong ducked behind the tree trunk. Slugs chewed into the tree bark, but Charlie remained untouched. The Cong cautiously peeked around the edge of the trunk. He saw O'Neal's empty M-16 hit the ground. The Green Beret had tossed it into plain view to be certain his opponent saw it.

"Chieu hoi!" O'Neal called out. At the time he was not certain what the expression meant, but he thought it was the Vietnamese equivalent of "I surrender."

O'Neal would later learn that the correct translation of *"chieu hoi"* was "open arms." The United States military offered an "open arms" policy to VC or NVA who willingly surrendered. These defectors were not punished, and many became scouts for the Americans. Whether or not the Vietcong behind the tree was familiar with this policy, he clearly understood that O'Neal had announced he wanted to surrender.

The man's lip curled with contempt for the American coward as he stepped from the tree and prepared to gun down O'Neal. A three round burst hit him chest and throat. The astonished VC collapsed, dying rapidly from the lethal volley.

O'Neal had gathered up the wounded GI's M-16 before tossing away his own weapon. He placed the rifle against his knee and reached for his first aid kit. O'Neal's mind raced over his training in battlefield first aid. He recalled the need to protect a gunshot victim from infection. Trying to dig the bullets out of the guy was too dangerous for an inexperienced soldier to attempt. O'Neal picked up the man's leaking guts and placed them on his abdomen.

"Take it easy, man," O'Neal told the wounded man. "Just hang in there."

He covered the wound with a field dressing. O'Neal propped the wounded man's feet on his helmet. He removed the GI's poncho from a field pack, and folded it into a pillow for the injured soldier, using his own poncho to cover the guy.

O'Neal heard shooting beyond his position, but he elected to stay put. If he ventured into the bush, his own men might shoot him down. Besides, he didn't want to leave the wounded GI. Suddenly, the shooting stopped. O'Neal saw two shapes appear among the trees. He held his fire, waiting to be certain whether the men were friends or foes.

"Holy shit!" a sergeant with a deep Alabama accent exclaimed. "Looks like you've been busy here."

"This guy's hurt bad, Sarge," O'Neal replied.

"Medic!" The NCO cried.

Moments later, a medic joined O'Neal. He examined the wounded man and nodded his approval for how O'Neal had taken precautions in case the poor guy started to go into shock.

"You give him any water, soldier?" the medic inquired.

"No," O'Neal replied. "I didn't think I was supposed to when a person has a belly wound."

"That's right," the medic confirmed. "Congratulations soldier. I think you probably saved this kid's life."

O'Neal smiled faintly and took a cigarette from his pocket. Only then did his hands shake. He staggered away from the medic and the wounded soldier. O'Neal fell to his knees and vomited in the grass.

William O'Neal made rank rapidly in 'Nam. His courage, skill, and ability to remain calm in a crisis soon earned him his sergeant's stripes. Less than a year passed before he was ordered to Saigon. The Army had decided he was ideal officer material. They wanted O'Neal to go to Officer Candidate School.

The slum kid from the Windy City had never thought of himself as officer material—and he wasn't sure he wanted to be an officer. Like most enlisted men, he had learned to regard officers as adversaries. "Us" and "them." Besides, O'Neal felt a certain resentment toward authority figures. The vast majority of young people do. Of course, he had already become a sergeant and thus commanded other men in the field.

The army gave him a weekend pass and a trip to Okinawa to think about the offer. O'Neal enjoyed the brief vacation from the tension and horror of the Vietnam war. He visited a few nightspots and slept in a hotel bed with clean sheets. Since he'd spent most of the last year in the bush, O'Neal had six month's pay to spend. He was smart enough to save about half of it, the rest spent in Okinawa. About a month's salary went to paying for hookers.

O'Neal had finally lost his virginity, although he was till very leery of Vietnamese hookers due to the stories of incurable veneral disease. Actually, he never learned for certain if black syphilis was real or just an exaggerated rumor. However, he'd never heard any tales of VD horror connected with Okinawa whores, so he humped away, without fear of getting anything that a shot of penicillin couldn't handle.

When the weekend was over, O'Neal was surprised to discover he was eager to get back to 'Nam, to return to the bush and the combat. It seemed insane. How could any man miss being in hell? But it was true. Maybe he felt needed in 'Nam. Maybe he simply didn't know what else he'd do with his life. Although he would have choked on the words if he tried to say them—he really wanted to make the military a career.

He decided to go to Candidate's School. After all, how many Chicago slum kids become honest-to-god United States Army officers? The challenges of OCS did not intimidate him. He had learned self-confidence in Vietnam, and he had also learned that he didn't know all the answers. The first rule of wisdom to learn is to realize there is always more to learn. He knew a commission wouldn't make him God, either. O'Neal didn't want God's job anyway. He had his hands full with his own.

O'Neal became a second lieutenant in a Special Forces team. Of course, he had to extend his time in the service from three years to five, but that was okay. He'd already served one year, and would probably have reenlisted anyway. The young lieutenant, barely nineteen-years-old, was assigned the dangerous job of point man in the bush. O'Neal accepted the duty without complaint, even though he thought he should see a shrink sometime in the future, because he knew the war should repulse him.

Not that O'Neal enjoyed killing. He didn't care much for the military dictatorship of South Vietnam either. Their brutal, heavy-handed tactics against Buddhist protestors disgusted O'Neal. Was President Ky trying to make the image of his government more appealing by such tactics? Didn't he realize that one of the arguments against American involvement in Vietnam was that the government of the South was no better than the Communists of the North?

Although the senseless destruction and suffering of the war disturbed O'Neal, he found the combat a fascinating paradox of terror and excitement. Adrenaline addiction can be as difficult to overcome or control as any narcotic. William O'Neal didn't really try. He didn't worry much about it either, and his sense of guilt gradually faded. Vietnam was where he belonged at that time and place. For O'Neal, this was his ultimate truth.

He was soon promoted to executive officer and received a battlefield commission to first lieutenant. As second-in-command of the team, O'Neal was primarily concerned with operations and intelligence. His group worked with the MACV/SOG (Special Observation Group). Often their missions sent them behind enemy lines in Laos, Cambodia, and North Vietnam.

Captain Walt Herald was team leader when two young sergeants named Caine and Fanelli joined the outfit. They fit in well with the team, although Caine was a bit moody and basically a loner, and Fanelli was a little cocky and got into trouble due to his big mouth, weakness for booze, and occasional dealings on the black market. But Fanelli was a valuable demolitions expert, and Caine had a superb rapport with the hill people, the Montagnards, and especially the Katu.

During a recon mission, Captain Herald and the team medic, Sergeant First Class Leonard Fowler, were killed by a VC ambush. Both men were machinegunned before they could fire a shot. O'Neal and Lan Cho, the team guide, swiftly opened fire on the Cong. Two died instantly, and two more bolted from O'Neal and Lan Cho, only to run into a crossfire from Fanelli and Caine, who nailed them with twin streams of M-16 fire.

The last VC dove for cover behind a clump of ferns. O'Neal blasted the guy's camouflage with 5.56mm rounds. The Cong screamed and tumbled into the open, both hands clutching his bullet-torn crotch. Caine finished the man off with a knife thrust to the heart. They buried their dead, and concealed the bodies of the enemy in a ravine.

"Do we go on with the mission, Lieutenant?" Fanelli had inquired.

"What do you guys think we should do?" O'Neal replied.

"Hell," Fanelli had chuckled bitterly. "This ain't a democracy, Lieutenant. This is the fuckin' army, remember?"

"You're in charge now, sir," Caine added.

"Let's just say I'd like your opinion before we continue," O'Neal explained. "That goes for you too, Lan Cho. Do we go on with the mission or turn back? Since our OIC and medic are both dead, nobody will blame us if we do."

"I not think Captain Herald would want us turn back?" Lan Chao answered. He was a Kit Carson Scout, a former VC who had defected to become a guide for American Special Forces. He never backed off from battle with his former comrades, and he had earned the trust of his American companions.

"Neither do I," Caine agreed. "Let's do our job, sir."

"Yeah," Fanelli grinned. "I say we go on too."

"Then it's unanimous," O'Neal said with a nod. "Let's go."

They accomplished the mission. The team returned to MACV/SOG with a camera full of film, photographs of NVA troop buildup along the border, and eyewitness accounts of enemy activity. As far as O'Neal knew, the army never acted upon this information. Had it been worth the lives of Captain Herald and SFC Fowler? Was it worth killing five men to acquire this data?

Fuck it. That was war. It never made much sense.

There was no right or wrong in war—only duty and survival.

O'Neal was promoted to captain and became the new leader of the team. A West Point graduate named Lieutenant James Wentworth III joined the team as the new XO. He was an odd character who liked to talk about Civil War battles and Japanese samurai. Still, Wentworth was a fine officer and a helluva fighting man.

The team reached a new peak level of efficiency with O'Neal, Wentworth, Fanelli, and Caine as the core. Four slightly eccentric and extremely dedicated men, with very different backgrounds and personalities, they became the best in their field. They became known as the Hard Corps. It was said the Vietcong themselves had first christened the team with their nickname. Four hard guys who never backed down.

In 1973, American troops were going home, and only a small Defense Attaché Office remained. The Hard Corps had been disbanded. Fanelli had already been sent "back to the world" after being wounded in Combat. Caine had vanished shortly after the death of his Katu wife. The guy simply sneaked off to the jungle. Technically he was AWOL and officially listed as MIA. O'Neal and Wentworth were sent stateside. The war was over as far as the U.S. military was concerned. It was something they had all prayed for—including the men of the Hard Corps. There had to be more to life than jungle warfare and a constant struggle to survive.

O'Neal quickly lost interest in a military career after Vietnam. Without a war to fight, the army was just a lot of rules and regulations. Toy soldier bullshit had never appealed to O'Neal. He finished his enlistment and resigned his commission. It was time to become a civilian, and learn to live a normal life all over again.

But O'Neal didn't find civilian life to be paradise.

The antiwar protesters were still public heroes. People distrusted Vietnam vets. Television programs and movies depicted them as drug-crazed lunatics and kill-crazy psychos—walking timebombs ready to explode.

William O'Neal's parents had died while he was in 'Nam, but he returned to Chicago because it was home. He tried to join the police department, but his application was rejected with no reason given. Afterward, O'Neal noticed a couple of plainclothes detectives following him. He put up with this for one full week. Finally, then confronted them.

One cop pulled a gun when O'Neal approached, but the 'Nam vet looked at the detective's snubnose .38 and smiled. He was used to opponents armed with AK-47s and F-1 handgrenades. A shitty little revolver with an undersized barrel didn't make much of an impression on the former Green Beret.

"Jesus," the cop muttered. "You *are* crazy!"

"What do you guys want?" O'Neal inquired.

"None of your business," the other cop replied. "You came up to us, punk. Not the other way around."

"Why are the cops following me?" O'Neal asked.

"Who said we're cops?" the second cop asked.

"I'm from the Southside, jack," O'Neal replied. "I can recognize a plainclothes cop by looking at his shoes and the way he carries himself. Show me a guy who tries to act nonchalent and swaggers like a bully at the same time, and I'll show you an undercover Chicago cop."

"Got a big mouth, asshole," the cop with the gun snarled. "You know, I can shoot now and plead self-defense later. Another Vietnam vet goes wacko. Open and shut case."

"Yeah," O'Neal shrugged. "I suppose you can do that. Will you at least tell me why you're following me?"

"We got orders," the other cop answered.

"I understand orders," O'Neal nodded. He simply turned and walked away.

O'Neal never knew why the cops had followed him. Probably just checking up on local crazies who might cause trouble . . . with Vietnam vets at the head of the list. Maybe they thought he'd lead them to a heroin dealer or an illegal gunrunner. There wasn't much he could do about it. If he made a formal complaint against the department, if would be dismissed as from another fucked-up Vietnam vet.

He was turned down for other jobs. Some employers were quite vocal about their reasons. He was called a "baby-burning fascist" by a guy who had opposed the war. A WWII vet called him "a sissy bastard," telling him that "Americans knew how to win wars when I was in the service, but now they've got a bunch of dopehead losers like you."

"Too bad you weren't in 'Nam to help us out," O'Neal commented dryly.

"Why don't you go get a fix, junkie," the surly WWII vet sneered. "Your yella streak is startin' to stink up the joint."

O'Neal finally got a job as a bartender. It was easy work. He just poured the drinks and listened to the customers tell him their troubles. He kept his mouth shut, occasionally nodding or shaking his head while he listened. O'Neal didn't talk much. He had little to say. How could he tell anyone that even 'Nam had been better than being treated like a leper? That being shot at was better than being a stranger in his own country? God, they'd put him in a fucking straightjacket.

He had kept in touch with a couple of his Army buddies, including Wentworth. In 1974, Wentworth came to Chicago to visit him—he'd also resigned from the service. Since Vietnam and the Hard Corps, it wasn't the same. They sat up all night, drinking beer and talking about "the good old days," when they still felt they had something to live for. Even something to die for. Neither man had yet reached his thirtieth birthday, yet they talked as if the best years of their lives were in the distant past. As if they were old, tired men, waiting to die.

"What if we could resurrect the Hard Corps?" O'Neal suggested.

"And do what?" Wentworth scoffed. "Play war games every Saturday afternoon?"

"We do what we were meant to do, Jim," O'Neal replied. "We'll fight wars. Only this time, we'll choose what cause we want to fight for, and how we're going to fight for it."

CHAPTER 7

"ALL RIGHT," O'NEAL began as he confronted Trang
Nih. "I'd like to know what the hell is going on. Start
by telling me about this Captain Vinh."

"Captain Vinh Chi Lam is a professional assassin,"
Trang Nih explained. "The section of the Vietnamese
State Security Service he works for is the counterpart of
the KGB's *Morkrie Dela* or "Blood Wet" department.
Vinh's specialty is hunting down enemies of the Com-
munist government of Vietnam. He has already killed
several freedom fighters: two in Thailand, three in
Europe, and at least two here in the United States."

"Jesus," Willis rasped. "You didn't tell me nothin'
about a bunch of killers tracking you guys down!
Neither did the fuckin' CIA!"

"We had hoped we'd thrown him off our trail,"
Trang Nih sighed. "But Captain Vinh has never been
known to fail."

"The guy's human," O'Neal stated. "And human beings can fail. Hanoi wants you pretty bad to send one of their best kill-experts with plenty of back up. How many troops do you think Vinh has?"

"I don't know," Trang Nih admitted. "Hanoi has great faith in the captain. If they feel he needs them, they might give him a thousand men."

"Shit," Willis muttered. "We're as good as dead."

"No we're not," O'Neal assured him. "I doubt if Vinh has a thousand guys out there. Too many men for a single junior officer to command. Especially a Commie-trained officer."

"Oh, don't give me that 'we're better than them' bullshit," Willis snapped. "Next you'll tell me we'll be okay 'cause God's on our side."

"Look, we've got some advantages too," O'Neal said.

"I would like to hear them," Trang Nih admitted.

"Okay," O'Neal replied. "Vinh doesn't know much about us. If he did, he would have sent in more men and struck from more than one direction. He also doesn't have aircraft or he'd launch an aerial strike and blow us away. He doesn't want to alert every cop and military unit in the state, so he'll try to keep the fighting quiet as long as possible. So he won't be eager to blow the shit out of us with the big guns unless there's no other way to take us out."

"I had hoped there would be more to your list of advantages," Trang Nih sighed. "But I suppose we should be grateful for what we can get, under the circumstances."

McShayne opened the door to the head shed. Fanelli entered, half dragging Jim Wentworth across the threshold. The Hard Corps XO was conscious although his legs were still wobbly. O'Neal uttered a sigh of relief and helped Fanelli carry Wentworth to a chair.

"He regained consciousness and insisted on walking," Fanelli explained. "He's still sort of dazed, but I think it's just a scalp wound."

"I'm all right," Wentworth insisted. "Just give me some time to rest and clear my head."

"You're going to the dispensary," O'Neal replied, checking the bloodstain at the top of Wentworth's bald pate. "We'll check for a possible concussion . . ."

"And what if I have one?" Wentworth asked, with a thin smile. "You planning to put me on the bench? No way, Bill. You're going to need everybody, and you know it."

"I hate to admit it, but you're right," O'Neal said. "But I still want to check out your hearing and eyesight."

"I'm gonna get back with Steve," Fanelli announced. "The enemy's still out there and I figure they'll be back for more any minute now."

"Willis," O'Neal turned to the black man. "Go with him."

"What if . . ." Willis began, but he decided there was no point in arguing with O'Neal. "If I live through this, the goddamn CIA better give me a raise."

Willis followed Fanelli outside. McShayne checked the monitors. The enemy had retreated, but they had almost certainly regrouped beyond the reach of the compound security devices.

"Trang Nih," Top began. "How did Vinh get his agents into the country? Don't tell me they all sneaked in with the legitimate refugees."

"Some probably did," Trang Nih replied. "But we believe most of Vinh's people slipped across the Mexican border with groups of illegals. Once across the border, the Communist Vietnamese are assumed to be Southeast Asian refugees. No one associates them with illegals or enemy agents."

"Clever," Wentworth commented. "It fits too. Not many people would believe the Vietnamese government could manage something like this."

"That's probably why they even get away with it," O'Neal replied. "Now, let's take a look at that wound and start planning our strategy."

Captain Vinh inspected what was left of the assault force under his command, stationed at the fenced borders of the compound. Vinh was perturbed by the setback. He'd sent a dozen men into the base, and only one had come back alive. Whoever was helping Trang Nih, they were far more powerful than Vinh had suspected.

Eleven men had died, but Vinh had many more—and he wouldn't be so careless next time. He was determined to complete his assignment, find his quarry, and "terminate with extreme prejudice."

Vinh had been a troop commander with the Vietcong during the war and had specialized in sabotage operations within Saigon and other South Vietnamese cities. He'd also gotten plenty of jungle combat experience in the battle zones of Southeast Asia. Vinh was good— very good.

After the war, Vinh was highly decorated for valor and achievements beyond the call of duty, by the Communist government of the new Democratic Republic of Vietnam. He received a commission as an officer and assigned to military intelligence.

The Soviet Union took a special interest in Vinh. He traveled to the U.S.S.R. and attended the Patrice Lumumba University—a school for foreign-born individuals recruited to serve the interests of the KGB and Soviet-inspired Communism. The university was named in honor of Patrice Lumumba, an influential African Communist active in the Congo during the sixties. Its graduates included Mohammed Boudia, a Palestinian terrorist leader active in Western Europe in the '70's, and Illyich Ramirez Sanchez—better known as the legendary "Carlos, the Jackal."

Vinh learned much in Moscow. He studied foreign languages, world history, and the cultures of Western countries. He learned the macabre skills of espionage, and the finer points of assassination and sabotage. He graduated with honors, and returned to Vietnam to become Hanoi's number one hitman.

It was appropriate, Vinh thought, that he had been chosen to terminate Trang Nih. The most wanted man in Communist Asia would be eliminated by the Vietnam government's best hunter. The task was more difficult than Vinh had expected, but this didn't discourage him. The captain enjoyed a challenge. He wasn't very happy about losing eleven men to the American "gangsters" in the compound, but that didn't matter. Trang Nih and his allies were as good as dead.

However, Vinh found it more difficult to track and kill his quarry in the United States. His last target had been a refugee freedom fighter named Nguyen Phan, who had fled from Vietnam to the Chinatown section of New York City.

Apparently Phan had reason to suspect Hanoi had sent agents to kill him, because he avoided the Vietnamese ghettos which had cropped up across America. New York is a city where people ask few questions—an ideal place for a man to hide. But it is also a city with too many people and too few police to protect them.

Ban Ban, Vinh's right-hand man, had hired three Puerto Rican youths, and paid them with a packet of Golden Triangle heroin—and a promise of a whole kilo after they murdered Phan.

Vinh's sources learned that Nguyen Phan left his tenement house only to go to the small grocery store on the corner. Ban Ban told the three young hoodlums to take him out. When Phan emerged from the store one evening, the trio were waiting for him. The Asian was a small, slight man, and the youths were confident they could handle him without working up a sweat. One of them asked Phan for a light.

Nguyen Phan produced a matchbook, opened it and struck a match. The hood with the cigarette suddenly grabbed Phan's wrist while another punk drew a switchblade. Phan reacted immediately, twisted his wrist and used the flaming match to ignite the others in the matchbook. He adroitly dropped the improvised torch down the first hood's open shirt. The burning fibers of the polyester shirt shrunk and clung to his torso like napalm. The conflagration rose to envelop his unkept hair.

The switchblade artist lunged at Phan, but the tough Asian moved to keep the burning human torch between them. As a martial artist, Phan was a one trick pony, but he was clever and fast. He side kicked the burning figure in the shoulder and sent him sprawling into the knife artist. Then he backfisted the blademan to the temple. The young tough dropped like a stone.

The third hood wasn't idle. He pulled a Saturday Night Special from the back of his belt and tried to zero in on Phan. The Asian was desperate and felt that the only source of safety was his tenement building. The gunman stood in his path.

Phan simply collided with the punk. The cheap handgun barked and a bullet creased Phan's leg. Both men tumbled to the ground. The Vietnamese grabbed the youth by the hair and smashed his face into the concrete three times. Teeth and blood flew from mouth and nose. Phan scooped up the punk's pistol and ran to his apartment.

Vinh and Ban Ban observed the scene from their vantage point across the street. The former Vietcong commander believed in assaulting a target quickly if the first attempt failed, while the victim is still off-balance. Vinh sighed. He had hoped to make the assassination look like a street crime, but the hoods had failed. He ordered Ban Ban to take care of the three incompetent punks in the alley. Vinh would see to Phan personally.

The Hanoi hitman peered through the Bushnell scope mounted on a .22 caliber AR-7 rifle. He aimed the weapon at the window to Phan's apartment and waited. Vinh knew Phan would draw the window shade to conceal himself within his little station of alleged safety. Vinh's only concern was the possibility that Phan might stand clear of the window while he pulled down the shade.

Nguyen Phan's face appeared in the window, reaching for the blind. Vinh squeezed the trigger three times, firing the semiautomatic rifle as fast as the mechanism allowed. The first .22 round struck Phan in the forehead, between the eyes. The second drilled through his upper lip and split his jawbone. The third slug hit Phan in the throat. Since all three bullets had been dipped in cyanide, it was assured that Phan would not survive.

Ban Ban had returned to Vinh's side, his trophy knife in hand. He wiped blood from the razor edge as he gazed wishfully at the window to Phan's room. Vinh knew what his partner was thinking.

"No," Vinh said with a firm tone. "We have to leave quickly."

Ban Ban frowned. He already had two bloody human ears in his jacket pocket. He had hoped to claim Nguyen Phan's ears for his collection, but he had to settle for only one set that night. Pride had stopped him from claiming the incinerated Puerto Rican hood's ears or those of the one with the fractured skull, but Ban Ban had finished off the dazed switchblade artist. In Ban Ban's scheme of values, punk ears were a worthy and deserved addition to his macabre collection.

The New York mission had not been entirely to Vinh's liking, but at least he hadn't lost any personnel. The three young hoods didn't count. Vinh would have probably killed them even if they had succeeded. Recruiting local scum for assignments was a regular part of Vinh's schemes. After these individuals completed their duties, they were expendable. Very expendable.

Ban Ban had spent twelve hours driving through the small towns that bordered Puget Sound in order to recruit Vinh's most recent accomplices. He had finally found two men willing to sell their soul for a promise of Golden Triangle dope.

"Money talks but dope screams," Jacques, a small, dark man had commented.

His partner, a beanpole named Slim, had nodded in agreement. The pair were perfect for Vinh's needs. Totally unprincipled, unpatriotic, and devoted to nothing save their heroin habit. The monkey on their back had robbed them of any scruples or honor either had ever had.

The two American low-lifes had even helped steal an eighteen-wheeler, truck for Vinh's crew. The tractor trailer was big enough to carry a hundred men. A large group of Asians might have attracted attention in the state of Washington, but nobody thought much of a big rig driven by two Caucasians.

The truck had arrived, bringing reinforcements for Vinh's second assault on the compound. His men were armed to the teeth. Vinh gave them an hour to talk among themselves. This would help them develop self-confidence in themselves, and as an effective unit. This could be a key factor in combat.

Ban Ban smiled at his commander. Vinh Chi Lam was an impressive man, powerfully built, with excellent reflexes and a shrewd mind. His golden eyes filled his men with confidence, an ability which made Vinh a born leader. His training by the KGB had helped Vinh perfect this gift to influence and manipulate others.

"Now we will kill the traitors and their damned American pig allies, yes?" Ban Ban asked eagerly. He carried an M-79 grenade launcher with several cartridge grenades inserted in harness loops. The "blooper" had long been his favorite weapon—one shot could kill a dozen men.

"Not yet," Vinh replied. "Our quarry isn't going anywhere, comrade. Before this night is through, they will all be dead. Of that, there is no doubt."

Ban Ban nodded, certain his captain was correct.

He had never known Vinh to be wrong about such matters.

CHAPTER 8

AFTER CHECKING OUT Wentworth's wounds as best they could, O'Neal and McShayne decided he was fit for duty. The Hard Corps commander called Fanelli and Caine to join the others for a war council. Trang Nih and Franklin T. Willis also participated.

"Trang Nih has been telling me everything he knows about a Commie killer named Captain Vinh," O'Neal told his troops. "Apparently that's who we're dealing with. Son of a bitch is a pro. Very professional. Very ruthless. Joe, you remember reading that article in the newspaper about those Southeast Asians who were killed in San Diego?"

"Yeah," Fanelli replied. "We figured it was a drug related hit. Probably Triad."

"That was Vinh's first attempt to kill Trang Nih," O'Neal stated. "You recall that there were two white guys killed? Those were a couple of American scum hired by Vinh. It seems he recruits locals whenever possible. So if you happen to come across any non-Asians in the forest, don't assume they're good guys.''

"Anyone who'd help a Communist savage doesn't deserve to call himself an American," Wentworth hissed with contempt.

"They'll be all-American corpses if we get hold of 'em," Fanelli commented.

"Vinh tends to hit fast, and follow up with another hit immediately," Trang Nih explained. "That's what he did in San Diego. When the shotgun killers burst into Psar Phumi's apartment and opened fire, we knew Vinh would follow with another attack immediately. He did. They fired a grenade at us."

"Psar Phumi's apartment?" Caine raised his eyebrows. "Does he have any idea how they found out you were meeting with your allies at his residence?"

"No, he doesn't," Trang Nih replied. "In fact, we were a bit suspicious of Psar Phumi after that incident. You see, he wasn't in his apartment at the time of the attack."

"Interesting coincidence," O'Neal frowned. "What makes you think you can trust him now?"

"He explained that he had been ambushed by Vinh's men on his way to our meeting," Trang Nih answered. "The two men with him were killed and he received a bullet wound on his left arm. He barely escaped with his life."

"So he says," O'Neal muttered. The cynical mercenary leader wasn't inclined to trust anyone under such circumstances. "Must not have been much of a wound. Psar Phumi doesn't have his arm in a sling, let alone a cast."

"The bullet creased his arm," Trang Nih said. "I've

124

seen many bullet wounds before. I've no doubt that's what caused his wound. I also find it difficult to believe Psar Phumi would betray us. He is Cambodian. You know how much his country has suffered under the Communists. Even more than my people or the people of Laos. The Communists have slaughtered three million Cambodians since 1975.''

"We know about that," Wentworth remarked sourly. "But I'm not so sure how many other Americans do. The news media barely mentions the genocide in Cambodia."

"Yeah," Fanelli added. "You don't hear many of those 'peace advocates' who protested American involvement in 'Nam talk about what's happened in Southeast Asia since '75."

"Let's take care of personal survival for now," O'Neal said sharply. "We'll solve the rest of the world's problems later."

The Hard Corps commander turned to Trang Nih. "The fact Psar Phumi is a Cambodian doesn't mean he couldn't be working with the Communists. After all, there are Cambodians *participating* in the genocide within their own country. A person's nationality doesn't guarantee they've got halos—any more than it means they've got devil's horns."

"What about Qui Nhung or the others?" Trang Nih asked. "They were with me at Psar Phumi's apartment when the killers attacked. Do you really think any of them could be traitors?"

"If they didn't know what sort of tactic Vinh would use, they wouldn't know they'd be putting their ass on the line by betraying you," O'Neal replied simply. "Of course, when the shooting started, even a spy among your people would start shooting back to save himself.

Anyone of them could be a spy for Vinh. And—face it, Trang Nih—one of them *is*."

"I've been wonderin'," Willis began. "How did Vinh find out where we landed? I mean, I can see how one of the passengers could have sabotaged my chopper, but I don't see how they signaled this gook fucker . . . uh, no offense, Trang Nih."

"None taken," the Vietnamese assured him. "I've occasionally referred to the NVA and Vietcong as 'gooks' myself. It isn't a Vietnamese word, and I don't think it's English. I always wondered where you got that term from."

"It's Korean," McShayne, a veteran of the Korean conflict answered. "It's a slang expression. Means about the same as 'guy' or 'dude' in English. And to answer your question, Willis, the saboteur on the chopper probably had a radio homing device attached to the bomb. It signaled Vinh before the bomb exploded. No more helicopter. No more transmitter. The evidence was probably vaporized by the blast."

"What we have to do now is prepare for Vinh's next move," O'Neal insisted. "And he'll hit us again. I don't think he's gonna back off. Judging from what Trang Nih says, there's a real good chance he'll hit us sooner rather than later."

"Wait a minute," Willis said suddenly. "You guys got two choppers here, right? So why not fly us outta here? You got a Bell UH-1D? I'll fly it. Big enough to haul all of us outta here . . ."

"You forget the enemy has grenade launchers," Fanelli reminded him. "Maybe rocket launchers too. They could shoot us outta the sky before we could get clear of the compound."

"Yeah," Willis admitted grimly. "You're right."

"All right," O'Neal began. "Everybody has personal weapons, but we'll also need to get out the M-60 machine guns, mortars, grenades, and the rest of our more powerful weaponry."

"If we start firing mounted machine guns and setting off explosives we're gonna draw attention," Fanelli reminded his commander. "We could find our balls hangin' in the wind, with the cops and the feds ready to cut 'em off. Don't expect any help from Old Saintly either. His only concern will be keeping the Company from being associated with us."

"I said to get the heavy stuff out," O'Neal explained. "I didn't say we'd use it—unless we *have to*. If it comes down to a choice between being slaughtered by Vinh's unit or risking some confrontations with the authorities later, I say we go with the latter."

"Yeah," Caine agreed with a thin smile. "After all, they'll have to catch us before they can arrest us."

"For their sake," Wentworth said with a shrug. "I hope they don't try it."

"Let's worry about that when and if it happens," O'Neal urged. "For now let's . . ."

"Sorry to interrupt, sir," McShayne announced, watching the surveillance monitors. "But company's comin' again."

"Which direction and how many?" O'Neal asked, moving to the monitors. He saw the shapes moving across the screens. Only two monitors showed any movement. "Looks like they're coming from the east again."

"We've only got two cameras left on that side," McShayne stated. "First group took out a couple of 'em. Could be more of 'em where the cameras are out. Microphones don't help much. These guys are quiet when they sneak around in the dark. Real quiet."

"Switch on the motion detectors on the east side," O'Neal said. "That ought to give us an idea of how many opponents are heading toward us."

The motion detectors were not used as a regular form of surveillance at the compound because large animals —deer, elk and McShayne's dreaded bears—could activate them. However, no large animals would remain in the immediate vicinity of a large group of humans. McShayne activated the detectors and examined the shapes that appeared on a separate monitor.

"A dozen or more," Top declared. "All coming from the east."

"Doesn't make sense," Wentworth commented. "Vinh's obviously got enough people to strike from more than one direction. It's poor tactics to assault a base on only one front."

"Vinh knows that as well as we do," O'Neal assured his men. "The sly bastard is trying to trick us. He knows we've got surveillance gear out there. His men know to look for the cameras now and they spotted them before and took 'em out. But they don't even seem to be looking for the cameras now."

"Yeah," Wentworth agreed. "Vinh wants us to think he's going to strike only from the east. He's probably got other reinforcements positioned, waiting for orders to move in."

"Let's let him think his idea worked," O'Neal announced. "Trang Nih, Willis, you two stay here. Set up a machine gun nest. Maybe two. There are areas prepared for this already. You'll find the sandbags that form horse-patterns: south, north, east and west. Set one up at the east, in case the enemy reaches the heart of the compound from that direction. Set up the other nest at the north post. That one is close to the west post, so you can change position in a hurry, if necessary.''

"And if you have to use the M-60's," Fanelli added, "use the bipods. None of that *Rambo* shit. You know, shooting from the hip? That might work okay in the movies, but a mounted machine gun is supposed to be fired while mounted."

"Hey, I was in the Marines, remember?" Willis snapped, annoyed by Fanelli's remark. "And I was in 'Nam, man. Don't give me a crock of shit about basic handling of weapons."

"Top," O'Neal continued, ignoring the other men's conversation. "You try to supervise Trang and Willis, keep an eye on the monitors, and set up a couple of mortars."

"Thanks, sir," McShayne growled. "Do I gotta do all three at the same time?"

"Aren't you used to doing five things at once?" O'Neal smiled.

"Yeah," McShayne shrugged. "I guess I am. No sweat, sir."

"Good," O'Neal said with a nod. "Jim and Joe, you'll come with me. We're going to meet the advancing troops coming from the east."

"You must have something special planned for me, Captain," Caine commented, his poker face not revealing whether this appealed to him or worried him.

"I want you to set up some surprises for anyone who tries to close in on us from the north, south or west. Especially north and west. I think those are the more likely directions that a large force of enemy assault troops will come from. More cover among the trees to the west and that damn hydroelectric generator to the north is an ideal strategic target. Vinh will probably want to cut off our power. That reminds me, Top . . ."

"Get the emergency generators ready," McShayne said with a sigh. "No problem, sir."

"Then everybody has a general idea about what to do," O'Neal declared. "Grab your gear and let's move."

CHAPTER 9

JAMES WENTWORTH III entered his cottage and yanked open a guncase. The lieutenant had lots of personal firearms and he needed a replacement for his H&K assault rifle, lost when the enemy grenade bowled him over. Fortunately, Wentworth still had his .45 Colt and *wakazashi* short sword which was in his belt when the explosion occurred.

Wentworth glanced over the weapons in the gunrack. These included a Remington semiautomatic shotgun, a Franchi over-under trapgun, a Weatherby .300 Magnum bolt action rifle with a Bushnell scope and an M-16 assault rifle. However, he selected a Belgian *Fusil Automatique Leger*, better known as an FAL. Manufactured by the Fabrique National Herstal, the FAL is one of the most widely used and highly respected military weapons of the Western world. Wentworth's FAL was already equipped with a Starlite scope and silencer.

He smiled slightly as he raised the rifle and shoved a twenty-round magazine into the well. The hunt was about to begin, Wentworth mused, as he chambered the first cartridge. There had been many others before. The hunt was something Wentworth understood very well. He had been a hunter all his life.

As a youth in Oklahoma, James Wentworth III had enjoyed hunting trips with his Uncle Harmon. They hunted rabbit, deer, and game bird. The Wentworths did not believe in killing for trophies. They enjoyed their blood sports, but ate what they killed. Like all good hunters, the Wentworths did not take life without reason—although they were quite proud of their ability and skill.

The Wentworth family believed in honor and integrity. They were a very old family who had been proud to call themselves Americans since the time of the Revolutionary War. They were fighting men and they never missed a war. They had fought the British, the Indians, and the Mexicans in Texas. It had been the only available armed conflict at the time.

The Wentworths fought for the Confederacy during the War Between the States; the family had settled in Oklahoma, which didn't take sides, but once again, the Civil War was the only one available. Geography determined which side the Wentworths fought for.

A family legend claimed that some members of the Wentworth clan had lived in Virginia, and had fought for the Union. Supposedly, two Wentworth men clashed on the battlefield at Gettysburg. One was a Confederate, the other a damn Yankee. They were cousins, but they allegedly looked enough alike to be twin brothers. Fellow soldiers could only tell them apart by the color of their uniforms. The Reb eventually stabbed the Yankee with a bayonet. He watched his own face stare up at him and die.

Wentworths were with Teddy Roosevelt and the Rough Riders in Cuba. They fought in World War I, where James Wentworth Sr., the grandfather of James III, was a highly decorated veteran.

His son, James Wentworth II, later fought "those damn Huns" again during World War II. By then the "Huns" had become "damn krauts" or "fuckin' Nazis." James II was promoted to major by the end of the war. He later commanded a battalion of troops during the Korean Conflict. He retired as a full colonel. Naturally, the Wentworths were all officers, West Point graduates since the place had become a military academy. At seventeen, James III was looking forward to carrying on this family tradition.

Uncle Harmon Wentworth and James III went hunting on a sunny afternoon in July that year. They bagged two wild turkeys, both shot by young James. Harmon and his nephew had become very close after James' father died when the boy was fourteen. They spent many hours together, mostly talking about the state of the world and military history.

Uncle Harmon was also a World War II veteran, in the Pacific theater. He had been among the occupation forces in Japan after the war, and got to know the Japanese people, learning their language and culture. Many of his closest friends were Japanese—men who would have killed him during the war.

"I wonder how many of the Japanese soldiers I killed might have become my friends had we met in Tokyo after the war," Harmon told his nephew. "You know, soldiers don't start wars. We just have to fight them."

Uncle Harmon told James many stories about the Japanese samurai. The courage, discipline, and skills of these legendary warriors fascinated the youth. He studied *akido* and *kenjutsu*—Japanese fencing. James loved Japanese culture. They loved beauty and art and they were highly civilized, yet, the Japanese were also a warrior people, incredibly fierce in combat.

This paradox was not unlike the culture of the American South, and the Wentworth family in particular. The Chinese call it "yin and yang." Everything must have its opposite in order to exist. A warrior race often has a fine culture to balance their killing arts and deadly skills.

"How do you feel about the war in Vietnam, Jim?" Uncle Harmon inquired as they marched across the meadow, carrying their rifles and the dead game birds. "A lot of young people think the war is wrong."

"I'm going to West Point, Uncle Harmon," Jim stated. "And I'm going to fight in Vietnam. It's my duty, sir."

"I figured you'd feel that way," Harmon sighed. "But I hope you think about it. Our soldiers are getting a dirty deal in Vietnam and anybody who comes back alive will get a dirty deal from an ungrateful public."

"I can't believe that of America, sir," Jim replied. "Sure there are protesters and critics of the war. That's a phase. It won't last and those folks are just a noisy minority anyway."

"I hope you're right," Harmon said, shaking his head. "For your sake, Jim."

James Wentworth III went to West Point. He possessed much higher than average intelligence, and he excelled in his studies. He was in splendid physical condition and already had a black belt second dan in akido. He was an excellent marksman and gutsy as hell. Not surprisingly, Wentworth graduated with honors and went on to jump school, continuing his training as an officer in the Green Berets. Wentworth's only concern was that the war might end before he got to 'Nam.

He needn't have worried. The war was still going at fever pitch by the time Second Lieutenant Wentworth arrived in Southeast Asia. His first week in Saigon was uneventful, but he was soon in the bush and his first firefight.

It had been a typical hit-and-run Vietcong strike. The enemy struck from the cover of trees and elephant grass. A soldier next to Wentworth caught a bullet in the side of the jaw. The slug shattered bone and teeth, ripping the guy's lower jawbone off. Blood splashed Wentworth's field jacket as he dropped to the ground, trying to unsling his M-16. The wounded soldier fell beside him, twitching in agony and pawing at what remained of his face.

The American patrol returned fire. Bullets raked the bush without effect. Sniper fire erupted from behind the U.S. troops. Two soldiers screamed and fell, bulletholes spilling blood from their backs. Wentworth and a couple other troops turned and fired in the general direction of the VC ambusher. God, it seemed hopeless. Wentworth was a crack marksman, but he couldn't find the goddamn target. He didn't even see the muzzle flash of the VC's weapon. Shaky fingers clawed his leg. Wentworth glanced at the horribly disfigured face of the soldier on the ground beside him. Blood still flowed from the ragged bottom of the man's shattered face. His tongue flopped loose among the crimson pulp where his jawbone had been. The guy's upper lip curled back to display the single row of teeth that remained in his mouth.

The poor devil was mutely asking for help, Wentworth realized. But what could he do for the man? Wentworth removed his first aid kit and put a bandage around the terrible wound. The soldier pounded the ground with his fists and wept. Wentworth felt like crying too. He couldn't cry, he couldn't allow anything to fog his eyesight or his judgement. The wounded soldier clutched at Wentworth's hand.

"I gotta be able to use both hands to use my rifle," Wentworth told him gently. "Hang on, soldier."

The lieutenant pulled the man closer and leaned the soldier's blood-drenched head against his abdomen. The wounded man clung to him, seeking comfort in the closeness of a fellow soldier, relying on Wentworth to protect him. Wentworth tried to control his breathing. His heart was pounding like a jackhammer inside his chest.

Long seconds crept by. Charlie did not strike again. Several American wounded groaned. At least two soldiers were already dead. A medic crawled to Wentworth and the injured soldier. He examined the man briefly and gave him a morphine injection.

"I thought you weren't suppose to give drugs to a man with a head injury," Wentworth remarked.

"So sue me for malpractice, sir," the medic growled. He was a staff sergeant, but a grizzled veteran of the war. "If this guy has a bone shard in his brain he's either gonna die or be a vegetable regardless of what I do. So I reduced the poor bastard's pain. Hang around, sir. You'll start wantin' to shoot up morphine every day to take away the pain."

"What does that mean?" Wentworth demanded.

"It means you got a lot of fuckin' pain here, sir," the medic replied. He started to check on another patient, but turned to Wentworth again. "By the way, you did good with that man, sir. You did all you could."

"Sure," Wentworth muttered. His voice sounded very small and weak.

The VC had fled from the area. A search turned up the body of one slain opponent, dressed in black pajamas. His comrades had managed to strip him of weapons and supplies before they fled. Charlie had lost one man, but five Americans were down and badly hurt. It wasn't supposed to be like this, Wentworth thought. The enemy didn't fight and didn't give them an opportunity to fight back. It wasn't fair . . .

Wentworth shook his head, annoyed by his own naive notions. Of course it wasn't fair. This was war, not a goddamn rugby game. There were no rules . . . at least none for the Vietcong or the NVA to worry about. They didn't give a damn about the Geneva Convention. The people of North Vietnam weren't crying for blood when NVA officers slaughtered civilian villages, but Lieutenant Calley was accused of being a war criminal by his fellow Americans. Okay, if he committed the My Lai Massacre, maybe the title fit, but nobody seemed to give a shit how the NVA behaved. Nobody cared about the victims of the Vietcong or the Pathet Lao. Nobody was accusing any of those motherfuckers of war crimes.

Wentworth recalled his conversation with Uncle Harmon. He had told his nephew there would be no glory and that American GI's were getting a raw deal. Uncle Harmon was right. Wentworth would recall other comments made by his uncle. Future events would prove that the man's insight rivaled the predictions of Nostradamus.

There were other battles, endless confrontations with the hit-and-run tactics of the VC. These usually ended with more American casualties than the enemy sustained. But Wentworth claimed the lives of more than a dozen VC during his first year in 'Nam. Four of these had been during a single battle.

American troops assisted the ARVN forces in strikes against Communist bases in Cambodia in April of 1970. Lieutenant Wentworth was among them. A Red patrol confronted Wentworth's group near the border. The young lieutenant was point man. He spotted the first enemy soldiers a split second before the shooting started.

"Down!" he yelled to the other U.S. troops.

They dropped to the ground as the NVA and Cambodian Commies opened fire. Streams of 7.62mm slugs sliced air above their prone forms. Wentworth returned fire. He saw a 'Cong gunman's head recoil when a rifle round crashed into it.

American and Communist troops slithered through the elephant grass toward one another. Each spotted opponents and opened fire. Wentworth blasted a three-round burst into the chest of the closest Red gunman. He swiftly turned his M-16 on another target and triggered another volley. The Communist soldier cried out and dropped his AK-47, but he bolted away and dove into the elephant grass for shelter.

The other American troops exchanged shots with the NVA and their Cambodian comrades. Men fell on both sides, but neither patrol retreated. Instead they closed in and soon engaged in fierce hand-to-hand combat.

A GI shrieked as a Cambodian soldier lunged with a bayonet attached to the end of a Type-56 assault rifle. The blade plunged into the American's guts. Twisting the bayonet, the Cambodian tore a grisly slit in the American's belly. Intestines slithered from the wound like eyeless snakes. Another GI quickly avenged his wounded pal. He stamped the buttstock of his M-16 into the base of the Cambodian's neck, cracking the vertebrae on impact.

Another Cambodian charged from the elephant grass and thrust a bayonet at Wentworth. The guy had appeared so suddenly and closed in so quickly that Wentworth didn't have time to use his M-16. The Green Beret lieutenant parried the thrust with the barrel of his rifle and slammed a sidekick to the Cambodian's kneecap. The Asian grunted and stumbled off balance.

Wentworth slashed the barrel of his M-16 across the man's throat. The Cambodian dropped his weapon and clutched at his throat with both hands. Wentworth hit him with the butt of his rifle to the temple. The man fell and Wentworth stomped a boot heel into the bone between the Cambodian's eyes—and made certain the guy never got up again.

The lieutenant turned to see how his men were holding up. Dead Americans and Asians littered the ground. An NVA soldier had knocked down a GI and was about to finish him off with a bayonet lunge, but another American soldier jumped the Asian from behind and pulled him away from the fallen GI. He rammed a knee into the Vietnamese Commie's balls and forced him to drop his weapon. Then the GI wrapped an arm around the Asian's throat and planted a knee in his back to pull the man to the ground and throttle him.

Another GI had pinned a Cambodian Commie to the ground and buried a bayonet blade in his opponent's chest. The man Wentworth had wounded and disarmed had wandered from the bush with his good arm held high.

"Chieu hoi!" he called out, announcing his desire to surrender.

An NVA officer made certain the man didn't get his wish. The Red team leader aimed a Tokarev pistol at the would-be defector and fired three rounds into the man's upper torso. An American gave the officer a dose of his own medicine and shot the NVA commander in the back. The Communist performed a wild dance for a second or two, then fell on his face.

Suddenly, an NVA soldier bolted from the grass. He held a Type-56 by the barrel and swung it like a bat at Wentworth's head. Apparently the guy's weapon had jammed so he used it the only way possible. Wentworth raised his M-16 to block the enemy attack, but the force of the blow ripped the rifle from Wentworth's grasp.

The Vietnamese trooper swung his rifle at Wentworth again. The Green Beret dodged the slashing T-56 and quickly moved forward. He seized his opponent's wrists. The NVA twisted his trunk and tried to jab the gunbutt at Wentworth's face.

Wentworth suddenly swung a forearm under the guy's chin and simultaneously swept a foot against his ankle. The enemy soldier lost his footing and crashed to the ground. The Type-56 fell from the guy's fingers. He lashed a kick at Wentworth, but the American dodged his boot. The NVA rolled away and sprang to his feet, as Wentworth reached for the .45 Colt on his hip.

The NVA trooper froze, his hands poised like twin axe-blades, feet braced in a horse-stance. Wentworth stared into the other man's eyes. He nodded and raised his empty right hand to chest level. His left hand guarded his groin. The Colt pistol remained in its holster.

"Come on," Wentworth invited. "This might be the closest thing to a fair fight either of us will get during this war."

The enemy soldier may not have understood Wentworth's words, but he clearly understood the challenge. He attacked, feinting with his left hand to distract Wentworth while he snap-kicked at the American's groin. Wentworth's left palm slapped the kick aside.

The NVA slashed a karate chop at the American's neck. Wentworth blocked with a "praying mantis" technique. His right hand snared the Asian's wrist while he stabbed the stiffened fingers of his left under the guy's ribcage.

The NVA trooper groaned. Wentworth held his opponent's wrist with his right hand and grabbed his elbow with his left. Then he pulled with one hand, pushed with the other, and pivoted. The startled NVA soldier suddenly found himself hurtling to the ground. The guy rose slowly, his fingers scraping the earth until he touched a rock. His hand scooped it up and he quickly hurled the stone at Wentworth's head.

The Green Beret ducked. The rock sailed above his head. The Vietnamese quickly rushed forward and swung a boot at Wentworth's face. The American sidestepped the kick and stepped forward, ramming both fists into his opponent's torso. The double punch caught the man off-balance and knocked him to the ground. Wentworth bent a knee and dropped into the dazed NVA's mid-section, landing with all his weight behind the blow.

The Vietnamese gasped, breath spewing from his body. Wentworth balled his fists, the middle fingers bent, knuckles jutting out like blunted horns. He smashed them into the NVA trooper's skull, caving in the sphenoid bones. The man's body twitched once and lay still.

"Jesus, sir," one of the American GI's rasped. "You sure fucked up his day."

Shortly after the battle by the Cambodian border, Wentworth was reassigned to a Special Forces team headed up by a captain named William O'Neal. Wentworth had some doubts about the man. After all, O'Neal wasn't a West Point graduate and he *was* from

Chicago. They raise gangsters there. Of course, O'Neal had earned his rank the hard way—on the battlefield. OCS or not, O'Neal certainly had experience and he had been in Vietnam almost three years longer than Wentworth.

The men under their command were a bit odd—especially Steve Caine. A loner who would have probably gone AWOL in a regular unit, Caine fit in as well with the team as he would ever fit in anywhere. The man was a superb warrior and he was good with the Montagnards. Maybe too good. There was something primitive about Caine. He would never be truly regimented and able to conform to military life. Perhaps this bold spirit appealed to Wentworth. He liked the guy.

Fanelli was a bit crude in a slum kid's way, but he was very tough and far more intelligent than he seemed at first meeting. Fanelli was courageous in battle and very skilled with explosives. He seemed to dislike the word "sir" and referred to officers by their rank instead. That didn't bother Wentworth. The best soldiers in elite fighting units were always more individulalistic than the regular troops.

Wentworth was the team intelligence officer. He gathered information and evaluated it. The lieutenant was good at his job, but he favored active missions to sitting in camp discussing strategy. This feeling was shared by the other members of the outfit. And they spent a lot of time in the field, mostly behind enemy lines, taking on some of the most dangerous missions of the Vietnam conflict.

They were the Hard Corps. It was a title Wentworth took pride in. Despite the horror and frustration of the war, the lieutenant felt he had truly found his place in the world. He and the other three were brothers as surely as if they had come from the same mother.

142

But Uncle Harmon had been correct about the war. America would not win. The politicians and public opinion about the war saw to that. Troops were being pulled out of Southeast Asia, and in the 1970's American involvement was finally coming to an end. The Hard Corps was half dissolved by the time O'Neal and Wentworth returned to the world. O'Neal planned to get out of the service, but Wentworth chose to stay in uniform.

Vietnam had been enough war, even for a Wentworth. Uncle Harmon had told him the truth. It had been a bitter, terrible experience. Wentworth knew that he needed to put it behind him now. The Army wanted him to teach a course in military intelligence at Fort Benjamin Harrison. That sounded like a good way to readjust to life in the United States.

He was transferred to "Uncle Ben's Rest Home." The nickname suited the base, in Wentworth's opinion. Fort Benjamin Harrison largely consisted of military schools for AIT (Advanced Individual Training) of military personnel. Fresh troops, just out of Basic, came to the classrooms. Wentworth felt as if he was talking to aliens. None of them had been to Vietnam. None of them knew what it had been like.

Wentworth doubted that the authors of the military intelligence textbooks had ever been to 'Nam either. Some of the material was obsolete—thirty years behind the times. Wentworth hated the damn textbooks and he hated teaching classes. He had always been a scholar, but the classroom just didn't mean anything anymore. Why teach the students about military intelligence anyway? So they could get involved in another war that Washington and the United Nations would prevent them from winning?

Besides, in order to operate intelligence operations

successfully, one had to be able to maintain security. That seemed more difficult than ever. The Watergate hearings had started and politicians were busting their balls to get ahold of classified information which they could take to the press and expose.

With guys like that around, Wentworth thought, how the hell can you hope to maintain security? How can intelligence personnel expect to do their job when their names might wind up in a front page story about covert operations abroad?

Wentworth spent his spare time playing chess and *go,* a Japanese board game of strategy. He practiced martial arts at a *dojo* in Indianapolis and he went target shooting once a week. He took a course in Russian, and started to read, write, and speak it. But all the busy work didn't make up for the empty feeling in the pit of his stomach. It seemed all his enthusiasm for life ended in Vietnam.

He finally resigned his commission and left the service. Maybe O'Neal had been right. An army without a war is just rules and regulations. It's like a racehorse that isn't allowed on the track.

When Wentworth became a civilian again, he learned how very true Uncle Harmon's final prediction about Vietnam had proved to be. The public wanted to forget Vietnam, and they didn't feel any need to acknowledge the sacrifices of the Vietnam veterans. No permanent monument was built to honor those who gave their lives during the conflict—or the 2,494 MIA's—until November 12, 1982, almost ten years after Americans withdrew from Southeast Asia.

By then Wentworth had already met with O'Neal in Chicago, and the Hard Corps had been reborn as a team of international mercenaries. For Wentworth, this had been welcome salvation from a world that had been slowly crushing him.

Wentworth hurried from the cottage to join his fellow teammates. It was time to once again adopt the role of hunter—although Wentworth realized they would also be the hunted. That is the nature of war, and James Wentworth III wouldn't want it any other way.

CHAPTER 10

THE INVADERS APPROACHED from the east side of the Hard Corps compound. William O'Neal watched them come through the lenses of a pair of TH 70 Nitefinders. The Hard Corps commander was impressed. Even with the special goggles, they were well-concealed. He was barely able to see their camouflaged shapes.

"Vinh's people are pretty good," O'Neal whispered to James Wentworth III and Joe Fanelli. "Well-trained jungle fighters out there."

"I guess Hanoi cares enough to send the very best," Fanelli replied, checking the silencer attached to his M-16. He had also attached an M-203 grenade launcher to the underside of the barrel. He figured he'd have to remove the noise suppressor before he used the launcher or the 40mm shell might strike it and explode in his face.

"They're still using weapons with silencers attached," Wentworth commented as he peered through the Starlite nightscope mounted on his French FAL rifle. The Starlite gave him greater visibility in the dark than O'Neal's Nitefinder. "I count sixteen, but there might be more."

"That's probably a pretty safe bet, Jim," O'Neal said as he unslung a silencer equipped M-16 from his shoulder. "It sure looks like the boys in Hanoi are pulling out all the stops to get Trang Nih."

"And take out anybody else who gets in their way," Fanelli added. "This is the biggest *dinky dau* shit we've gotten into since 'Nam."

Nobody could argue with that. "Dinky dau" is a military slang term (a perversion of the Vietnamese term *dien cai dau)* meaning "crazy." It was a dinky dau mess, no two ways about that.

"Okay," O'Neal told his men. "Try to avoid making noise. Joe, don't use that launcher unless it's an emergency."

"I'd say it's already an emergency," Fanelli muttered. "But I know what you mean. I won't use the grenade launcher unless I *really* have to. Just remember, they've got things that go boom too."

"I remember," Wentworth assured him, jerking a thumb at the bandage wrapped around the top of his head.

"Let's try to take at least one of these suckers alive," O'Neal ordered. "We'll have to spread out in order to cover enough territory to be sure none of them slip past us. Try to stay within each other's sight. If you get a chance, Jim, wing one of 'em and then cover me when I move in to bag him. Okay?"

"Got it," Wentworth said with a nod.

"Party time, Captain," Fanelli said, watching the invading troops creep closer to the Hard Corps position.

"So get the door prizes ready," O'Neal replied.

The Hard Corps trio separated. Fanelli went north, O'Neal south, and Wentworth stayed put. Thanks to the Nitefinder goggles, O'Neal and Fanelli were able to move through the darkness with ease, avoiding bushes and stepping on twigs. The enemy did not appear to have any night vision gear. The moon was a thin crescent in the sky, and dark clouds blocked out most of the stars, so the night goggles were a definite advantage for the Hard Corps.

Since the odds were almost six to one in favor of the enemy patrol, the Hard Corps would need every advantage they could get. Actually, the odds were probably a lot worse. The sixteen men Wentworth had spotted were probably just a fragment of Captain Vinh's assault force.

The enemy drew closer. Most of them wore night camouflage uniforms. Others wore brown and green camies. Some even wore matching hoods and scarflike face masks, similar to the headgear worn by the legendary *ninja* warriors of Japan. The Hard Corps trio could camouflage themselves better than the invaders because they concealed themselves and then waited for the enemy to close in. A bush that stays still is less obvious than one that walks.

Two of Vinh's trigger men walked past Fanelli's position without seeing the tough Italian-American. Fanelli lay on his belly, his lower body covered by loose branches, head and shoulders concealed within the limbs of a fern bush. He couldn't see much as he peered between the thick stems, but Fanelli could see the legs of Vinh's men. That was enough for now. For the moment, he was more concerned about staying out of sight than seeing his opponents.

O'Neal was concealed in a similar manner. He wasn't as close to the invaders as Fanelli, but close enough. They formed a more or less V-shaped pattern. Two enemy scouts took the point and the others formed columns behind them. The enemy was alert, glancing from side to side and occasionally looking over their shoulders. One man stared directly at O'Neal's hiding place.

The Hard Corps commander stiffened. He held his breath and clutched the frame of his M-16. Suddenly, his cover seemed transparent. He expected at any moment to feel the invader's bullets crashing into the bush. But, the man's head turned away, and his attention moved to another direction.

Suddenly, the same man howled in pain and tumbled to the ground. He clutched his right leg. Blood seeped between his fingers. Wentworth had shot the guy with his silenced FAL. The other invaders scattered. One grabbed the wounded man and dragged him to the cover of a thick spruce tree.

Wentworth tracked the progress of another opponent, watching the man through the Starlite scope. He triggered the FAL twice, pumping two 7.62mm slugs into the upper torso of his chosen target. The invader's body twisted about and crashed to the ground. Wentworth quickly changed position and switched his FAL selector to full auto.

The enemy began to fire at the faint muzzle flash of Wentworth's silencer-equipped FAL. Bullets slashed into the ground and whipped air as the mercenary hurtled away, rolling to cover behind a boulder. His heart pounded and he breathed deeply, trying to control his fear. Wentworth was once again using the ancient samurai technique of *zazen* breathing. He pressed two fingers to the point on the abdomen known as the *hara*, inhaled through his nostrils, and exhaled from his mouth.

"Nice try," he whispered, referring to the invaders' attempt to kill him. "But you'll have to do better than that."

Wentworth eased his FAL around the corner of the big rock and scanned the area for the enemy. The two scouts were slowly crawling toward his position. They were probably grateful to still be alive and assumed Wentworth hadn't seen them yet. They were wrong. The Oklahoma sharpshooter had chosen targets toward the rear of the enemy formation because the Hard Corps wanted to reduce the likelihood that any of the enemy would escape. They specialized in search and destroy operations, and they didn't believe in doing a half-ass job.

Joe Fanelli had suddenly found himself with a lot of action on his hands. Two of the enemy assault force had dashed straight for his fern camouflage for cover. One man practically ran over Fanelli's body, but the mercenary suddenly rose from the ground.

Holding the M-16 like a pugil stick, Fanelli struck his opponent's Mini-14 rifle. The force of the blow sent the Asian's weapon flying from his fingers. Fanelli quickly delivered a hard buttstroke to the man's face. The guy dropped as his startled comrade fumbled with the safety catch of his MP5 submachine gun. The Asian killer wasn't familiar with the Heckler & Koch blaster.

He paid for his clumsiness with his life. Fanelli hit him with a three-round burst of 5.56 mm slugs in the face. The man's features dissolved in a crimson smear, and his brains burst from the back of his shattered skull.

His corpse fell and Fanelli whirled to confront a third invader.

The M-16 coughed through its noise suppressor and a trio of high velocity lead rain ripped the guy's chest and slammed his heart and lungs into oblivion. The gunman hopped backward and landed in a twitching heap. Fanelli turned his weapon toward the remaining invaders beyond the bush. None of them seemed to have noticed Fanelli's brief battle with their comrades.

Then the callused edge of an oriental hand chopped Fanelli between the shoulder blades. The unexpected blow drove him to his knees. Pain bolted from his spinal cord to his brain. White light flashed before his eyes. A boot lashed into the M-16, kicking it from his grasp.

"Que lam!" the Asian snarled, as he kicked Fanelli in the face.

The American sprawled on his back. His head throbbed as if construction workers were pounding his skull from the inside. His vision blurred for an instant, but cleared in time to see the Asian killer standing above him. The man's face was a mask of cold rage. Blood oozed from his left eyebrow and a bruise near his temple showed where Fanelli had hit him with the buttstroke. *Not hard enough,* the American thought, as he watched his opponent draw a Puma hunting knife from a belt sheath.

The Asian held the knife like an icepick, the blade jutting from the bottom of his fist. American and European fighters generally use an underhand grip, and tend to regard the overhand as the sign of a novice. Many Asians knifefighters use the overhand because of their martial arts training. Anyone who has taken on one of these blade artists knows better than to scoff at their style.

Not that the guy planned anything fancy with his

knife. He simply intended to plunge the blade into Fanelli's chest, and finish him off before he could recover from the stunning blows he'd received. The Asian bent over Fanelli and raised his knife.

Fanelli lashed out a kick. His boot caught the invader in the kidneys. The Asian groaned as the blow knocked him off balance. He still struck out with the knife. The sharp point stabbed dirt near Fanelli's right ear. The American whipped a backfist to his opponent's face. The Asian tumbled sideways, rolled, and swiftly climbed to his feet.

Joe Fanelli also scrambled upright. His head ached and the forest seemed to sway before his eyes. The tough Italian-American blinked quickly to clear his vision. The Asian knife artist held his weapon ready, poised to attack.

The obvious defense was simply to draw the .45 Colt from leather and shoot the bastard. Fanelli would have been happy to do just that, but his opponent was less than six feet away, close enough for the knife artist to cut him to ribbons before he could draw his pistol. The Asian was waiting for Fanelli to make his move, well aware that he still had the upper hand in their duel.

He expects me to go for the gun, Fanelli thought quickly. *So I won't disappoint him.*

Fanelli's right hand hovered near the butt of the holstered weapon. The Asian saw the move, but failed to notice Fanelli's left hand slide into a pocket. The knifeman lunged and slashed his blade at Fanelli's right hand, planning to slice off his fingers as soon as the .45 cleared leather.

But Fanelli suddenly jerked away and dodged his opponent's blade. His left hand emerged with his NATO pushbutton knife. The blade snapped into place and Fanelli jabbed quickly. The Asian screamed as Fanelli's blade pierced his right arm just above the elbow.

Fanelli hooked a kick into his opponent's lower abdomen. The Asian groaned and nearly doubled up, but he managed to toss the Puma to his left hand and lashed out at Fanelli. The American jumped away from his adversary's blade. With a *kiai* cry, the invader swung a roundhouse kick at Fanelli's knife hand.

The merc weaved his blade away from the flashing boot and cut the guy's calf muscle with a quick slash. The Asian attempted a clumsy lunge and desperately swung a crossbody karate chop with his wounded arm. Fanelli ducked beneath the whirling limb. His opponent followed with a knife thrust. Fanelli side-stepped out of the way and switched his NATO pushbutton to his right hand.

The Asian tried a backhand knife slash, but Fanelli suddenly stepped forward and plunged his blade between the guy's ribs. The Asian yelped in pain. Fanelli chopped the side of his left hand across his opponent's wrist. The Puma dropped to the ground. Fanelli twisted his knife in the invader's flesh and yanked it free.

Blood spilled from the enemy agent's side, but Fanelli hardly noticed. He rapidly moved behind his adversary and stabbed him in a kidney. The Asian uttered a feeble sob and began to sink to the ground. Fanelli didn't take any chances. He grabbed the guy's hair and quickly drew the razor edge of his NATO knife across the invader's throat. At last, he allowed the man to fall to the ground and die.

Fanelli's knees were weak and his head still throbbed. His cheekbone felt as if it had a shard of broken glass lodged in it. He wondered if the Asian had broken some small bone in his cheek. *Worry about it later,* the American told himself, as he staggered to his fallen

M-16 and retrieved the rifle.

The other members of Vinh's hit squad had been busy with problems of their own. Wentworth had continued to fire down at the invaders. His FAL raked the Asian killers with full auto destruction. One assassin's head blew apart from a trio of 7.62mm slugs to the cranium. Another bolted for the cover of a tree, but Wentworth tagged him with another three-round burst that smashed his spine.

Two invaders dashed for shelter, heading straight for death as O'Neal cut them down with a volley of M-16 fire. But the enemy responded with their own weapons. Silenced firearms spat flames and ugly rasping noises as bullets sizzled toward the mercenaries' positions.

Wentworth heard the lead smack against stone as projectiles struck the boulder. He ducked for cover as bullets chipped chunks from the rock. Ricocheted slugs screamed against the boulder as Wentworth huddled behind the rock. He clenched his teeth and cursed under his breath.

The Hard Corps XO was in a dangerous situation, but far less hazardous than his two teammates, who didn't have the advantage of a large, solid cover. The boulder was effectively bulletproof. It would stop anything short of a grenade or a motor round. The bushes used for cover by O'Neal and Fanelli wouldn't stop any bullets.

Wentworth was more concerned about the lives of his fellow Hard Corps warriors than for his own safety. Of course, he had drawn a lot of enemy fire away from his teammates and he had already taken out three opponents and wounded a fourth, but that still left plenty of invaders for O'Neal and Fanelli to cope with. Drawing enemy fire? Big deal. One or two men with automatic weapons would be enough to keep him pinned down and out of action.

No way, he thought. *No way are these sons of bitches going to keep me from my duty. No way am I going to let my blood brothers face this alone.*

He fished a small penlight from his pocket and snapped it on. Wentworth tossed the penlight away from the boulder. The light bounced and whirled as the instrument rolled. Since both sides were using silenced weapons, the enemy was watching for the muzzleflash of the Hard Corps's rifles. When they saw the rapidly moving penlight dance in the darkness at the knoll, the Asian hitmen assumed it was the muzzleflash from a noise suppressor.

Vinh's followers also assumed the "weapon" belonged to the sniper on the knoll. They immediately shifted the aim of their weapons and fired in the direction of the penlight. The steady beam of light soon betrayed the tiny flashlight and the Asian killers realized they had been tricked. But the diversion had bought Wentworth two and a half seconds, more than enough time to scramble from the boulder and roll to a new position.

Wentworth prepared to continue picking off opponents one by one, but two shapes suddenly rose to the summit of the knoll. The enemy scouts had continued to approach the lieutenant's position. Wentworth had been so busy trying to help cover his partners, he had completely forgotten about the two men who had been steadily closing in to take him out.

The closest man carried an M-16 rifle slung to his shoulder and held what appeared to be two sticks in his fist. The other scout had an Uzi subgun in his fists. The latter presented the greatest immediate threat. Wentworth snap aimed and fired his FAL. A three round burst shattered the scout's face and turned his brains into gray ooze that splattered into the night.

With an angry shout, the guy with the sticks charged. He lashed out with his weapon. One stick was attached to the other by a short horse hair rope. A *nunchaku,* Wentworth realized, an instant before the sticks struck the barrel of his FAL.

The *nunchaku* is a flexible device, originally a rice flail used by farmers throughout the Orient. It is also a superb hand-to-hand weapon, very fast, elusive, and capable of breaking bones with even a glancing blow. Although generally associated with Bruce Lee and other kung fu artists, the *nunchaku* can be incorporated in any style of fighting, and it is deadly in the hands of an expert.

One stick whirled around the barrel of Wentworth's FAL. The scout seized it with his free hand and trapped the rifle, using the sticks and horsehair rope to create a vicelike grip on the merc's weapon. The Asian quickly rammed a hard sidestick to Wentworth's midsection. The blow staggered the Hard Corps XO as his opponent yanked the *nunchaku* and ripped the FAL from Wentworth's grasp.

The enemy scout tossed the rifle aside and advanced with his *nunchaku* whirling, the loose stick cutting a series of figure eight patterns in the air. The Asian wanted to take Wentworth alive. He might have to break a few bones, but the guy appeared to be confident he could accomplish the task without killing the American merc. The way he handled the *nunchaku* suggested his confidence was well-deserved.

Wentworth grabbed the hilt of his *wakazashi* and drew the samurai short sword from its scabbard. He held the weapon in an unorthodox overhand grip, the foot-and-a-half steel blade extending from the bottom of his right fist. Wentworth met his opponent's charge, slashing his sword in a figure eight pattern similar to the assassin's own *nunchaku* strokes.

The tactic surprised the assailant. Wood struck steel. The flail stick was chopped in half by Wentworth's whirling blade. The Asian tried to back away from Wentworth, aware that his opponent wasn't the "cowardly weakling" that all Americans are supposed to be according to Hanoi.

Wentworth didn't let him escape. The merc stepped forward and slashed a backhand sword stroke across his opponent's belly. Blood spewed from the deep cut as the Asian staggered and howled in agony. Wentworth reversed his grip on the sword hilt and struck again. The blade of the *wakazashi* sliced through the wounded man's neck and decapitated him. Both head and body tumbled down the knoll.

William O'Neal hadn't been able to use a boulder for cover or a penlight for a diversion when the enemy began pumping rounds into the bush he was using for cover. The Hard Corps commander had only one choice of action. It was simple, desperate, and based more on reflex instinct than conscious strategy.

O'Neal rolled furiously, firing his M-16 with a steady stream of full auto slugs. He didn't aim, and he didn't pay much attention to any single target. For the moment, O'Neal was more concerned about simply keeping the enemy occupied than shooting them. He glimpsed the shapes of two or three enemy invaders diving to the ground. Another shape convulsed in a twitching death dance, a line of bulletholes streaked across his chest.

The Hard Corps commander came to a halt, pointed

his M-16 at a disoriented Asian opponent, and fired the last three 5.56mm rounds from the magazine. The bullets burned into the Vietnamese hitman's solar plexus and tunneled upward to blast his heart to bits.

Two more enemy gunmen approached. O'Neal triggered his M-16. The "click" of the empty weapon sounded like the key unlocking the door to Death. The two Asian gunmen aimed their weapons and prepared to open fire. O'Neal glared at them and left the M-16 on the ground. He rose slowly, but did not raise his hands.

"Xin ong lam on," O'Neal began, addressing the Vietnamese men in their native language. "Please, allow me to die standing up."

"Co chul!" one of the gunmen replied. "Agreed."

"Toi rat doi on," O'Neal bowed. "You have my gratitude."

The Hard Corps commander stood straight and raised his head. The knot of fear in his belly wasn't as hard as he thought it would be. Long ago O'Neal had accepted the fact he would die on the battlefield. He knew he would not live to a ripe old age. The idea of death didn't frighten him. It happened to everyone and O'Neal wasn't egotistic enough to think he'd be an exception.

"Sure hope they're good shots," he muttered, waiting for the bullets to crash into his body.

Automatic fire erupted. O'Neal flinched. An involuntary gasp escaped from his lips. His hands jerked upward, moving to defend himself. It was an absurd reflex reaction, trying to ward off bullets with flesh.

But O'Neal's body hadn't been ravaged by high velocity projectiles. One of the two Asian gunmen suddenly dropped his weapon and fell on his face. Three ragged bullet holes marked his back between the shoulder blades. The other Vietnamese killer turned to face Joe Fanelli. The mercenary's M-16 smashed three more 5.56mm rounds into the Asian's chest.

The Hanoi hitter was tough. He staggered and fell to one knee, but still tried to point his MAC-10 machinepistol at Fanelli. O'Neal drew his Colt pistol and fired two rounds with speed and accuracy worthy of an Old West gunfighter. Fanelli also unleashed another volley of M-16 missiles. The Asian was slammed by five bullets. His head and upper torso looked as if a pride of lions had had them for lunch.

"You okay, Captain?" Fanelli called out.

"Yeah," O'Neal replied, scooping up his M-16. "Thanks to you, Joe. Watch yourself. There's more of 'em around here."

"Not many," Fanelli replied.

"Only takes one to kill you," O'Neal reminded him.

The Hard Corps commander remembered the invader Wentworth had shot in the leg. Better take care of him now, he thought. O'Neal took the empty magazine from his M-16 and replaced it with a fresh mag. He told Fanelli to stay undercover and watch for opponents. Then O'Neal headed for the spruce, where one of the invaders had dragged the wounded man at the beginning of the firefight.

O'Neal approached slowly, slithering behind a column of bushes to conceal his movement. The lone figure of the injured Vietnamese lay by the base of the tree, his back resting against the trunk. The guy seemed to be alone. A CAR-15 was propped against the tree near his right arm.

The man's comrades might have simply abandoned him as wounded and unable to walk. Pretty cold-blooded behavior, but they might also be using the wounded man as a lure. O'Neal assumed the latter. Soldiers are soldiers regardless of nationality. Captain

Vinh might not give a shit about the lives of his men, but most soldiers feel a strong bond of loyalty toward their brothers in uniform.

The Communist doctrine of Southeast Asia was hardhearted and callous, but the people there aren't much different than elsewhere in the world. Not really. O'Neal knew that the belief that orientals do not value human life was bigoted nonsense. The family is very important to most Asians. Governments and national duty usually take a backseat to doing what's best for the family.

Unfortunately, what was best for the family often required soldiers to march off to war in order to avoid shame or, in the case of dictatorships like Vietnam's, to avoid the family punishment for having a traitor as a son, brother, or husband. The VC had recruited a lot of personnel by threatening their families. The government of Hanoi was probably still using that tactic for getting men to act as agents and saboteurs.

The men the Hard Corps were fighting probably didn't know much about their mission, and they'd probably rather be home with their families. Most probably didn't belong to the Communist Party or care much about politics one way or the other. Most were victims of a system they did not understand.

War is always a dirty business, O'Neal thought. The Hard Corps would have to kill the invaders for self-preservation. Half of fighting is just trying to stay alive. O'Neal considered it a pity that strangers must fight and die in obscure battlefields for a cause none of them really understands. Vinh's men were victims of circumstance, but they also threatened the lives of the Hard Corps and Trang Nih's group of freedom fighters.

O'Neal suspected the wounded man by the tree was being used to bait him. That meant one or more of

Vinh's men was probably lying in wait, ready to ambush anyone who tried to capture the wounded invader. O'Neal slowly scanned the area, searching for evidence of concealed enemies . . .

He noticed a branch that jutted from a bush near the tree. Something was odd about it. The branch looked like two branches tied together. O'Neal wasn't certain, but he thought the "branch" might be a camouflaged rifle barrel. He aimed at the bush and triggered his M-16. The silenced rifle sliced a trio of 5.56mm slugs into the bush, a couple inches above the suspicious branch.

A voice groaned and the body of the Vietnamese ambusher tumbled from the bush, his chest riddled by bulletholes. The wounded man grabbed his CAR-15 and swung the weapon toward O'Neal's position. The Hard Corps commander had no choice. He fired at the gunman before his opponent could aim the carbine. The top of the man's head popped open like a jack-in-the-box. Brains splashed the treetrunk and the man's body slumped lifeless at the base of the spruce.

"I thought you wanted to take one of them alive," Fanelli commented as he approached O'Neal.

"You can't always get what you want," O'Neal said with a shrug. "Why'd you leave your post?"

"They retreated," Fanelli answered. "If they come back, there'll be more of 'em. Besides, you figured this was pretty much a diversion from another assault from another side of the compound. I figured you'd want to regroup and either head back to base or form a defense here, in case the enemy follows up with another strike. That's Vinh's MO, isn't it?"

"But don't count on him following it," O'Neal frowned. "Vinh is a seasoned commander. He'll try to avoid being too predictable. Looks like you took a few lumps, Joe.''

"Oh?" Fanelli touched the welt on his cheek. "Had a little hand-to-hand with one of the enemy. You should see the other guy, Captain."

"No thanks," O'Neal replied.

CHAPTER 11

CAPTAIN VINH CHI LAM was frustrated. His second hit team had apparently been no more successful than the first. This wasn't like fighting the army of South Vietnam, which often lacked organization and initiative. Whoever these Americans were, they were very good.

Vinh remembered fighting Americans in Vietnam. They were always straddled by restrictions, but they were very tough, very clever, and often seemed to do their best when things were worse. The enemy holding the compound were certainly doing well. Too damn well. Battlefield intelligence reports indicated an American had been transported from the first firefight on a stretcher. Only one of them was wounded, but Vinh did not know how badly. This was small comfort, since Vinh had already lost almost thirty men since the conflict began. Most frustrating.

Jacque and Slim, the two junkie hustlers, were dumbfounded and shocked by the intensity of the military action going on around them. They hadn't bargained for anything on such a large scale. Shit, they figured the gooks had hired them to drive the truck so the dudes could rouse some dope dealing competition. They hadn't reckoned on getting involved in a goddamn war.

So far Jacque and Slim had not been actively involved in the fighting. But that could change if Vinh decided to employ the two American dopers. Not that they minded helping the former Vietcong kill fellow Americans. Neither man was very patriotic. And four kilos of uncut heroin would do a lot to soothe what consciences they had.

"It's my own ass I'm worried about," Slim told Jacque. "If you had any brains, you'd be worried too, man."

"What makes you think I ain't worried, shit brains?" Jacque replied as he squatted by the eighteen wheeler. "What you gotta keep in mind about these or-ientals is they value honor, and they got no respect for a man who can't keep up his macho. So do your best to suck it up tight."

Ban Ban glared at the two round-eyed occidentals with disgust and loathing. He wanted to send the pair into combat, use them as cannon fodder to flush out the enemy. Let Americans kill other Americans. Captain Vinh had vetoed this plan. He claimed the two junkies could provide a more valuable service.

Of course, Ban Ban followed Vinh's orders, although he didn't like it. He'd like to kill all Americans. Every man, woman and child. He couldn't understand why the Soviets hadn't launched missiles armed with thermonuclear warheads to blow them all to bits.

He fingered his trophy pouch full of shrunken ears, collected over the years from the bodies of his slain enemies. Ban Ban remembered how his adopted father, a farmer in Vietnam, had first told him about the custom of collecting ears from dead soldiers. The idea had intrigued and amused him even as a boy.

Ban Ban had no memory of his natural parents or his real name. All he knew was that they had been killed while he was still an infant. Then he was adopted by the farmer. For five years, he lived with his adopted father, and these had been the happiest years of his life.

"Be careful little one," the boy's adopted father cautioned him. "Don't stray too far. I can not watch you while I am working."

The bronzed and weathered man shooed the toddler back onto the dike between the higher and lower sections of the rice paddie. They lived in a rural settlement, too far from the Mekong Delta to be part of the large plantations owned by the wealthy growers.

The peasants eked out a living for themselves, with barely enough left over to barter for city goods. It was a hard life, but the peasants didn't mind. It was the same lifestyle their families had known for centuries.

Sometimes the farmer would have to leave his adopted son with women from the village. But then there were times when the pace of his labor was not so urgent, when the farmer was not planting rice or harvesting it or repairing dikes for the monsoons to prevent flooding. He would take the boy along with him and watch the hours measure the day until it was time for the evening meal. Then the boy would listen to the farmer's tales of his travels and experiences as a youth.

The farmer's name was Ngo Diem. His mother was originally from Burma. When World War II broke out, Ngo was a young man, looking for adventure. His mother heard from her people, the Kachins in Burma, that the Americans were organizing members of her tribe as resistance fighters against the Japanese. The Americans were also paying them in gold.

She arranged that her son be met by relatives. The family concurred that her arrangement was a better choice than waiting for the young man to be conscripted by the occupying forces of the Japanese and put into a labor battallion.

Ngo was sent to Burma where his uncles taught him how to fire their musket rifles. His experience during World War II consisted of waiting for Japanese soldiers to ambush them. The Kachin tribesmen cut off the ears of the dead Japanese and sold them to the Americans for gold.

Ngo related these tales to the boy from day to day, and once he even showed the lad the musket he had used during the war. The farmer lovingly unwrapped the piece from oil rags, used to maintain it from tropical moisture. The musket was of ancient design, but not itself an antique. The Americans had tried to introduce the Kachins to more modern rifles that were in greater supply, but the traditional tribesmen would not accept them. Thus, the Americans had traditional muskets newly manufactured and flown to Burma for the Kachin resistance forces.

The tiny, shriveled black prunes that the farmer showed his son didn't look like human ears, but the boy was certain his adopted father would never tell a lie. He was fascinated by the macabre trophies that Ngo Diem kept in a leather pouch.

The first incursions of Vietcong were sporadic, as they made their transit through the tiny village where Ngo and his son lived. The VC would tell the villagers of their long journey, bringing them supplies from the north. They spoke of transporting war materials as if they were performing a religious pilgrimage. As time went on, the sporadic trickle became a steady stream. Instead of backpacks with one or two motor shells the porters were pushing bicycles with bamboo frame braces weighted down with about a hundred kilos of cargo. The 'Cong had become a highly effective human railroad.

Every day brought more of the Vietcong through the village. Their polite entreaties became outright demands.

"Ngo Diem," one of the VC addressed the farmer, "you must perform your patriotic duty. Merely feeding us from time to time is not enough."

"From time to time?" Ngo Diem displayed a bitter smile. It had been months since he had enough rice left over to barter for the few luxuries that brightened their lives. The boy's few playthings had worn out or been lost and there was nothing left to replace them.

"You must also make a journey to the north," the 'Cong leader harangued him. "You are strong and you can be spared from your farming for a while. These are hard times, comrade. We must all make some sacrifices."

The guerrillas were still trying to win the hearts and minds of the people. They had not yet begun their infamous efforts to destablize the population by systemically murdering civil servants, mayors, teachers, and tax collectors to try to "urge" villagers to join the "people's revolution."

The Vietcong traveling the Ho Chi Minh Trail were becoming so effective at resupplying their comrades close to Saigon that the U.S. Air Force was directed to interdict the supply route. At first the flights of B-52 bombers looked for large concentrations of Vietcong.

The aircraft also carried chemical agents to denude the heavy tropical foliage because the 'Cong could be detected more easily without their protective tree cover.

On one of the endless, bright, sunny days between monsoon seasons, the boy was attending his first session of school some distance from the site, where his adopted father labored.

Suddenly, he and his classmates heard the thunder fall from the sky. Five-hundred pound bombs from one flight of B-52's obliterated one square mile, overturning earth and rendering the landscape unrecognizable. When the boy returned to his home, he exhausted himself looking for some sign to tell him he was in the right place. He searched in vain until dark for his father, wandering between the newly formed sinkholes.

Thus, when the boy lost his adopted father, it was not directly due to the actions of the Vietcong. These circumstances would have a great effect on the choices he would make in the future.

Most of the farmers had been warned to relocate by the government, but the pressure from the Vietcong for them to stay was just as intense. In the end, to choose either path became a death sentence. Making no decision at all was far easier.

As the bombings continued, the Vietcong took away everything they could carry from the destroyed land, including the seven-year-old boy. They sought new trails on which to carry their cargos to the south.

The fighting against the ARVN intensified, and the 'Cong didn't know what to do with the boy. A few of them genuinely cared for him and tried to keep him fed and clothed. He was watched by the women of a village where members of the VC worked at masquerade jobs during the day. But when night fell and they became guerrillas again, the boy became very excited. He knew an attack would begin somewhere soon. The Cong were amused by his cries of *"Ban ban!"* Vietnamese for "clash in battle." This eventually became his nickname among the 'Cong. Ban Ban decided he liked his new name.

After a couple of years, Ban Ban was big enough to serve as an ammunition bearer for the 'Cong. He joined the VC on several missions and saw the results of more jungle bombings. He came to the conclusion that the Americans were his mortal enemies and the Vietcong was his family.

The black pajama-clad 'Cong soldiers moved in a steady, disciplined dog trot toward the headquarters of the unit located at a village in the Mekong Delta. There, a muscular young VC sergeant with golden eyes met the team.

"Sergeant Vinh," a VC trooper reported. "The Americans have begun their sweep."

"Did you spot the ARVN unit?" Vinh Chi Lam queried.

"I've noted their location on the map," the soldier replied.

"Now that we know their location, we don't have to worry about them anymore," Vinh mused. "They will stay put even if ordered to the contrary."

Vinh's contempt for the ARVN troops was based on his own observations. Many times he had watched an American Special Forces advisor as the Yankee exhorted an ARVN officer to attack when the moment was right because the Vietcong had been outmaneuvered by the American troops. All too often, the South Vietnamese units were told by their officers to avoid confronting the enemy. Instead, they would head for where the fighting was lightest, and the looting most plentiful. Vinh felt confident he could count on their unintended cooperation.

As for the American forces, that was another matter. But even they had their weaknesses. Whereas the "vulnerable child" ploy no longer functioned to paralyze the ARVN soldiers, it never seemed to fail to immobilize the Yankee dogfaces.

"Have you found a child to use in tricking the Americans?" Vinh asked.

"Not this time, Sergeant," the soldier replied. "The parents of this village have lost three children in the last month. They have successfully hidden the others."

"Didn't you tell them that the savage, incompetent Yankee soldiers shot their children by mistake?" Vinh blustered.

"The villagers replied that it didn't matter who was responsible," the private replied. "They said they are going to make certain it doesn't happen again."

"Cowards," Vinh growled with disgust. "Find Ban Ban. We are going to need some advantage facing those American troops."

"*Mau Lin! Mau Lin!*" Ban Ban yelled. "Hurry! Hurry!"

He and his companions played a game around a pool of water that had formed within a bomb crater. As usual, he had appointed himself the leader over the younger children, the only ones who would put up with his bullying.

He lined the children up in mock squad formation and made them stand at attention before sending them off into the tropical ground cover to hide. Suddenly one of the children's mothers ran along the pathway from the village.

"Come quick!" she yelled. She made a quick nose

count and called out for a missing child. "Government soldiers are coming with Americans. There is going to be a battle. Come back to the village. We must hide."

"I am not afraid!" Ban Ban replied. "I will fight with the Vietcong. They are our friends. If you were patriotic, you would do the same."

She shooed him away and herded the children off. The woman was as fearful of the 'Cong as she was of the coming battle.

"You are a foolish little boy," she called to Ban Ban as she and the children hurried away. "I cannot be responsible for you."

The Vietcong private found Ban Ban doodling pictures in the mud with a stick. He told the boy that Sergeant Vinh needed him. It was to be the first of many such requests that Ban Ban would hear for the rest of his life. He eagerly followed the soldier back to the VC unit, occasionally glancing over his shoulder for the enemy.

Sergeant Vinh deployed his squad behind the tree line and told Ban Ban not to show himself until he felt a tug on the piece of twine tied to his ankle. The American troops were the main danger. They were a squad of U.S. Army soldiers on a search and destroy sweep, seeking to catch the 'Cong in a pincer movement, and force them into the arms of the entrenched ARVN troops.

Ban Ban waited, sitting in the tall grass. He waited for the signal which would allow him to risk his life for the VC.

The American soldiers grew wary and hesitated as they neared the treeline. Sensing something might be lurking among the trees, a sergeant in the patrol ordered one of his men to lob a blooper round into the forest. Vinh saw the soldier break open an M-79 and check the 40mm fragmentation shell inside. That was enough for

Vinh. He jerked the twine tied to the boy's ankle.

Ban Ban stood up and walked parallel to the line of advancing soldiers. He stopped and turned his head as if he had just noticed them. His eyes brightened with his best plastic smile as he waved at the Americans.

"Hold it!" a green trooper from Canton, Ohio, cried out. "He's just a kid!"

"Fire that weapon!" the American sergeant told the PFC with the blooper. "That's a direct order!"

Those were the last words the NCO ever uttered. The hail of gunfire from the treeline cut down eight of the eleven troopers, including the sergeant.

Two hundred yards away, the radioman from the platoon to which the squad belonged called in for his commanding officer. When Lieutenant Andrews learned what had happened, he ordered another squad to reinforce the first.

The Vietcong had finished off the remnants of the first patrol and gleefully looted the bodies of the dead Americans. Ban Ban noticed that one piece of equipment had been left behind. He rolled over the dead PFC who had manned the M-79. The boy pried the blooper from the dead soldier's bloodstained fingers. Barely able to lift the weapon, Ban Ban cradled it in both arms and followed his companions into the bush.

"Look what the boy has brought us!" Corporal Phong, Vinh's assistant squad leader declared. "A grenade launcher!"

"Ban Ban!" yelled the excited boy. "May I keep it, Captain Vinh?"

Vinh had not become a sergeant without being able to think on his feet. He was more accustomed to motivating adults than children, but decided that one technique might work well with the boy.

174

"You have done your squad a great service by recovering such a valuable piece of equipment, Private Ban Ban," he declared. "Even though the honor is yours, you will have to let Corporal Phong operate the launcher for you until you are older. You must grow strong to handle such a weapon. However, we shall allow you to carry ammunition for him. It is a very responsible and important position, Ban Ban."

The boy was already tired from carrying the M-79. He realized he was going to need help and decided that being an ammo bearer was better than being nothing at all. Best of all: Sergeant Vinh had called him Private Ban Ban! Until now, he had had no status in the group —now he mattered at last.

Suddenly the Vietcong heard the sound of approaching jet aircraft. Their world erupted into a ball of fire. It was by chance that any of them escaped with their lives. Ban Ban recalled the sea of flames for the rest of his life. He remembered choking from lack of oxygen. He remembered his hair burning as he staggered from the inferno, the grenade launcher still in his grasp.

Sergeant Vinh found the boy and carried him away from the site of the airstrike. As soon as the boy could breathe, he began to sob inconsolably. After Vinh dragged and carried Ban Ban three kilometers, he fell to the ground exhausted.

"I will kill all Americans," Ban Ban sobbed, heartbroken that, once again, those close to him had been killed by American bombs. "I am not afraid. I am not afraid."

There were no other survivors from Vinh's unit. Since his group had been decimated, Vinh was given a new assignment by Hanoi. He was to work even closer to enemy lines—within Saigon itself.

"What will we do now, Sergeant Vinh?" asked Ban Ban, as the two slowly and stealthily made their way toward the capital.

Vinh found it difficult to formulate an answer that would make sense to the boy. At last he said, "You and I will travel disguised as father and son. When a suitable opportunity presents itself, we will harass the enemy and destroy his ability to make war on us."

The language used by his superiors about his new assignment had been very brief and to the point. Vinh was to perform sabotage, assassination and terrorist mass murder.

"What do I get to do?" Ban Ban asked.

"You will be of great value to me posing as an adorable child," Vinh explained. "First, you must refrain from calling me sergeant."

"Shall I call you father?" the boy suggested uncertainly.

"In the interests of our mission," Vinh replied with great seriousness. "I'm afraid that will be necessary."

"Oh!" the boy smiled. "That won't be so hard."

Vinh had been trained to regard any sentiment as weakness that would only delay the eventual triumph of the revolution. But he saw no harm in fostering the illusion of that sentiment in the boy, since it might at some point be useful. Yet, he needed to rationalize in his own mind behavior containing family ties that could be considered emotionally normal. He wanted to avoid confused notions about his goals. As long as the boy did nothing that wasn't expected of him by others, he would be useful. It didn't matter what illusions Ban Ban allowed himself to believe in.

"We will pose as a country peddler and his son," Vinh explained. "If you learn your lessons well, I will allow you to carry explosives for me, and I will teach you how they are used.''

On their journey to Saigon, Vinh had grilled Ban Ban incessantly about the boy's new identity. He skillfully interrogated the boy about his past, and used the information to weave new identities for both of them. Thus, the deception would be very hard to penetrate in a casual street interrogation.

After they arrived in Saigon, the pair stole a cart, and day by day, gathered the cast-offs of the city. They lived by bartering and through the generosity of the American troops toward the boy.

Vinh made contact with his Vietcong underground and was assigned his first targets. On their first mission, Vinh rubbed some local chile pepper into the cheloid tissue of one of Ban Ban's old burns. The pepper made the tissue red and swollen. Then Vinh obtained a small container of chicken blood, to be applied liberally to the boy's head at the proper time.

Now they were ready. Sergeant Vinh pulled the cart up outside a bar frequented by American soldiers. He had double-checked himself to make certain he had discarded all weapons that day, except for two throwaway grenades. There would be no incriminating evidence to link him to the bombing.

Outside the bar, Vinh instructed Ban Ban to hold a fragmentation grenade for a moment. The Vietcong NCO held a white phosphorous grenade in his fist as he checked Ban Ban's burn. It appeared fresh, very red and swollen. Vinh nodded with satisfaction and pulled the pin from his willie peter grenade, lobbing it through the bar door.

Clouds of flaming dust spewed into the street, but Vinh and Ban Ban had already stepped clear of the blast area. The screams of agony within the bar were welcome music to Vinh and his young accomplice. The VC sergeant snatched the other frag grenade from the boy's hand and yanked the pin. Any survivors would try to seek an exit. Vinh tossed the grenade across the threshold to insure they would find only death.

He motioned for Ban Ban to lay on the ground. The second grenade exploded. The impact knocked Vinh to the ground, but he quickly lashed a kick to the cart and knocked it over. Then he opened the vial of chicken blood and applied it to Ban Ban's scalp and forehead. The bar was burning vigorously now and the screams from inside had ceased.

"My child!" Vinh wailed for the sake of any passersby who might be called upon as witnesses. "Please help my child!"

The Saigon police soon arrived, closely followed by the American MP's and a television crew. The newsmen carefully recorded the magnanimous behavior of the MP's, who put the wounded Vietnamese child and his father in the first ambulance at the scene. They were whisked away from the area even before the American GI's were extracted from the bombsite.

When the police interrogation team arrived at the hospital, the brave lad and his father were nowhere to be found.

Weeks passed. The "father and son" team gathered intelligence about the daily habits of possible assassination targets. Sometimes Sergant Vinh would stand watch, noting American truck convoys carrying ammo. Ban Ban waited to be sent as a runner to notify VC teams waiting to ambush the GI's.

Ban Ban's terrorist education was not neglected. He learned to read French, Russian and English from packets of plastic explosives. He improved his Vietnamese by reciting propaganda leaflets left by the Vietcong. He learned geography and civics by following public officials about the streets of Saigon. And he studied his mathematics with great care, by estimating such things as a two minute fuse, and the precise distance needed from a target for an assassination to survive the detonation of plastic explosives.

He was slowly shaped into a well-honed tool of the Vietcong. From time to time, Sergeant Vinh would take bets from his fellow VC on the chances that Ban Ban would survive his next mission. Vinh figured he couldn't lose. He would get the money if the boy lived and, if he was killed, he would be relieved of his tiresome duties as a babysitter.

Ban Ban turned fifteen during the fall of Saigon. Shortly thereafter, Sergeant Vinh was made an officer. It almost broke the young man's heart to see his hero depart for further training in the Soviet Union, but Ban Ban had distinguished himself to such a degree that he was made a corporal in the newly established local militia. His only regret was that there were no more Americans to kill.

Ban Ban soon found his duties boring and spent his off-duty hours hanging out with remnants of the Saigon Cowboys, the motorcycle riff-raff that had found no place in the new society. They specialized in harassing people who had worked for the Americans, but had not been evacuated.

Then his hero returned from the Soviet Union. Ban Ban was informed by the commander of his unit that he was being reassigned to his former CO. Vinh was forming a new team of special operatives.

In truth, Ban Ban had worn out his welcome with the militia. His appetite for savagery and his total paranoia of anything American made him difficult to work with.

A new city was rising out of the turmoil following the victory of the north, and his fellow militiamen were glad to see Ban Ban depart. Now they could get some work done.

Ban Ban also had work to do. He had collected one hundred and forty ears so far, and he hoped to reach two hundred on his new assignment in the United States.

CHAPTER 12

CAINE FINISHED PREPARING a bed of punji stakes and covered it with some loose brush. This was the last of a number of boobytraps he had prepared. Enemies were coming toward the compound. He didn't hear them approach, but he sensed them, as a sleeping snake senses the presence of a bird that lands too close.

He slipped into the shadows and waited for the enemy to draw closer. From the south, Caine heard the elongated crack of a 5.56mm round, and nodded with grim satisfaction. An enemy had discovered one of his surprises.

The shot he'd heard had been fired from a stainless steel tube. The trap gun was hidden in a small fern, near a narrow dirt road, and had been detonated by the force of a man's foot, which shoved the tube down and rammed the end of a cartridge into a nail, which then acted as a firing pin. The bullet drove upward through the invader's foot, severing muscle and spraying his pant leg with blood. The projectile cut more flesh, split his tongue, and lodged in his brain. The man died noiselessly.

Not so silent was the victim's partner, who jumped back, retreating from his comrade's fate. But he found death has many forms. Stepping backward onto a false platform of brush, he fell into a shallow pit lined with punji stakes. In this case, the sticks all pointed inward. The man's weight carried his foot sideways to sharp points that dug deep into his flesh, and deeper as he tried to pull his leg free.

His cries of anguished terror brought a third raider to abandon his line of advance. He dashed into the forest into a piano wire snare propped open by two slender shavings of pine, which gave way at the slightest pressure. The wire noose tightened with a snapping force in direct proportion to the man's momentum. As it constricted around his neck, the wire cut off his breathing, sliced neatly through his windpipe and carotid arteries, and left a dripping crimson gash where his throat had been.

A line of enemies from the north were drawn by the screams of the trapped victim. Caine waited for them, unseen, as the three men walked just past him. His first arrow punctured the last man's kidney. He couldn't even scream as he fell dying to the ground. The curare tip had caused muscle paralysis to set in, and cut off his voice.

The two remaining men were momentarily unaware of the fate of their companion, just as Steve Caine had planned.

He launched his second arrow when the second man in the line bent forward to duck under a large branch. When his body was inclined forward, the arrow split his backribs and sliced up the trunk to pierce his heart.

A sinister but effective principle of jungle warfare is that killing the enemy is not enough. It must be done with style and efficiency, to terrorize as much as possible, to demoralize and confuse the enemy.

Thus, Caine left the third man alive. When the invader finally turned around, he found his two comrades lying dead. He gasped in horror and amazement, then turned and fled. The man would return to his comrades and tell them what happened. The fear-inspired caution might make the invaders slow their advance, or even cause a retreat.

However, Caine soon spotted another group of interlopers who seemed determined to keep on coming. He noticed they were positioned near another set of traps. The Hard Corps merc raised his M-16 to his shoulder and aimed carefully.

Although a highly trained marksman, Caine let off a seemingly indiscriminate stream of 5.56mm rounds according to the principles of area fire. The multiple projectiles hit two men. One invader's arm was severed at the elbow. The second was hit in the upper thigh. The sudden spurt of arterial blood in a geyser from his femoral artery splattered his comrades as the man lay screaming in agony.

The hail of lead served to drive the surviving men to seek cover. The first was lucky. He hit the ground and encountered only a soft bed of pine needles. One of his comrades was not so fortunate. He landed on a punji stake which punctured his abdomen. His efforts to disengage himself slowly degenerated into nothing more than a reflexive wriggling that continued after he was dead.

Another invader had flopped down on a trio of punji stakes, puncturing his chest and throat. He died within seconds, a pool of blood forming around his corpse.

Only two members of the group survived. They retreated as fast as possible, as Caine coolly moved to another position.

His previous missions within the compound were paying off. Caine knew the 500 acres better than anyone. He had planned his boobytraps carefully, and selected his ambush spots based upon his knowledge of the forest. Moving into his new position, Caine lowered himself to the ground and seemed to disappear. Motionless, he waited.

Five minutes passed before he heard enemy footsteps. At least four men, Caine reckoned from the sound of their boots. The infiltrators walked past Caine's unseen figure, as he rose from his camouflaged blanket, a convincing cover with a layer of dirt, pine cones, and blades of grass. Caine unsheathed his survival knife and jumped the four from behind.

The first stroke with his razor sharp blade sliced through the nerves at the base of an unsuspecting opponent's neck. His spinal cord severed, the man dropped like a stone. One of his comrades started to turn, a MAC-10 machinepistol in his fist. Caine moved in swiftly, and slashed the top of his opponent's gun hand. Cut tendons robbed the hand of muscular control.

Two horizontal slashes across the man's neck finished the job. Blood jetted from the slit carotid and jugular. Caine tripped the dying man to get him out of the way. The guy hit the ground face down in a puddle of his own blood.

The survivors were suddenly aware of Caine. One of them moved to flank him in order to keep the Hard Corps pro from performing the same maneuver. The other hastily unslung his CAR-15 from his shoulder.

Never a man to be chained to a single method, Caine

momentarily abandoned his cold steel and pulled his silencer-equipped Colt automatic. He snapshot the closest man, drilling a .45 caliber slug between the Vietnamese assassin's eyes. The orbital bones cracked and the man's eyeballs exploded from their sockets before his corpse hit the ground.

Caine felt a bullet from the second man's carbine whiz past his ear. Fear shot up his spine, but this only increased the speed of his reflex reaction to the near brush with death. Caine quickly shifted aim and took out the attacker with a 250 grain hardball messenger of death. The bullet crashed into the guy's sternum, driving bone splinters into his heart.

The sound of the battle drew more invaders to the scene. Three Vietnamese killers converged on the area and discovered the bodies of their four slain comrades. One of them glanced overhead at the limbs of a tree above, but he saw only a pine branch dipping gently in the wind.

Steve Caine concentrated on thinking "like a tree" as he moved his arm in rhythm of the shifting wind. He had first read about the ability to melt into one's surroundings from a magazine article about the *ninja*, the legendary espionage agents and assassins of Japan, but his actual instruction in the technique had been given to him by his brothers among the Katu. Like the *ninja*, the Katu were also masters of camouflage and concealment, and Caine had learned his lessons well.

He waited a moment, then aimed his silenced pistol and pumped a single .45 round into the top of an invader's skull. The man's head burst like a blood filled lab jar smacked by a sledgehammer. Another opponent looked up just in time to receive a bullet in the face.

The third and last gunman raised his Uzi and fired

into the branches above. The invader's weapon was also equipped with a silencer. It rasped harshly as 9mm slugs raked the pine tree. But, Caine's body did not come toppling down.

He had already dropped from the tree limbs and landed quietly on the far side of the trunk. The invader was still peering up at the branches, confused and puzzled by his inability to locate the Hard Corps ambusher. Caine quickly rushed his opponent, pushing down on the enemy's Uzi with one hand and with the other driving the blade of his survival knife into the man's throat.

Caine held his opponent to the ground and waited for the final convulsions of death to cease. Then he wiped the blood from his knife on the dead man's shirt, and returned it to the belt sheath on his hip. He slowly rose and glanced about for more attackers. He had no doubt there would be others.

CHAPTER 13

CAINE HAD NOT always been a deadly killing machine, but he had always been a loner.

"I'll try to get to see you more often, little Stevie," the boy's father, Richard Caine had said, apologizing to him. It was a promise much easier to make than keep. His sales job with a large restaurant supply corporation was supposed to have been an eight hours a day, but the corporation fell on hard times. They had let go many of the junior people, and senior salesmen like Richard Caine had to take over their duties.

Initially the corporation's shift from hourly wages and commission to a fixed salary seemed to be an upgrading of the position, but, Richard Caine soon realized the true reason for the switch. It was a lot easier not to pay an overtime differential, but simply write the extra hours into the new job description to be worked at straight time or perhaps no extra pay at all. The legal language describing the new position satisfied all applicable state laws. The company had been very careful of that.

The father's absences did not sit well with his wife, Corinne, the mother of his five children. He was never around to listen to her reports about the kid's progress —or to share in their disciplining.

Steve Caine was the youngest of the children. His mother came to regard him as more of a nuisance than a blessing. And Richard never got to spend as much time with his youngest son as he would have liked.

With little emotional encouragement from his family, Steve always felt awkward at school. The other school children expected him to join their social and physical rough and tumble, but because he didn't keep up, he was marked as the odd man out.

It didn't take the school bullies long to zero in on Steve Caine. His mother was frustrated beyond her ability to cope when he came home, week after week, with torn and dirty clothes, his face bloodied, injuries often requiring bandaging. Gentle admonishments gradually turned into severe threats, and later, beatings.

Steve asked a girl out shortly after entering high school. She laughed in his face. Crushed, he didn't get up the nerve to try again until his senior year. He received rejection after rejection. Steve started to feel he was lucky when the girl didn't laugh or threaten to have him arrested if he ever bothered her again.

But Steve was determined to continue and eventually asked Becky Koljeck if she would go with him to the Senior Prom. Only the social pressure of not having a date for the big event prompted her to seriously consider his request. Three days later, after checking with her parents for permission and thinking the matter over carefully, she accepted.

If misery loved company, they were natural partners. Becky had expectations about boys, love, and marriage from television soap operas and her gossip at school. Whereas she did not encourage all of Steve's advances, neither did she discourage them. The relationship progressed as fast as Becky was capable of adapting.

"If you really love me, Steven," she said breathlessly in the back seat of the car, "you will do the right thing and marry me before we go any further."

Steve was definitely ready for something new, for success instead of failure. He wanted to live the American dream as badly as she did. When he asked her to marry him, he hoped it would be the beginning of a new and better life. Becky's mother was pleased by the news, but her father was distrustful.

With an attitude of hopeless optimism, the newlywed couple bravely tried to stick it out. But Steve didn't have a job, and he wasn't having any luck trying to find one. Neither of them even knew how to balance a checkbook. Neither understood the responsibilities of adulthood. Finally, panicked and filled with despair, Becky returned to her parents.

Completely devastated, Steve began drifting. At first it seemed that the crowd of homeless street people welcomed him into their ranks, but the less social aspect of that element soon marked him as easy prey.

"Leave my sandwich alone, you skinny shithead," the burnt out boozehound bellowed at Steve, inside the Salvation Army soup kitchen.

He did his best to try to intimidate the young man out of his free lunch, but failed. The derelict conferred with two of his buddies and the three of them decided to teach Caine a lesson. They waited outside for Caine to walk into ambush.

It was not the first fight Steve had encountered on the road. He had been sternly advised by his newfound friends that he had better learn to fight back because he was now at the bottom of the barrel. With there was nothing left to be taken from him, the hyenas of the street would settle for a pound of flesh, if only to break the monotony and work off some of the frustrations of their lives.

Caine left the soup kitchen on that cold winter day and headed for a boardinghouse, where he found a place to stay in return for day labor. The three tough drunks had their territory staked out. One saw him approach and signaled the other two, who moved to cut off Steve's escape.

Their gait was unsteady, but Steve Caine knew the bums still constituted a real threat, especially if they managed to knock him off his feet. There are no Queensberry Rules on the street. You do what you have to in order to survive.

Caine struck out with his foot, kicking the first opponent in the balls. He then flanked the man, who was crouched in agony, drool dripping from his chin, and shoved him into the next attacker. The second man's head careened off the wall behind them, leaving matted hair and blood on the textured brick surface as he slid to the pavement. Steve turned to face the last opponent.

The hobo shattered a half-empty bottle of cheap wine over the youth's skull. The blow to the ridge of his brow opened a messy but shallow scalp wound, but otherwise had little effect on Steve. Blood poured down his face as he launched himself at the bum. Then he was on top of the guy, punching him in the face, watching brown stained teeth pop from the man's mouth. He was still slugging away at the fallen opponent when the cops dragged him away.

Steve Caine wasn't much to look at, decided George Thomson as he inspected the young man through the hatchwork wire safety glass of the interview room with the county jail. The thin kid was dressed in castoffs, and appeared sullen and distrustful. But the ten year veteran probation officer sensed there was something special about Caine. The kid had an above average level of spirit and intelligence, but he just wasn't doing anything with it. Goddamn waste, Thomson thought.

According to the arrest report, Caine had been attacked by three derelicts and given back far better than they could take. He was either a man on his way to becoming a vicious killer, Thomson decided, or somebody who had merely defended himself with everything he had.

George reviewed the boy's family history again in his mind. Caine was the product of the middle class, the youngest of five children. That, and the subsequent data, could mean anything to the untrained eye. But, for Thompson, the positive points in Steve's case seemed to out-weigh the negative.

"Probation interview?" Caine said with a shrug. "Looks like you've already got me pegged. I don't need any probation. Put the alkies on probation. You probably will anyway."

"Listen to me, Steve," George Thomson began. "Let's get something straight before we start the interview. The name of this little talk doesn't necessarily mean you're gonna get probation. But, the information I gather here might make the difference, not only in how severely you're judged, but also whether you are found guilty of any crime at all. Just do your best to give me straight answers."

After the explanation, the boy quieted down and settled back. As the interview progressed, Thomson felt his sixth sense kick up. He began to put his finger on the positive influences in Steve Caine's life. Although he was withdrawn, Caine was an avid reader, but not necessarily the material assigned in school. Steve idolized his absent father, making up excuses for all the man's shortcomings.

Thomson decided by the end of the interview that all he could do was give Caine another chance, and exert a little pressure on him to take it.

"I can see you're not so full of hate that you would reject any opportunity given to you," Thomson told Caine at the end of the second probation interview.

"What do you mean by that?" Steve asked. "I don't see any opportunities."

"All I want you to do is give this some thought before you answer," Thomson said. "I have some contacts, friends from my time when I was in the army. If you were to join the military voluntarily, it would give the judge an excuse to cut you loose and keep you out of the stir. But if you do, you've got to play it straight with these guys, especially in Basic. It's no picnic."

"Tell me about it," Caine chuckled. By the end of the second interview he had become more relaxed, even jovial, under the influence of the firm but confident individual in front of him.

"Think about it," Thomson urged.

At the preliminary hearing, the judge addressed Steve severely.

"You are a sorry sight for a young man with his whole life ahead of him," he began. "But you choose to spend it brawling in the street with derelicts. On the basis of your probation interview, I have decided to give you one more chance. You can attempt to defend yourself against a charge of assault or promptly enlist in the United States Army. The armed forces will make a man of you. If you want to fight, Mr. Caine, do it in Vietnam."

Caine had heard about what happened to young men in prison. He heard about being attacked in the showers and cornholed by five hardened convicts who didn't care what the prison did to them since they would never get out of jail anyway. That plus the friendly prodding of George Thomson, made up Caine's mind for him. He told the judge he'd go.

The military wasn't so bad for Caine. All he had to do was follow orders. The threats and shouting of the drill instructors was no big deal. He had been through far worse. The physical demands and pressures were no problem. He simply accepted the training and did what the sergeants told him to do.

By the end of Basic Training, Caine decided to opt for the Special Forces. What the hell, if he was going to get killed in 'Nam he might as well do it right. He didn't honestly give a shit anymore. Let them kill him over there in some rice paddy. It didn't matter anyway.

Despite his "fuck it" attitude about his own life, Caine did remarkably well in Jump School. He also received praise for his physical and mental accomplishments. Not much, of course. The army never gave big praise unless they wanted you to re-up. Still, it was enough to encourage Caine to try harder and do better. He polished his brass, shined his boots, and hardly ever left the barracks on the weekends, when most soldiers headed for town to get drunk or get laid—preferably both. He graduated with honors and went to 'Nam as a private first class.

"Hey Caine," a fellow squad member began as they zipped up the bodybag of one of their buddies, to get the corpse ready for the Graves Registration personnel. "Don't this shit ever bother you, man?"

"I think of it this way," Caine replied in an effort to mollify the distraught man. "I had a clearer picture of what I was getting into than most of you guys did. For me, this is a step up from the life I had back home."

"I hate to think of what that must have been like," the other man muttered. "But I guess that would make you look at things a lot different."

Amidst the physical destruction and emotional turmoil going on around him, Steve Caine soon found that he was beginning to get his "sea legs" on this voyage of discovery. With his own misery on the wane, he began to turn his attention to the people around him.

Never before had Steve Caine been a part of a group, but he genuinely cared about his fellow GI's—especially the other Green Berets. There is a special kinship between men in combat. Caine wasn't very good at expressing his feelings, but he was willing to risk his life for the sake of his fellow soldiers, and that was enough. He also came to care for the Vietnamese, whose lives were being destroyed by the conflict.

As a boy, Steve Caine had never done well in school, but he discovered he had a natural talent for languages. He soon began to understand significant portions of the Vietnamese he heard on the street and among the South Vietnamese troops Special Forces he worked with.

His sensitivity increased, and his outlook broadened. He was astonished to find that there were people whose lives were far more wretched than his own had been. Even worse than the misery-filled existence of the war-weary Vietnamese. Caine's Special Forces unit was assigned to make contact and establish relations with the primitive tribesmen who occupied the central and northern highlands of Vietnam. They were known as the Montagnards, or " 'Yards" for short. "Montagnard" was a French word for mountaineer.

Caine was fascinated by the Montagnards and the rich history of the area. The group his unit had been ordered to make contact with were especially interesting. They were called the Katu. To their neighbors, "Katu" meant savage.

The Katu were a primitive people, as alien to the American soldiers as beings from another planet. But Caine tried to learn everything possible about the tribes, even before his unit met the Katu. Unfortunately, Sergeant Victor Dymally seemed to think the Katu should simply do as they were told. Caine knew that attitude wouldn't go far with the Montagnards, and it might turn the Katu against them—and the Katu were not a people one wants for an enemy.

"These Katu are a tough nut to crack, aren't they, Caine?" the sergeant commented. "I knew the minute I first tried to convince those Vietnamese to move into our protected villages that I wasn't cut out to be a social worker. But, the regular gooks were easy compared to these people."

"Well, Vic," Caine replied after considering the team member's remark. "I know you saw that tree they cut down and left across the path of their village. That meant the whole village is *dien* or taboo because of an unclean death or sacrilege or some other reason. I told you about that at the time. But you didn't even offer to pay the fine they asked for . . ."

"It was my judgement that our contact mission was more important," Dymally responded defensively. "Getting them organized against the Vietcong is a life and death matter. It's for their own good, Caine."

"They don't have any reason to believe that when we don't show any respect for their customs, Vic," Caine insisted. "You also tried to drum up support for our programs with the villagers of lesser status before enlisting the aid of the tribal elders. That was really a slap in the face to the whole tribe."

"How come you pick up on these things so quick, Caine?" Dymally asked, mulling over Steve's points in his mind. "I don't see why a bunch of primitive savages who don't even wet farm their rice could be as important as organizing the city dwellers."

"I try to stay current with our briefings," Caine answered. "From what I've been able to learn, winning the 'Yards over to our side is essential to our war effort because even though they're only a small, primitive part of the Vietnam's population, they occupy half of its total land area. Another thing to consider is that they have no ideological ties to the Vietcong. So if you and I play our cards right, we could develop a valuable military asset here."

"Maybe you're right," the sergeant admitted. "We'll see, Caine. We'll try your way for a while."

Caine absorbed all the knowledge he could on the Katu. Aside from his army briefings and the people themselves, his greatest source of knowledge was a chaplain who was also an amateur anthropologist. After hearing of Steve's interest in the tribe, the chaplain couldn't seem to help him enough.

"I wish all the Green Berets would study these people like you do, Steve," the chaplain declared. "It might well save a soldier's life one day. But I don't want to ignore the good you're doing for the Katu by making their lives more understandable to your teammates. They are God's creatures, just as we are. I can't help believing that what we are doing for them will one day put pluses on our celestial balance sheet."

The Katu were distrustful of the Vietnamese soldiers and were more willing to associate with the Green Berets. But Steve Caine established a special rapport with the Katu, showing respect for their religion and culture. He learned their customs and language, and they soon came to regard him as a friend.

The Vietnamese and most of the other Montagnard tribes were terrified of the Katu, but Caine found them to be fascinating. The Katu were fierce and individualistic, yet curious, and eager to learn about new things as long as one did not try to change their traditional lifestyle.

Caine became closer and closer to the Katu. He learned much from them: how to track, set traps and snares, handle a bow and arrow, find drinkable water, and many other valuable survival skills. He also fell head-over-heels in love with Tran Mai.

By this time, Caine had become a member of the Special Forces outfit headed by Captain Herald and Lieutenant O'Neal. Herald was a bit worried about Caine "turning native," but figured no American would be crazy enough to throw away Western civilization to make a life among savages. O'Neal knew his men better than the captain. He wasn't so sure about Caine. The guy was strange enough to do anything.

Steve's fellow Green Berets regarded his infatuation with the girl with skepticism. Most figured it would be another in-country marriage. When the final bugle sounded and the Americans left Vietnam, Caine would dump his bride and jump on the first plane available back to the real world.

But that wasn't what Caine was thinking at the time. Caine persuaded one of the village elders to act as an intermediary between himself and Tran Mai's father, as was customary, so that the respective families of the bride and groom could meet and share an engagement feast at the time of the full moon. Caine asked the chaplain, who shared his interest in the Katu, and Joe Fanelli, one of his closest friends among the Green Berets, to accompany him in gathering the bridal price, which consisted of cloth, brass gongs, pots, and jars.

Fanelli and Caine had hit it off quickly, although they were an odd couple in most respects. Fanelli was quick to pick a fight and quick to forget the reasons for it, whereas Caine did his best to try to understand a situation and only employed violence as a last resort. Fanelli was often loud and rowdy, but Caine tended to be reserved and quiet. Yet, both were brave men, dedicated Green Berets, and more than that—good friends.

"Now you've got a pot to piss in, Steve," Fanelli remarked after they had haggled over one particularly large item of porcelain and finally purchased it from a village merchant.

Caine took Fanelli's friendly ribbing in a good natured manner, but he did request that Joe avoid doing anything new or unusual among the Katu unless he checked with Steve or the chaplain first. This was as much for the Katu's protection as Joe's. The life of the tribe was deeply affected by perceived spiritual consequences of everyday village life.

"What's so special about getting the right rooster?"

Fanelli asked Caine as they neared the end of the nuptial scavenger hunt. Steve explained that the prospective groom must produce a live rooster with which to consult the spirits.

"So what is so important about his feet?" Fanelli continued. "Does it have to be pedigreed?"

"No," Caine explained. "The sorcerer we hire to consult the spirits will cut off the right foot of a living rooster and examine the claws, which must be normal and mesh correctly, or the marriage is thought to be in trouble from the beginning."

"A *live* rooster?" Fanelli wrinkled his nose with disgust. "That's fuckin' nasty, man. I mean, don't they at least give the bird a shot of morphine first? Maybe get him good and drunk?"

"The rooster doesn't get a purple heart either," Caine replied dryly. "Look, Joe. Don't make waves about the Katu customs. That's just how things are done."

"Well, in Jersey you get a lot further greasing the palm of a sorcerer than playing around with a chicken foot," Joe muttered.

"This isn't Jersey," Caine reminded him.

"No shit?" Fanelli said with mock surprise.

Steve Caine and Tran Mai's engagement of six months had been relatively short in comparison to the normal Katu waiting period, which could extend beyond two years. When the night of the marriage ceremony arrived, Fanelli was taken aback by the rhythmic beat of the drums and the haunting throb of brass gongs, pulsating through the wet, dark jungle. It created an unforgettable sensation of being transported back into time.

"I hope these guys don't practice human sacrifice," Fanelli said, only half-joking as a shiver ran down his spine.

"They do," Caine answered in all seriousness. "But not very often."

"What?" Fanelli glared at him.

"Don't worry," Caine assured him. "The blood hunt is only engaged in as a last resort and only after a great deal of consultation with the spirits. Of course, now that you mention it, they do prefer the blood of foreigners over their own people."

"Blood sport with people?" Fanelli shook his head. "You're kiddin' me, aren't you?"

"Not at all," Caine insisted. "Having been on a blood hunt improves a Katu's attractiveness to the ladies as a potential marriage partner. About a year ago, before you got here, a group of Vietcong wandered into the area. They didn't know anything about the customs of the Katu or about the taboos that must be observed. They wandered into the village uninvited and accidentally desecrated a family burial vault.

"One of the village elders was afraid that they would wander off before the necessary meetings could be held to decide their fate," Caine continued. "If the VC got away, the Katu might never see them again. In that case, the entire village would have to be abandoned and the people would be forced to live in the jungle without shelter for a year or more. The village elder wanted a quick solution, so he contacted the padre and a representative of the Green Berets. We were called in to take care of the situation. Between us, we greased the skids and got the whole process moving. The Berets were picked to accompany young men of the village on a blood hunt. I learned a lot about tracking from watching the Katu that afternoon."

"*You* took part in the hunt?" Fanelli stared at Caine.

"Yeah," Caine said with a shrug. "Anyway, there were five Vietcong. Two of them were dead before we found them. They stumbled into animal traps. Impaled on stakes. They were the lucky ones. We helped corner the other three and the Katu went to work on them. There was nothing we could do to stop them. It was their business. Their law. We were just along for the ride. It is customary for the members of the blood hunt to dip their spear points in the blood of the living victim and apply it to their bodies like warpaint . . ."

"That's real interesting, Steve," Fanelli said. "But I don't need to hear any more."

"You asked," Caine reminded him.

Caine caught sight of Tran Mai, whose quiet beauty entranced him. Her skirt extended from below her breasts down to her knees. It was made of black cloth with red stripes. She had discarded her short-sleeved, V-neck overblouse to signify her status as a married woman. She wore a long gold bracelet comprised of one piece of coiled metal, which reached from elbow to wrist. Around her neck she wore a choker made of white, yellow and red-orange beads that Steve had never seen her wear before.

She also wore a necklace of large, black and white beads, with tiger claws and the heavy beaks of horn-billed birds. The hog tusk comb that normally held her jet-black hair in a bun had been replaced by one made of shining copper, with a bamboo spray attached to the top for the festive occasion.

Tran Mai gave Caine a proud smile and quietly joined him. Her father approached the couple. Because the temperature at night was chilly, he wore a long blanket of blue cotton wrapped around his shoulders, and a sturdy cloth vest with interlinked gold rings beneath the blanket. This was more decorative and less functional than the garment he usually wore, with iron rings instead of gold. This served the Katu warrior in a manner similar to that of a European coat of chain mail. Her father was a stocky, muscular man, and adorned with tatoos from head to toe.

"Mai karo kah, amah?" Caine asked. "Are you well, Father?"

"Huan, Karo ahkoon," the man who was now Steve Caine's father-in-law replied. "I am well, my child."

Steve Caine hoped to take Tran Mai back to the States with him or possibly stay in Vietnam if the Communists were defeated. There was so much he could share with the Katu. So much they needed. So much *he* could learn from them in return. Besides, the Katu were Tran Mai's people. He didn't want to take her from them unless he had to.

In 1972, the United States began to withdraw troops from Vietnam. No large troop replacements were coming to replace them. American involvement in the Southeast Asian conflict was finally coming to an end after more than two decades and five presidents.

Caine began to lay the groundwork to get his wife out of the country. As the forces of the U.S. Military Assistance Command retreated to their points of disembarkation, the NVA made incursions into territory formerly controlled by the Green Berets. Now, Captain O'Neal decided to relocate the Katu village to one of many steep valleys and assigned Caine to accompany the village elders to a suitable spot, where the signs could be read by a sorcerer.

The party had been at the site for less than a day when Lieutenant Wentworth appeared. The officer's manner was most urgent.

"Sergeant Caine," he declared. "The captain needs to see you right away. I'll cover for you here."

"Yes, sir," Caine replied, confident that Wentworth

would be able to manage. The lieutenant's affection for Japanese culture had refined his manners and his sensitivity for the beliefs of others.

Because a trail had been blazed through the jungle on the party's way, it took Caine only one hour to hike the two miles back to the Special Forces camp. A grim Captain O'Neal met him there.

"I have some bad news, Steve," the CO began slowly. "While you were gone, the village was overrun by the NVA. Tran Mai was among the casualties."

Caine's eyes glossed over with tears. O'Neal placed a hand on the NCO's shoulder and added, "I'm sorry, Steve," O'Neal bit his lip and then blurted out. "She's dead."

Caine trembled slightly. His breath escaped with a ragged gasp. He closed his eyes and tears trickled down his cheeks. Caine remained stiff-backed at attention although O'Neal had addressed him informally. At last he spoke.

"Request permission to lead a react team, sir," Caine declared.

"I think you ought to sit down . . ." O'Neal began.

"Please, sir," Caine insisted. "I want that react team."

"Permission granted," O'Neal said. "But don't get careless. Remember you'll be responsible for the lives of others."

An impromptu blood hunt with a contingent of Katu villagers started stalking Tran Mai's killers. By daybreak, they had found the NVA and slaughtered the entire patrol. Steve Caine killed several men personally, but he was still devastated by the loss of the woman he loved.

In 1973 the last of the American troops were leaving 'Nam, except a small group at Saigon. The Hard Corps unit was among those finally able to go back to the world. But Steve Caine was not among them. He had disappeared into the jungle and joined the Katu. Caine's war in Vietnam was not over yet.

The Katu accepted Caine as a brother. He taught them about modern weapons, and they taught him to set snares and man traps. He taught them to read a map and compass. They taught Caine to move silently in the dark, and use natural camouflage.

Soon the Katu became one of the most effective resistance groups in Southeast Asia. They ambushed NVA troops, set boobytraps, and rigged trap guns. The Katu killed hundreds of Communist troops, but to little avail.

And the NVA killed Katu as well. After a while, Caine wished only to keep the rest of the tribesmen alive and to hold onto the memory of his love for Tran Mai. In the end, the latter was all he could succeed at.

Finally, only Steve Caine and his brother-in-law Kimet remained alive, a situation that wouldn't last long. Kimet was hit by shrapnel from an enemy grenade. He was mortally wounded, but Caine tried his best to keep the Katu warrior alive, as they hid beneath an overhang of bushes, shivering in the clammy fog-laced night.

"Kimet," Caine implored the man. "You've got to keep these dressings on your wound. They have power to kill the infection."

No matter how persuasive he tried to be, Steve could not convince the Katu warrior to swallow the capsules, or accept bandages. Kimet believed it was wrong to use foreign medicine. He thought the Katu should use only herbs and lustral waters to kill the demons of illness. The Katu closed his eyes and began to pray to the spirit world.

Kimet died shortly before dawn, his head resting in Caine's lap. The American dug a shallow grave with his knife and buried his last comrade-at-arms. He was alone again.

By 1975, Saigon had fallen. South Vietnam was conquered by the Communists, and Laos would soon follow. Caine decided that to continue fighting would be senseless. He headed west, and eventually slipped across the Laos border into Thailand.

Once more a drifter, Caine wandered about seeking employment of any sort. Then he heard of a group of mercenaries who planned to recruit men for a mission into Laos to rescue alleged American POW's from a prison camp there. Caine thought he'd had his fill of fighting and war, but the mission was a spark, reminding him of the one thing he was good at, and he decided to check out the offer.

To his astonishment, the mercenaries were Captain O'Neal, Lieutenant Wentworth, and Sergeant Fanelli. The Hard Corps was reunited once more.

CHAPTER 14

O'NEAL, WENTWORTH AND FANELLI had returned to the Hard Corps headquarters after their battle with the invaders at the east portion of the compound. They called to Trang Nih and Franklin Willis to hold their fire. The Vietnamese freedom fighter and the black chopper pilot were stationed at a machinegun nest with an M-60 and 800 rounds of ammo. John McShayne was also ready to greet them.

"Glad to see you all got back in one piece," the top sergeant declared, adjusting the strap of his M-14 rifle. "The bastards have taken out most of the cameras, so it was tough to figure how things were going from the microphones."

"We drove the enemy back," O'Neal announced. "But not for long. How's Caine doing out there by himself?"

"Well, he ain't lonely," McShayne answered. "Cameras are mostly out of order at the north and south too.

The enemy has moved in from both directions, just like you figured, sir. Motion detectors suggest more than two dozen are closing in. Some of them have already met either Caine or his boobytraps or both. Microphones picked up screams, moans of agony, that sort of thing.''

"No way to know if any of those sounds might be from Caine himself," Wentworth said grimly.

"I don't think Steve would scream if you stuck a hot poker up his ass," Fanelli commented. "But he's sure in trouble. We gonna help him, Captain?"

"We're not gonna leave him out there to fight alone," O'Neal confirmed. "You two load an M-60 onto a jeep and go give him a hand."

"An M-60?" Wentworth raised his eyebrows. "Does this mean we aren't concerned about making noise anymore?"

"It means we're more concerned with staying alive, Jim," O'Neal replied. "Take grenades and whatever explosives you want, Joe."

"Now you're talking," Fanelli said eagerly.

"The enemy isn't going to hold off on explosives and heavier artillery much longer," O'Neal explained. "Since the noise pollution level is going to increase anyway, we might as well try to beat 'em to the punch."

"Makes sense to me, Bill," Wentworth confirmed.

"You guys get ready to move," O'Neal continued. "I'm going to . . ."

"Oh, sir?" McShayne interrupted. "Got somebody on the radio you might want'a have a few words with. It's Old Saintly."

"Damn right I want'a talk to him," O'Neal growled.

The Hard Corps commander stomped into the head shed and headed for the radio. He grabbed the microphone.

"This is Deep Six," O'Neal said, using their present code name with the Company case officer. "CO speaking."

"Hello, Deep Six," St. Laurent's voice boomed from the radio receiver. "I trust the visitors arrived. Over."

"Goddamn right they did," O'Neal told him angrily. "What the hell did you think you were doing when you sent them here without telling us shit about it? Saintly?"

"Watch what you say on the radio, Deep Six," St. Laurent warned him.

"Fuck you," O'Neal replied.

"The FCC disapproves of profanity on the air," the CIA man stated. "I think it might be a felony . . ."

"Fuck them too," O'Neal snapped. "Did you know those guys you sent are being hunted by Charlie?"

"Charlie?"

"Yes. Charlie." O'Neal commented. "It's a nickname for the Vietcong. Remember?"

"The Vietcong?" St. Laurent sounded surprised. "What kind of cigarettes have you guys been smoking lately?"

"Very funny, asshole," O'Neal replied gruffly. "Maybe if you hadn't decided it was April Fool's Day, we wouldn't be fighting for our lives now."

"Against the Vietcong?" the Company man scoffed. "In the state of Washington? Come on. I don't even think the Vietcong exist anymore."

"You'd sure feel different if you were here, Saintly," O'Neal assured him. "There was a double agent for the Communists among the visitors. Son of a bitch managed to lead the enemy to us . . ."

"Hold on," St. Laurent interrupted. "You're violating security, Deep Six."

"You goddamn well *raped* our security, Saintly," O'Neal countered. "Don't bitch to me, pal. You know

we don't meet with clients here. Why the hell didn't you use regular channels?''

"There was a pressing need to get the visitors to you as quickly as possible to try to arrange an agreement before they left the country.''

"In other words, you knew they were being stalked.''

"I didn't think the enemy would try anything at your base,'' St. Laurent explained. "It seemed the safest place for them.''

"A good idea at the time, huh?'' O'Neal snorted. "Think again, Saintly.''

"I wish you'd stop calling me that.''

"I wish we weren't under siege,'' O'Neal replied. "But unless you've got a connection with the Tooth Fairy, wishing isn't gonna do us a hell of a lot of good, Saintly. Fact is, the visitors' enemies aren't lightweights. They've got us surrounded and they're trying to kill us. Luckily for us, it's turned out the other way around.''

"You mean you've actually fought with these people? How many of them are you up against?''

"Beats the shit outta me,'' the Hard Corps commander admitted. "We haven't taken time for a body count, but I figure the other side has suffered about thirty losses, but these motherfuckers are still coming. That means there are still plenty of 'em left to fight. Shit, Saintly. We've got a battle going on *right now.*''

"That seems hard to believe,'' St. Laurent said. "How could that many foreign agents get into the country? How could a second rate Third World nation manage something like that?''

"You know American security sucks,'' O'Neal replied. "You know that as well as I do. Goddamn KGB owns beach property in California. They use such powerful transmitting equipment at the Soviet Embassy, they scramble legitimate transmissions."

"You keep talking that way and I'll end this transmission pronto, mister," St. Laurent said sharply.

"None of that's classified, Saintly. It's all been printed up in national news magazines and detailed on network TV news. It's no secret that American intelligence is shitty. I'm not blaming you, Saintly, but it's the truth. As for how the enemy did it, I don't really give a damn about that. It's happening. That's all that really matters."

"Okay," the CIA case officer began. "I'm not sure what I can do, but I'll try to help you somehow."

"Thanks, but I'm not sure we can stand any more help from the Company."

"I'll see what I can do," St. Laurent assured him. "Meantime, hang in there."

"You think we have a choice, Saintly?" O'Neal laughed bitterly. "Look, I've got to get back to work . . ."

"Of course," St. Laurent replied. "I understand."

"You don't understand shit," he muttered with disgust, ending the transmission.

CHAPTER 15

JOE FANELLI SLID behind the wheel of the jeep. *Shit*, he thought. *If I'd gone into demolition derbies professionally, I might be rich by now.*

"Then again," he said aloud. "I might be dead."

Fanelli had driven in a boot-leg demolition derby the weekend before he enlisted into the army. About a week after he dropped out of high school and spent all his money. He figured he had to find something to do with his life. Going to war sounded better than going to jail . . . which is where a lot of kids he went to school with wound up.

More than half the kids Joe grew up with in Jersey City were either in Juvenile Hall or buried before they reached seventeen years of age. They were the assholes in gangs who got caught with stolen merchandise or weapons. The idiots who OD'd on heroin or got their dumb asses blown away trying to rob a liquor store. The folks in Fanelli's neighborhood didn't generally have

213

long life spans, unless they were very clever or kept themselves locked in their homes at night with a shotgun handy.

Joe Fanelli hailed from Jersey City, New Jersey. It was once a thriving city of half a million near the Hudson River. But, when the factory economy slowed, there were a lot of people without a job or much chance of getting one, hanging around the streets and looking to come by a fast buck any way they could.

After Fanelli's father injured his back and went on disability, life got steadily tougher and more desperate for Joe. He got into plenty of fights. He had plenty of scars from these battles, but he dished out plenty of the same. In some ways, Joe could accept that it was "better to give than to receive."

A washed-up boxer at the YMCA had tried to talk Fanelli into going into boxing. Joe had quick reflexes and he was good with his fists. The Golden Gloves would be his ticket out of the neighborhood, according to old punchy, as he wiped snot from a runny glob of flesh that used to be a nose, before it got rearranged in the ring.

Sure, Fanelli thought. Look what boxing did for old punchy. There was a great future in getting your head punched in. Sure. Managers and promoters gobbled up profits. More often than not, boxers wound up in two-bit jobs washing bottles or sweeping floors. Some wound up on skid row or busting up people for the mob. No thanks, jack.

Joe was clever. He was too smart to take a one-way road to nowhere. He wasn't going to box his way out of poverty or get work with the mob, running numbers or selling pot. A lot of kids he grew up with were connected with "the Family" one way or the other.

Great opportunity that was, too. Join the Mafia and

belong to a fucking *capo* for the rest of your life. He pulls the strings and makes you dance. Great life. And who gets busted? Not the big guys who run everything. Not the big-time button men who can do a hit and take a vacation in Vegas until the heat dies down. The big guys had high priced lawyers and judges in their pockets. The little dealers and small time runners were the ones who got nailed. Fanelli didn't intend to serve time. No fucking way.

So, at the age of seventeen, Joe decided to quit high school and join the army. He knew he'd probably go to Vietnam, but that was okay with him. Hell, at least ten kids he had gone to school with had been killed in the streets of Jersey. Staying in the city seemed almost as dangerous as going to war anyway.

Joe remembered stories he'd heard from the guys in the VFW Hall. They talked about the battles they fought, the women they screwed, and the grand reception they got when they came home from World War II. He concluded that if he went to 'Nam and killed some gooks, he would win a medal, come back to the States to a tickertape parade and lots of new opportunities. People busted their butts to give jobs to war heroes. They became politicians, like Ike and JFK. They became movie stars, like Audie Murphy. They had the world by the ass.

Sure Vietnam wasn't popular now, but Fanelli figured WWII wouldn't have been popular either, if the Japs hadn't attacked us at Pearl Harbor. Or if people hadn't found out that little shit Hitler was baking Jews in ovens and killing millions of people.

Ho Chi Minh was probably doing the same stuff or planning to. Not with Jews, maybe. But, Ho was probably doing that sort of thing to somebody and when it came out, Vietnam vets would be heroes, too.

Joe Fanelli planned to get right in the middle of the conflict. A regular John Wayne from Jersey. That would show everyone in the neighborhood what Joe Fanelli was made of. It would show his father, who'd become a drunken bum after he failed to bribe a union official to give him even a day job off the books.

He just drank cheap wine and bitched about the goddamn niggers. "Those goddamn niggers were all on welfare and drove around in brand new Caddies," he claimed. "Goddamn niggers were gonna ruin the country."

When he wasn't complaining about black freeloaders and Jewish bankers—who really ran the country, according to him—Joe's father was telling his son what a good-for-nothing little shit he was. He said Joe would never amount to nothin' cause he was just like his mother. At least Mom got out. Joe was getting out too.

But, first he had a demolition derby to win. Fanelli and some of his pals put some money together to buy a battered old Ford Galaxy. It didn't run very well, but it was built like a tank. They welded pipes to the fenders and bumpers and knocked out all the glass. They put iron strips around the radiator to protect it, in case somebody got cute and welded an I-beam ram to the front of another car. Demo derbies could get pretty mean.

Joe and his buddies headed for the illegal contest grounds outside the city limits. Fanelli drove his bruiser into the makeshift arena, near a rural wrecking yard. Fanelli was ready to take on all comers, including the Talbot brothers.

The Talbots were the local champions. The Talbots claimed they could whip anybody in demo warfare—especially some goddamn dago punk with a piece of shit jalopy. Joe wanted to show those bastards, just like he wanted to show everybody in Jersey, that he was a real man.

Joe Fanelli hadn't matured enough to realize that the only opinion about him that really mattered was what he thought of himself. He didn't realize his macho gestures and desire to impress others proved more about his own insecurities than it did about his courage. He was determined to prove he was a gutsy little guy, better than anyone twice his size.

"The clutch wasn't worth shit," Peter Mancini, one of Joe's friends, explained. "so we replaced it. The rest of the powerplant should hold up 'til the race is over."

"I'll treat her like a baby," Joe assured him sarcastically. "Did you get the bet in on time?"

"Yeah," Pete answered. "Put one hundred bucks down with the bookie. The odds are pretty high against us, so if you can pull this off, we'll go home with a nice piece of change."

"Not to mention the contest money," Mario Bianco added.

The derby started out with ten junkers of various sizes and descriptions. The Talbot brothers showed up with a Rambler Matador. The car looked pretty formidable, and the Talbots themselves seemed to be burly, backwoods hicks. Jake and Bobby Lee Talbot had enough bulk on them for four guys—and less brains between 'em than a retarded cocker spaniel.

Joe depended on his superior speed and maneuverability to survive the early minutes of the derby. He had fat, low profile tires mounted on the front of the Galaxy, so he could maintain steerage when his wheel wells were reduced in size by frontal impact. The Talbots' Matador was solidly built and well-reinforced. They used musclehead tactics, attacking the opposition head-on more often than not. It was considered smarter to ram the other guy's radiator with the trunk of your car, which was far less liable to enough damage to put you out of the competition.

Every time Talbot tried to outmaneuver him, Fanelli would apply power and dodge around the slower cars. When Joe had to turn, he did it at high speed, maintaining a power-on four wheel drive. Talbot always ended up swinging out of control, sliding sideways.

After he lost the Matador in a turn, Joe pointed his vehicle toward the outer barrier, and aimed his trunk at the next oncoming auto. He slammed the gearshift into reverse and smashed into the Olds with his fender, taking advantage of the sharp rear corner of his Galaxy. The impact sent the Olds into a spin, which ended when the car crashed, nose-first, into the barrier.

The crowd cheered as metal hit metal and cars tumbled out of the contest. Smoke flowed from beneath the crumbled hood of one crippled vehicle. The driver bailed out and his friends soaked the engine with foam from a fire extinguisher. One by one the contestants were taken out of the derby until only three cars remained—Fanelli's Galaxie, Talbot's Matador and a Chevy Vega which had miraculously lasted through the punishing auto battle.

The Vega's luck ran out. Talbot vented his rage on the smaller Chevolet. The Matador rammed the Vega repeatedly until the impact turned it over on its side. Joe saw the I-beam jutting upward from under the radiator of the Matador. Talbot backed up for one more shot at the already-vanquished Vega. Fanelli put the pedal to the metal and steered the Galaxie backward until the precise moment of impact.

Talbot saw him coming and tried to speedshift gears to get out of the way. The obscene metallic grind testified to the stripping of teeth from first gear. Talbot quickly shifted into second, but his panicked application of excessive power only served to make his nearly treadless tires slip in the mud.

When the left edge of the Galaxy's rear bumper slammed into the Matador's radiator, the I-beam of Talbot's car stripped the bumper from Fanelli's auto cleanly away. This left Fanelli free to make his escape. He dodged around the derelict defeated vehicles like pylons in a slalom, staying ahead of Talbot's car until the Matador lost enough coolant from its ruptured radiator to seize up.

Fanelli won the derby, much to the delight of his friends, and to the astonishment of most of the spectators. Joe, Pete, and Mario collected their prize money. Five hundred bucks to be split between them—and there'd be four times that much in bets from their bookie.

"You greasy wops ain't goin' nowhere!" Jake Talbot snarled as he, his brother, and three other redneck assholes approached the winners.

"Sore losers?" Fanelli inquired, pocketing his cash.

"Gimme that money, you garlic-snappin' little shit," Jake insisted, fists jammed on his hips.

"Sore losers," Fanelli repeated, confirming what he had already guessed. Then he launched an overhead right to the bully's face and broke his nose.

More fists started to fly. Fanelli snapped his head away from Bobby Lee's fist and jabbed a left under the crud's heart. The Talbot boy gasped and Fanelli jabbed him on the chin, knocking him on his ass with a right cross. Pete and Mario were holding their own against two Talbot buddies while the third creep swung on Fanelli.

Joe's left forearm blocked a right cross and he rammed an uppercut to the punk's solar plexus, followed by a solid left hook and a ball-busting kick, which left the jerk writhing on the ground. He saw that Mario was losing ground against his opponent. Fanelli punched the Talbot pal in the kidney. The kid groaned and twitched from the blow. Mario hit him with a right to the jaw which spun the punk around to get another knuckle sandwich from Fanelli. Down he went, but Jake and Bobby Lee charged into the battle once more.

The latter didn't get too far. Fanelli kicked him in the face before the Talbot slob could climb to his feet. But Jake pulled a leather sap from his pocket and swung it into Mario's face. The Italian kid fell, moaning softly. Jake kicked the kid in the ribs.

"Try me, dick-licker," Fanelli invited, taking his switchblade from his trousers.

"Motherfuckin' wop!" Jake hissed as he swung the cosh at Joe.

Fanelli pressed the button and the blade snapped into place. He adroitly slashed Talbot's wrist before the cosh could connect. Jake screamed and dropped his sap. Fanelli quickly sliced the switchblade across his opponent's chest, cutting cloth and skin. Talbot had had enough. He bolted and ran for his life.

One of Talbot's buddies had seen too many TV shows and thought he could take a knife away from somebody, as if he was picking flowers from a vase. Fanelli cut the kid's hand and chopped off a finger in the process. The punk shrieked as blood spurted from the stump. The other members of Talbots' fan club decided the price was too great to continue the fight. They fled as Fanelli wiped the blood from his knife and put the weapon in his pocket.

"Jesus, Joe," Pete gasped. "Did you have to cut him like that?"

"Fuck him," Fanelli replied as he watched their opponents retreat. "I'm goin' in the army tomorrow. Cuttin' that sucker was good practice for when I get to 'Nam. Let's go spend some of this money, man. I want'a party before I join the Green Machine."

They spent the rest of the evening drinking beer, smoking cigarettes—a little pot as well as tobacco—and taking turns with a twenty-five year old whore. For twenty bucks she gave blowjobs. She'd lay on her back and moan in ecstasy for thirty. Fanelli had had her before and knew her thirty-dollar act was over-priced.

"Ain't you scared about going to 'Nam?" Mancini asked.

Fanelli lied and said he wasn't. He was young and foolish, but he wasn't stupid enough to think the war was going to be a barrel of laughs. If a man can't prove himself on the battlefield, where can he do it?

Fanelli got his wish. He joined the army and signed up to be a Green Beret, and almost didn't make it through Basic Combat Training because he talked back to a drill instructor. The sergeant threatened to break off a boot in his ass, but Fanelli knew the NCO's weren't allowed to hit trainees. Sure, a lot of them did it anyway, but Fanelli figured the DI wasn't dumb enough to risk a court martial by over-reacting to a slip of the lip.

Instead, Fanelli almost got an Undesirable Discharge for insubordination, but the company commander decided that the incident did not merit such strict punishment. So Fanelli got a written reprimand on his 201 file, stating that he had a problem accepting authority figures and lacked proper respect for his superiors. Of course, the same is true about most people to some degree.

Joe did well at everything else: marksmanship, field sanitation, physical training. He watched his mouth around the DI's, although the sergeants tried to provoke him. His temper had never been very good, but he managed to control it.

The drill sergeants were verbally abusive, put him on KP frequently, gave him extra duties, and ran him ragged. He was ordered to assume the front-lean-and-rest position, and told to do push-ups. Then the DI would stroll by and just happen to step on his fingers.

Fanelli had been warned that the next time he mouthed off to a superior, he would get worse than a reprimand. So, he swallowed his pride and accepted the abuse.

The army was a humbling experience for Joe Fanelli. He couldn't talk to the company commander or the AGI, so he just stuck it out until the end of BCT.

Jump School was even rougher. The DI's expected trouble from Fanelli after they read his 201. They rode his ass like a surf board to see if he'd slip up and get snotty again, but Fanelli realized what they were doing and tried to keep his opinions to himself. One thing Fanelli refused to do was call anyone "sir." He addressed others as "Sergeant," "Lieutenant," "Captain," "General," but never "sir."

Fanelli finally arrived in 'Nam. Saigon didn't seem all that different from New Jersey. There were shops and bars and whores who gave head for less than five American dollars. Fanelli didn't worry about the Black Syphilis he heard about when he was in the States. He figured that was a bullshit fairy tale to rattle a recruit's cage. Just like the stories about the "fuck you" lizard —a reddish brown reptile that was suppose to make a cry that sounded like someone saying "Fuck you."

How stupid do they think we are? Fanelli thought when he heard that story. He concluded that Black

Syphilis must be the same kind of crap.

Fanelli made Specialist 4th Class and had received acting sergeant stripes, but didn't really want them. "Acting jack" meant more work, more responsibility and no extra pay, but his CO insisted on it. He said it was Fanelli's chance to prove he could be an NCO, in charge of other men. Promised him he'd make E-5 for real if he did a good job, but six months passed and Fanelli still didn't get his stripes for real.

Then he was transferred to Captain Herald's outfit. He smuggled a pint bottle of whiskey into the Special Forces base. Herald made him dump his duffle bag and found the booze.

"Don't ever do anything like this again," the CO warned as he tossed the bottle to Lieutenant O'Neal. "If you want to get drunk, do it somewhere that won't endanger anybody's life except your own, soldier."

"Yes, Captain," Fanelli responded with a sigh.

"Your 201 says you have a problem with authority figures," Herald commented. "But you haven't been written up since Basic."

"Yes, Captain," Fanelli replied. He figured the less he said the better.

"Does that mean it just went away?"

"I guess so, Captain."

"So you like authority figures now?" Herald demanded.

"Come on, sir," O'Neal said with a chuckle. "Who the hell really *likes* authority figures?"

"Soldiers have to obey orders from their superiors," Herald insisted.

"So," O'Neal said with a shrug. "If Fanelli doesn't work out we'll just shoot him in the head and get another spec four."

Joe Fanelli stared at O'Neal. He wasn't sure if the

lieutenant was joking or not.

"Get him out of here," Captain Herald told O'Neal. "I don't want him in my hootch right now. Brief him about what his duties are, get him to his quarters, and haul ass back here, Lieutenant."

O'Neal took Fanelli outside and told him they would be heading north on a mission along the Laos border. The NVA had been sending supplies and advisers to the Pathet Lao. The Special Forces team was supposed to find the connection and terminate it.

"Fun assignment for your first mission, huh?" O'Neal remarked.

"It doesn't scare me," Fanelli told him.

"I hope you don't mean that," O'Neal replied. "If you're not scared, you must be nuts. We all get to be a little crazy after a while. This place is dinky dau city. But we still get scared. Having guys tryin' to kill you is a scary business, Specialist."

Fanelli was put in the same hootch with Sergeant Caine—a real E-5. Caine didn't talk much and he didn't care at all that Fanelli's bottle had been confiscated. Joe figured the guy must be an asshole. Didn't make any difference, since it was late and time to get some sleep.

Fanelli awoke suddenly in the middle of the night.

"Fuck you," a voice called.

"Knock it off, Caine," Fanelli growled.

"Fuck you," the voice repeated. This time Fanelli realized the sound was coming from outside the hootch.

"Caine, wake up!" Fanelli rasped as loudly as he dared. "There's somebody outside saying 'fuck you,' man."

"So you want'a hear it from me too?" Caine muttered. "Fuck you, Fanelli. Let me sleep."

"I'm serious," Fanelli insisted.

"That's just a lizard," Caine sighed. "You never

heard 'em before? Don't worry. You'll get used to it."

"Jesus!" Fanelli mumbled. "Where do I go to get checked out for VD, Caine?"

"Don't worry about that either," Caine replied. "There's a fifty-fifty chance you'll be dead by the end of the week anyway. Now, go back to sleep."

They trained for two weeks, studying maps and photographs. A Kit Carson Scout named Lan Cho accompanied the team. He was a former Vietcong who had defected to the Americans and had agreed to act as a guide for his former enemies.

Lieutenant O'Neal spoke Vietnamese fairly well and conversed with the man. Caine's Vietnamese was even better, but Fanelli didn't know more than a few words in the language. O'Neal announced that they would be moving out that night, with Lan Cho leading the way.

There were only seven men on the team: Captain Herald, First Lieutenant O'Neal, Sergeant Caine, Fanelli, Lan Cho, a Staff Sergeant Green, who was a medic, and a buck sergeant named Collins. The team soon found the junction where the NVA smuggled supplies to the Pathet Lao. It was time to terminate.

Herald and O'Neal hosed the Reds with 5.56mm rounds from their M-16's. The tumbling bullets ripped off one Pathet Lao's arm at the shoulder. Blood spilled from jagged exit wounds in the bodies of the Laotian commies and their NVA comrades. O'Neal lobbed a grenade into a group of enemy soldiers. The fragger flayed flesh to the bone, killing four men.

Caine used a NATO rifle with a scope to pick off two opponents hiding in the bush. The larger 7.62mm, 150 grain bullets were less apt to be deflected by jungle vegetation than the smaller M-16 rounds. Communists obediently dropped. Collins fired an M-79 blooper at the enemy, and launched a 40mm shell into a case of explosives in the NVA supply. The explosion wiped out nine North Vietnamese troopers, but also killed Sgt. Collins. Herald, O'Neal, and SSG Green were knocked down by the force of the blast. Two Pathet Lao closed in and fired their Type-56 rifles into Green, killing the staff sergeant medic before he could rise. They were preparing to finish off the two stunned officers when a grenade landed in front of them.

The Pathet Lao dove to the ground, unaware the pin was still in the grenade. Fanelli charged forward and blasted the Laotians with his M-16. A wounded NVA rose and tried to point his Soviet Kalashnikov at the Americans. Caine fired a single FAL slug into the man's forehead. It exited out the other side of his skull, spraying gray and white gelatin onto the broad leaves of the jungle plants behind him. Lan Cho found another wounded Laotian and cleaved his head open with the heavy blade of a jungle knife.

"Nice work, Sergeant Fanelli," Captain Herald told Joe. "Cute trick with the grenade."

"Thanks, Captain," Fanelli replied. "But I'm just a spec four."

"Not for long," Herald assured him. "I'll see to that."

Fanelli finally made E-5, and earned another stripe before Captain Herald was killed in a VC ambush. Lan Cho was also killed during another mission, when he triggered a trip-wire attached to a crossbow trap.

O'Neal was promoted to captain and became the new commander. The XO replacement was a career officer named Lieutenant James Wentworth III. Fanelli figured the guy would be a jerk. How many regular guys tack numbers onto the ends of their names?

But Wentworth fit into the outfit like he was born to it. The team functioned better than ever. They soon earned the nickname the Hard Corps—the toughest sons of bitches in 'Nam.

Fanelli got a two-week leave and spent it in Saigon, where he met some guys who owned a whorehouse and were interested in dealing some blackmarket cigarettes and booze. Fanelli used his ration card to buy half a dozen cartons of smokes and three gallons of American whiskey, and traded it with the pimps for a piece of the action at the whorehouse. They were unwilling to accept the deal until Fanelli assured them he could drum up more business among the horny GI's. He was as good as his word and brought in lots of business.

It was a profitable trade while it lasted. But CID (the Criminal Investigation Department) found out about Fanelli's racket, and "El CID" arrested him and brought him up for a Summary Court Martial. Though O'Neal and Wentworth testified as character witnesses, to Fanelli's war record, and to his courage in combat, he was busted to corporal, they took half his pay for six months and warned him that the next time he would get a Dishonorable Discharge—and at least a year in Leavenworth.

"No Good Conduct Medal for you, Joe," O'Neal commented after the sentencing. "What made you do it, you stupid shit?"

"Seemed like a good idea at the time, Captain," was Fanelli's only defense.

Back in the bush, Fanelli proved to be steadily better at his job. He learned to be a top-notch explosives expert and commo (communications) operator, as the team carried out mission after mission. Some of the guys attached to the outfit got killed or wounded, but it seemed that the main fighting men of the Hard Corps couldn't even be touched. Fanelli finally even got his stripes back.

Then the illusion of immortality was shattered. After the NVA launched an attack on the village of Katu tribesmen where the unit had been stationed, and Caine's recently-married wife was killed in the battle, Fanelli caught two bullets in the mid-section. The sergeant was sent to Saigon, treated at the hospital there and flown back to the States to recover.

Fanelli had been extraordinarily lucky. One bullet had cracked a rib and popped right out his side. The other had missed liver, spleen and kidneys. It passed clean through with a minimum of tissue damage. He recovered in a VA hospital, but didn't stay out of trouble.

Fanelli soon started a floating crap game with the other patients, arranged for liquor to be smuggled into their rooms, and even found a streetwalker who administered a special brand of bedside manner. Again, Fanelli was caught in the act.

Since he was a highly decorated combat veteran, however, with a Silver Star, two Bronze Stars and a Purple Heart, charges were dropped. Fanelli's ETS (End Term of Service) had almost arrived anyway. Since troops weren't being sent to 'Nam any more, nobody really wanted to bother with him. The Army didn't want to keep him either. The recruiter didn't even bother to visit.

In fact, after the hooker was banned from the hospital, nobody visited Fanelli. He received a few letters from Wentworth and O'Neal, but the news could have been better. Caine had disappeared when they started hauling out Special Ops. Technically he went AWOL, but the army listed Caine as MIA.

The war was coming to an end as far as America was concerned, and it was a virtual certainty the Communists would win. So many Americans had fought and died in 'Nam to try to prevent it, and now Washington had simply decided it was time to go home and call it quits.

Fanelli was released from the hospital and awarded an Honorable Discharge, in spite of all his fuck-ups. He returned to Jersey, where there was definitely no ticker-tape parade, and no congratulations for risking his life in 'Nam. But Fanelli couldn't sit around feeling sorry for himself. He finally found work as an auto mechanic.

But the problems began again. He started coming in late to work, generally suffering from a severe hangover. Then he showed up drunk on two occasions, and the third time he was fired for it. Soon Fanelli began drinking heavily. He was arrested for brawling in a bar, where he punched out three opponents and a cop, before another cop clubbed him senseless.

Due to his medical record at the VA hospital, the court sent Fanelli back there for observation, where he was labeled an alcoholic and sent to a treatment center. Therapy and counseling, however, seemed a waste of time. He disrupted the meetings so badly they barred him from further attendance, something virtually unknown in Alcoholics Anonymous.

"You expect me to believe in a Higher Power?" Fanelli had scoffed. "The only higher power I believe in is C-Four plastic explosives. God didn't help us in 'Nam and He didn't help us when we got back to the bullshit waiting for us here. Why the hell would He care about helping a bunch of drunks stay sober? Wise up, you morons. If there is a God, He just doesn't give a fuck."

His counseling sessions revealed more bitterness.

"I should have died in 'Nam instead of coming back to the World," he told his shrink. "That's what we used to call the U.S.—'The World,' where all our hopes were waiting to be fulfilled. Right? Fuck this 'World,' man. Let me out of here before the bars close."

Joe Fanelli's case seemed hopeless. He just didn't want to do anything but get drunk and try to forget about the world he lived in. The detox ward didn't know what to do with him. The answer arrived in 1975, with the coming of William O'Neal and James Wentworth III. They told the folks at the clinic that they had a forestry job lined up for Fanelli. He'd be out in the wide open spaces, with no booze and plenty of work.

When his psychiatrist interviewed Fanelli for the last time, the ex-Green Beret assured him that his friends would take care of him. They were old army buddies who were going to take him to Oregon or some place like that. They'd look after him and make sure he didn't drink anymore. The treatment center was glad to get rid of Fanelli, and they wished him good luck. More than a few whispered "good riddance" as well.

A few weeks later, O'Neal, Wentworth, and Fanelli headed for Thailand, where the Hard Corps had taken on a mercenary mission, the first of many. A number of families of MIA soldiers had pooled their money and hired the Hard Corps to check into a story about an alleged POW camp in Laos, where a number of American soldiers were supposedly held prisoner.

But they also had a personal reason in accepting the mission. Maybe—just maybe—they'd find Steve Caine in one of those tiger cases.

They found Caine all right, but not in a POW camp. He walked right into their "recruiting office" in a Bangkok bar, where they were trying to round up mercs for the mission. Through the grapevine, Caine had heard that they were in Bangkok.

They wept openly, unashamed of the tears, as the Hard Corps was finally reunited.

CHAPTER 16

JOE FANELLI DROVE his jeep along the logging road through the forest, in the direction where McShayne had detected Caine battling the enemy. If they didn't get to Caine quickly, his chances of survival would be worse than they had been in 'Nam. Fanelli speed-shifted through the gears of the sturdy little jeep, racing through the mud recklessly. He tried to stay left or right of the central hump of the washed out road. An occasional tree stump still poked above the center hump and could conceivably take out his transfer case, if he wasn't careful.

Of course, if one had asked Lieutenant James Wentworth III if Fanelli was being careful, the Hard Corps XO would have thought the question insane. As he rode next to Fanelli in the jeep, Wentworth was wondering if the sergeant had finally cracked up. In fact, Fanelli was taking some risks, but these were calculated, gauged according to the speed needed to assist Caine and his familiarity with the vehicle.

The jeep bounced off a bump in the road and plowed into the mud, just in time to regain traction for the next turn. Fanelli glanced across the jeep at Wentworth. He wondered if the lieutenant's head wound had jarred his brains. The guy was packing that goddamn samurai short sword again, as well as a large knife of similar design.

They had traveled five hundred yards from the lake and were now completely out of sight of the mess hall. Suddenly, a grenade flew from the treeline and exploded near the right front tire. It caused the speeding jeep to spiral through the air into the hemlock on their left. The trees cushioned the landing of the overturned vehicle, which gouged the damp earth and came to a smooth stop.

The attackers approached from the treeline. They smiled with satisfaction when they saw the still bodies of Fanelli and Wentworth, sprawled near the wrecked jeep. Four invaders covered two bolder comrades who marched forward and kicked the M-16 rifles beyond the reach of the motionless Americans.

"Ong di dau do?" one of the Vietnamese inquired with a chuckle. His comrades thought the question was very amusing and laughed at the joke. He had asked the still shapes where they were going.

An invader located the Hard Corps's M-60 machine gun which had fallen from the jeep when it crashed. He called this discovery to the attention of the other scum. Two of them joined him in examining the weapon, while another checked out the jeep, wondering if it would still run.

One of the ambushers drew a bayonet and grabbed Fanelli's left arm. He rolled the Italian Hard Corps warrior onto his back and prepared to bury the bayonet in his heart. Fanelli's right arm suddenly streaked forward, the NATO pushbutton blade ready in his fist. The blade snapped open and plunged into his opponent's right eyeball. Sharp steel sunk deep into the socket to pierce the man's brain.

Wentworth took advantage of the momentary confusion and swiftly rose. With a smooth, lightning fast draw, the *wakazashi* appeared in his hand. He continued the same motion and attacked the closest opponent. Slicing forcefully through the man's neck, Wentworth felt little resistance until the blade encountered the vertebrae. As he stepped around the man to engage his next enemy, the invader's limp head flopped backward, unrestrained by severed tendons and muscles. Twin geysers of blood shot up from the carotids.

The next invader turned and attempted to bring his Mini-14 to bear on the merc. The short sword moved in a two-hand grip from left to right, cutting cleanly through the rifleman's wrist. The startled gunman screamed and shook his weapon by the barrel held in his left fist, as if trying to dislodge the severed right hand from the pistol grip. The *wakazashi* swung right to left, cleaving through the man's abdomen. His guts spilled out onto the ground.

Another opponent tried to aim an Uzi at Wentworth, but held his fire because of the closeness of his mortally wounded comrade. Wentworth didn't give the guy time to reconsider. He threw the sword by its hilt. He realized the odds of this technique working were long and only hoped to distract the gunman long enough to draw his pistol.

But, the pitch scored far better than Wentworth had imagined. The tip caught the Vietnamese under the chin and sunk into his throat. The invader fell against a tree, his body rigid, the blade wobbling slightly as crimson spurted across the man's shirt front.

Fanelli had rapidly drawn his .45 ACP from shoulder leather and fired into the nearest attacker. The center-shot man went spreadeagle and flopped on the ground, a bullet hole marking the spot where the 230 grain projectile had stopped his lifepump.

A large Vietnamese, looking more like a Japanese sumo wrestler, lumbered toward Fanelli with his arms outstretched. The Hard Corps pro was still a bit dizzy from the car crash and found himself off-balance. He started to fall to the right as the huge Asian closed in from the left. Fanelli's left hand whipped out a .38 Special snubnosed Colt revolver from a holster at the small of his back. He fired the double-action piece upward into the oriental hulk.

Fanelli felt as if he was in the middle of a horror movie. The big bastard absorbed the first three rounds in the chest without stopping. He continued to slowly approach the fallen mercenary, determined to kill Fanelli with his bare hands. The snubnose barked twice more. The Asian's knees finally buckled, and he fell forward. Fanelli emptied the piece, putting the last 125 grain hollow-point round into the guy's face.

Wentworth held his .45 in one hand as he approached the corpse against the tree, the *wakazashi* still jutting from the throat. The blade had penetrated the man's neck and pinned him to the trunk. Wentworth yanked the sword free from the dead man's flesh and turned to Fanelli, stepping over the dying Asian brute, who was still clawing at the dirt near Joe's boot.

"Why did you shoot him six times, Joe?" Wentworth asked.

"Because this revolver doesn't hold seven bullets," the plucky Italian replied with exasperation. He was more than a little rattled by the big man's refusal to go down. "Tell you one thing, the next backup piece I get is gonna be a fuckin' Magnum. This guy just didn't wanna go down."

"He's down now," Wentworth stated.

Fanelli hit the cylinder release button, and with a flick of the wrist, ejected the spent shells. He pulled a rubber speedloader from an ammo pouch hooked to his web-gear, and inserted six fresh cartridges into the .38 Colt.

Suddenly a hail of automatic fire tore leaves from branches and slammed into one of the corpses. The two Hard Corps mercs didn't need a second warning. They dove behind the overturned jeep for cover.

Fanelli stared longingly at his M-16, which lay fifteen feet away, while the automatic fire continued unabated. Bullets hammered the thick sheet metal of the jeep and ricocheted across the dirt beneath. The raw smell of spilled gasoline assaulted their nostrils. Fanelli held his .45 overhead and fired two rounds in the general direction of the automatic fire. It was a hopeless gesture, but the situation seemed to merit it.

They couldn't leave their shelter without being chopped to pieces by the hail of full-auto death. If they stayed put, another grenade blast would finish them off or a single spark from a ricochet round would ignite the spilled gas.

Steve Caine moved across the familiar terrain of the forest, following the shifting sounds of battle. He carried the M-16 in one hand and a homemade spear—a stripped pine branch twisted into the hollow handle of his survival knife—in the other. His bow was slung over his shoulder, and he still had one arrow left.

As he rounded the ridge, staying carefully below the horizon, Caine saw the overturned jeep. He also spotted the two Vietnamese killers armed with assault rifles. One of the invaders was about to pull the pin from a grenade while his comrade continued to fire at the disabled vehicle.

Caine swiftly unslung the bow and drew an arrow. He aimed, notched the arrow to the bow, and fired as fast and sure a shot as he could. The curare-tipped arrow hit the enemy garbage between the shoulder blades and drove him forward onto his face.

The Hard Corps loner launched himself forward and hurled his spear, just as the second interloper turned to face him. The blade of the lance caught the startled Vietnamese under an upraised arm, splitting flesh between his ribs. The second man fell dying, and Caine closed in. Then he noticed the grenade roll from the corpse of the fellow he'd taken out with the arrow.

The son of a bitch had managed to pull the pin before the curare got him.

Caine dove for the live grenade, scooped it up and threw it away from himself and the jeep. He rolled for cover and let his jaw hang open, his hands over his ears. The exploding grenade sent a wave of red-hot shrapnel into the trees and showered the ground with twigs and pine needles. Caine rose quickly, M-16 in hand, searching for targets.

He spotted a number of invaders positioned to the north of the jeep. Caine switched the M-16 to full-auto and sprayed the area with 5.56mm rounds. He saw Wentworth and Fanelli dart from the jeep, scoop up weapons, and dash to the shelter of a rock formation.

A third grenade arched overhead from the enemy position. Caine hugged the ground, hoping his teammates were doing the same. A double explosion erupted as the detonating grenade ignited the gasoline from the punctured tank.

The pyrotechnic display from the burning jeep allowed Caine to maneuver to his partners' position. He silently slithered behind the pair. Fanelli gasped when he saw Caine. Although startled, Caine's appearance was welcome and also told them what the hell had happened behind enemy lines.

"What are you two doing here?" Caine asked.

"We came to rescue *you,*" Fanelli replied weakly.

"I see," Caine smiled. "Nice job. Thanks."

"Joe, you didn't forget the bipod," Wentworth said with mock surprise. He broke open the top of the M-60 and took an ammo belt from Fanelli. Wentworth carefully lined up the first round and snapped down the lid.

"We ready to rock and roll?" Fanelli inquired.

"In stereo," Wentworth confirmed, pulling back the charging lever to let it slam forward.

Wentworth manned the machine gun. Fanelli handled the ammo belt to make certain it didn't get bunched up and fail to feed into the weapon properly, while Caine called the shots. They sprayed the forest with high velocity projectiles. The heavy fire tore away ground cover, revealing the hidden enemy figures.

One enemy was shot in the act of lobbing a grenade. The blaster dropped from his hand as three 7.62mm rounds cut through his torso, and the grenade exploded among the invaders. Bodies scattered, many ravaged by the blast, while some dashed into the merciless blaze of the Hard Corps M-60. Only a few managed to escape and bolt deeper into the forest.

"That broke their backbone," Wentworth shouted, but he nonetheless decided to order a strategic withdrawal. They fell back on foot, moving toward the main base.

CHAPTER 17

CAPTAIN VINH, WHO had fought in jungles and cities, had been a manhunter for more than two decades. In the old days he had used crossbows and crude firearms made in jungle factories. Vinh had attacked large units of men with only one or two soldiers under his command. He'd lost some battles in the past, but he'd never experienced anything like the fighting now taking place in the Washington forest.

The Americans were far better-trained and better-armed than he had suspected. Of course, they knew the forest and could move about it better than Vinh's men, but that was hardly enough of an advantage to explain the defeats his forces had suffered thus far. There had to be more Americans at the compound than Vinh had first guessed. At least twenty or thirty of the Yankee devils.

Vinh decided it was time to try something different.

He had been taught psychological warfare by experts, and had studied methods of interrogation, intimidation, brainwashing, and "black propaganda," or spreading disinformation.

He turned to his communications officer, who had been monitoring the airways to detect police or military radio reports. They had eavesdropped on the conversation between O'Neal and St. Laurent. Vinh thought this information might be useful.

"Transmit on the same frequency the man referred to as 'Saintly' used earlier," Vinh instructed.

"That transmission came from Canada, Comrade Captain," the commo man answered. "Do you wish to contact this 'Saintly' person, or the enemy within the compound?"

"What do you think, you idiot?" Vinh snapped, regretting the remark even as he said it. He didn't want his men to see the effects of stress on him. Besides, the commo officer wasn't supposed to think, only to take orders. "Put me through to the enemy, Lieutenant. Use a low frequency to reduce the possibility of others picking up the signal."

"Yes, Comrade Captain," the commo man confirmed.

Using his excellent English, Vinh spoke into the field radio mike. "Charlie calling Deep Six," he said. "Come in, Six. Over."

"This is Six," O'Neal's voice replied. "What's up, Charlie? You want to surrender? Over."

"Hardly," Vinh told him. "We seem to have a stand-off, Six. Do you agree? Over."

"A little lopsided for a stand-off," O'Neal shot back. "We haven't got a single Zulu on this side, Charlie. How you doing? Get tired of seeing your boys come back to you in little pieces yet? Over."

A "Zulu" was a military term for a casualty. Vinh knew the term. His eyes hardened and his mouth tightened into a thin line.

"I congratulate you on that, Six," Vinh assured him. "I admire you and your men, but you must realize you can't go on this way forever."

"Just until the last one of your gang is dead, Charlie," O'Neal replied simply. "The way things have been going, that shouldn't take much longer."

"We can afford more losses than you can," Vinh stated. "You've done enough for your visitors."

"You must want Trang Nih pretty bad," the Hard Corps commander remarked. "You've sure paid a high price so far, Charlie. You'd be smart to go away and try again another day. Over."

"I wish I could, Six," Vinh said with mock regret. "We are simply soldiers, doing our duty. Trang Nih is a wanted criminal. I suppose he told you he is a freedom fighter against the Communist government. In reality, he is a thief and a murderer. He robbed money from the State Treasury of Vietnam and killed several guards in the process . . ."

O'Neal laughed in response. "That's a pretty sorry lie, Charlie. Even if I believed you, I don't think I'd get too upset about somebody ripping off your government."

"Why does Trang Nih matter to you at all, Six?" Vinh asked. "This man is a stranger to you. He isn't even a client. The one you call 'Saintly' sent him to you. You did not ask for this burden. For that reason, we shall leave you alone after you surrender Trang Nih to us. No retribution for the men you have killed. The war can be over, Six. You and I no longer need be enemies . . ."

"Knock off the bullshit, Vinh," O'Neal snapped.

"You can either back off or keep on fuckin' with us. That's up to you."

"Are your men's lives of so little importance?" Vinh demanded. "Have you so little regard for your own life? You owe Trang Nih nothing. Why risk your lives for him?"

"It's a matter of principle," O'Neal replied. "But I don't think you'd understand that."

"You must like your little compound, Six," Vinh said in a hard voice. "I hope you already have your graves ready because you are all going to die in there."

"Well, you know what they say about life," O'Neal replied. "Nobody ever gets out alive."

O'Neal switched off the radio. He didn't want to let Vinh get the last word. He turned to McShayne.

"What frequency did he call on us, Top?"

"Same as Saintly used," McShayne answered.

"Figures," O'Neal muttered. "Wait five minutes and turn the radio on again. Leave it on the same frequency. Vinh wants to play fuck-with-your-head-psychology, but that game can be played by two as well as one."

CHAPTER 18

"HOW THE HELL did I get into this?" John McShayne wondered aloud as he propped his elbows on the desktop and leaned his jaw into his hands.

The answer to his question probably began in 1950 when McShayne joined the United States Army. He had just missed being drafted into World War II, and he wasn't so sure he wanted to go to war anyway. Still, it seemed a good time to go into the service. GI's were getting lots of benefits. Public opinion of U.S. soldiers was still pretty high. Didn't seem likely there would be a war, but if it happened, it would probably be with the Russians.

It was a weird world, John thought. Five years ago, in 1945, the Soviet Union had been an ally of the United States. Most folks figured Stalin was a great guy back then. Nobody seemed terribly concerned about the fact Stalin's regime had slaughtered at least ten million Russians, Ukrainians, Siberians, and East Europeans. Stalin's genocide count was about five times greater than Hitler's. But people are willing to ignore a lot when they need allies.

McShayne was a big husky young guy who'd just turned twenty, and didn't have any definite plans for the future. He was a farmboy from Wisconsin who didn't want to spend his life plowing fields and shoveling horseshit. The army seemed like a way to learn about life, and figure out what he should pursue as a career. Even then he thought the career he might choose could turn out to be the military. Made sense to start there.

A good-natured youth with lots of muscle. McShayne completed Basic with greater ease than most. He went on to train in his new MOS (Military Occupational Specialty) as a motorpool mechanic. John had never thought of himself as being mechanically inclined, but he had always managed to get his father's tractor running, even in the worst Wisconsin winters.

Within a year after he enlisted, the Korean War broke out. That sent McShayne to Korea in time to participate in the battle of Pyongyang. It was warfare at its worst—a living nightmare with waves of Communist Korean and Red Chinese troops pouring down from the hills. They charged the Americans, brandishing various weapons, but the real threat was the sheer numbers of soldiers that swooped down on the U.S. soldiers.

A guy McShayne had known since Basic fell in front of him, most of his face shot away by enemy bullets. *Jesus*, McShayne thought. *What the hell am I doing here? I'm supposed to be a goddamn mechanic. My job is fixing up jeeps and tanks, not shooting people. I don't know these guys. They don't know me. This is goddamn nuts!*

But McShayne realized something greater than fear

and confusion on the battlefield. Why McShayne was there didn't matter—he *was there* and the other side was trying to kill him. Only self-preservation and looking out for his buddies remained.

He pulled an M-14 from his slain friend's grasp. McShayne had left his own weapon in the back of a truck. He aimed the rifle at the wave of humanity and opened fire. Bodies dropped all around him, as dozens of Asian opponents fell.

McShayne ran out of ammo. He grabbed the M-14 by the barrel as more Koreans and ChiComms kept coming. A North Korean officer skidded to a halt in front of McShayne and pointed a Chinese version of a Broomhandle-Mauser at the American. The big Norwegian-Scot struck out desperately with his rifle. The stock smacked the Mauser from the Korean's hand. McShayne followed with a backhand sweep, but the Asian ducked under the whirling weapon.

The Korean rammed a taekwondo-karate punch to McShayne's midsection. The ex-farm boy from Wisconsin was astonished by the force of the smaller man's blow. He staggered backward and the Korean chopped a rock-hard hand across his forearm, forcing McShayne's fingers to slip from the rifle barrel. The Korean's foot swung a crescent-kick which struck the rifle from McShayne's other fist.

A cross-body karate chop slammed the young McShayne across the chest. The blow knocked him off his feet and he fell to the ground next to a slain Korean soldier. The enemy officer raised a boot, about to stomp McShayne out of existence, but the American's hand touched the frame of a weapon lying next to the dead man. He quickly grabbed it and thrust the rifle forward. The muzzle and front sight of the barrel stabbed into the Korean officer's genitals, before he could complete the stomp. The guy shrieked in agony as sharp metal sliced into tender tissue.

McShane found the trigger and squeezed it. The recoil of the rifle snapped back into McShayne's shoulder. The bullet punched upward through the officer's balls and burrowed deep in his intestines. Overpowered by shock, the Korean collapsed to the ground, dying. McShayne rose to his feet with the enemy weapon in his fists. It was some sort of Chinese copy of an Enfield. McShayne was never quite sure what the hell the gun was, but it was very old, with a clumsy bolt-action and a kick like a liquored-up mule.

More North Koreans and ChiComms were shooting from the buildings of the North Korean capital, but some United Nations forces were now backing up McShayne's lonely little outfit. Fifteen other U.N. members had sent troops into Korea, although the United States had taken on the bulk of the burden for the "police action". The battle lasted for another hour or two before U.N. forces took the city. The following year, the Communists moved in and reclaimed Pyongyang. They would also move into Seoul, but American and U.N. troops would launch the absurd-sounding "Operation Killer" and drive the Reds out of Seoul.

McShayne was promoted to staff sergeant, then decorated for exceptional courage in the face of danger. Such attention startled John. He had simply done what he had to do at the time. That was how his father had raised him.

War was like that for McShayne. You simply do what you have to under the circumstances. He felt awkward about getting medals for doing that. McShayne even felt a little guilty about being awarded decorations and honors for killing other men. The young soldier hadn't thought about it much at the time. They attacked, he counterattacked, and they wound up dead instead of him. It had all happened so fast, he didn't consider the fact that he had actually taken the lives of others on the battlefield until after the fighting was over. He wasn't even sure how many of the enemy he had killed. Probably six or seven, he reckoned.

McShayne talked to an army chaplain about his feelings. The military minister assured John that he hadn't been rewarded for killing, but because his actions had been instrumental in saving the lives of many of his fellow soldiers. That made sense to McShayne—and he figured it was the only way to look at the situation without going crazy.

But McShayne wasn't the dumb country bumpkin stereotype. He was highly intelligent, and had remarkable ability with machinery. The army wanted to capitalize on his talent by teaching him to work on aircraft instead of land vehicles. The military had a new program for training personnel in mechanical maintenance of fighter jets and helicopters. Aircraft were becoming an important part of warfare.

During the Korean War, the first dog fights between jet fighters took place. Soviet MIG-15's gave the Communists an edge during the first year of the conflict, but the U.N. forces (with the Americans, as usual, taking the bulk of the burden) produced the F-86 Sabre, which proved highly successful against the MIG's. By the end of the war, about 800 MIG's had been shot down, but only 58 Sabres were destroyed in combat.

Also, for the first time helicopters played a crucial role in warfare. There hadn't been many choppers during World War II, but choppers were becoming more plentiful. Their ability to land or take off without a runway, maneuver without needing as much sky as a plane, and hover in a fixed position made the chopper a special piece of equipment with lots of potential.

The military clearly needed more aircraft mechanics to keep their new birds aloft. McShayne accepted the challenge, and returned to the States for training. More than a year later, he completed his special training, received a new MOS, and was assigned to an Army Airborne unit. His skills as a chopper mechanic were in great demand, and he quickly made Sergeant First Class. His rise in the ranks within three years was quite exceptional. McShayne figured if the army intended to treat him so well, he might as well stay for a while.

McShayne soon became involved with a lady he met off base. Like most young men, McShayne fell in love without a second glance. He courted Sara Holland for several months and proposed marriage. The couple were wed shortly before now-SFA McShayne got orders to go to Okinawa.

The couple had trouble adjusting to the change. McShayne enjoyed the adventure, but Sara missed her family and she didn't like Okinawa or the Japanese. She complained that the Japs had attacked us at Pearl Harbor, that they were a bunch of sneaky cutthroats. Her father had been killed in the Pacific during World War II and she blamed every single Japanese, regardless of age, sex or social status, for the deliberate murder of her beloved father.

McShayne tried to soothe her, but she soon started hating him for making her live among Jap murderers. She returned to the States, and a month later, McShayne received a letter from a lawyer. Sara had filed for divorce on the grounds of mental cruelty. McShayne did not argue.

The army became his home more than ever. He concentrated on his work and his life with the other soldiers. McShayne was well-liked and respected by his men. He was a war hero and possessed an all-important MOS. More chopper mechanics came into the Army Airborne unit, but McShayne was their NCOIC (Non-Commissioned Officer in Charge). The other mechanics looked up to him and regarded McShayne as a father figure, although he was only five or six years their senior. Most of the senior officers valued his ability and trusted his judgement. The army was a good place for him and he opted for another hitch in 1958.

McShayne spent his next tour of duty stateside. Both his parents died during that time, and, in grief, he drank himself into a stupor at the NCO club. When the sergeant-at-arms tried to throw him out, McShayne chucked the guy through a window. He punched out two more men before a half dozen soldiers restrained him.

With ten years of honorable service, they didn't want to bust McShayne's chops. The commander went easy on him. McShayne was simply fined and restricted to barracks for ninety days. The army could have burned him. McShayne had violated enough regulations, according to the Uniform Code of Military Justice, to cost him his career and a couple years in Leavenworth. But the UCMJ is so strict, ninety percent of the military personnel would be bounced out of the service if all the rules were enforced against everyone. The army doesn't crucify many people, but when it wants to, it can pound rusty nails through a man's hands, and leave scars that will last a lifetime.

America had already been involved in Vietnam for some time, and involvement there was escalating. More troops were being sent in, and McShayne was among them. The Americans were basically advisors for the South Vietnamese. Nonetheless, fourteen Americans were killed during the Kennedy years, and several had vanished; to this day their fate is unknown.

Then came the major escalations under the Johnson administration. McShayne was already in Vietnam and saw the changes occur, but the situation remained a no-win war. He correctly predicted it would be a long, terrible ordeal.

McShayne didn't see much of the bush. He spent his time in Saigon and at airbases, working on helicopters, and damned if those gunships weren't getting bigger and better. He had his hands full just keeping up with the changes. After fourteen years in the service, McShayne was made master sergeant, but shortly after his promotion, an NVA bombing attack blew up a chopper near McShayne's workshop. He was wounded by flying shrapnel. Two of his mechanics were also killed by the blast.

He returned to the States to recover from his wounds, but his request to return to Vietnam was denied. He was nearly forty and approaching twenty years in the service. They told him he ought to be thinking about retiring and collecting his pension.

McShayne didn't want to retire. He could stay in the Army for thirty, forty years—and he intended to. But that meant he had to learn about the newest addition to aircraft technology—if he wanted to keep his old MOS. Computers were rapidly becoming more important to the military. This was a whole new field for John McShayne, the farmboy from Wisconsin.

Most men McShayne's age would have shied away from a complex course in computer operations and programming, but McShayne still liked a challenge. He absorbed the new subject, fascinated by the advances in computer technology. In 1972, as U.S. troops were being pulled out of Vietnam, McShayne was sent to West Germany just in time for the Munich massacre at the Olympic Village. Black September terrorists murdered seventeen Israelis. This proved to be the preamble for a new wave of terrorist activity in Western Europe.

West Germany had more than its share in the early seventies. The Baader-Meinhof Gang, Second June Movement, German Red Army Faction, Turkish Gray Wolves, and a number of Palestinian outfits were keeping the authorities busy. Since American military personnel were also targets of terrorism, McShayne's newly acquired computer skills were put to work with S-2 Army Intelligence, instead of aircraft systems.

McShayne spent four years in Germany, then three as a sergeant major for command headquarters at a base in Texas. It was the end of a fine military career.

At the age of fifty, McShayne had spent two thirds of his life in uniform, and since he was still very fit and healthy, McShayne didn't want to retire. He had no desire to sit on his ass and collect a pension every month. He was still a soldier in his heart, but his fighting years were over.

With the United States Army, at least.

It was 1980, and the Hard Corps was recruiting mercs for a mission in Central America. McShayne learned about this through some covert sources he'd maintained among former military personnel who occasionally worked as soldiers of fortune. William O'Neal and James Wentworth were surprised when the craggy, middle-aged guy strolled in, looking for work as a mercenary.

"I know what you're thinking," McShayne had said with a smile. "You figure I'm too old for this sort of thing. You're right. I'm too old to run around in the goddamn jungle with a forty-pound pack on my back, but an army doesn't run on muscle and balls. You need organization, repair teams, maintenance of vehicles and equipment, communications, intel, bookkeeping, filing, and payroll management.''

''Uh-huh,'' O'Neal agreed. ''What job are you interested in?''

''Any or all of the above,'' McShayne answered. ''Hell, I've done 'em all before. And I can cook too.''

''You're hired, Top,'' O'Neal replied, already certain they had found the perfect first sergeant for the Hard Corps.

CHAPTER 19

AN ALARM SUDDENLY lit up on the wall, accompanied by a soft buzzer. McShayne bolted from his office to find O'Neal. The signal was from the stockade.

Somebody had just managed to break out of his cell.

William O'Neal leaned his M-16 in a corner and gathered up an Uzi submachine gun. The compact 9mm blaster was better suited for close combat. A shootout within the confines of the stockade would be at very close quarters. Close enough that an opponent might be able to grab a rifle barrel, and close enough to make wielding a longer weapon awkward. The short-barreled Uzi would avoid those problems, and supply O'Neal with plenty of firepower.

"What about the surveillance camera in the cell-block?" he asked McShayne as he shoved a 25-round magazine into the mag well of the Uzi.

"Whoever busted out of his cell already took out the camera," McShayne answered. "The monitor isn't receiving static, so I think he covered the lens with a blanket or something. What I can't figure out is how he broke out of a cell in the first place. He couldn't just pick the lock. Not even Harry Houdini could've done that. There's an electrical locking system that has to be switched off from the guard station outside the cell block. Unless that sucker's switched off, you couldn't open the cell doors if you had the keys."

"Yeah," O'Neal agreed. "I was here when we put the system in. If I can take the escapee alive, we'll ask him how he did it."

"You're not going in there alone, sir?" McShayne asked with a frown.

"You have to stay here, Top," O'Neal replied. "You're the best man to handle communications, monitor surveillance, and make coffee."

"Damn it, sir," McShayne complained. "You're the CO. You oughta let me go instead. They need you here to command this outfit."

"If I get killed, Wentworth will take command," O'Neal replied. "But we don't have a replacement for you, and it's vital we keep commo lines open. The other three are still out there fighting the enemy. If they need assistance we have to know about it. If Saintly gets off his CIA butt and gets reinforcements for us, we've got to know about it. And I've gotta haul ass before that prisoner gets away."

"Be careful, sir," McShayne urged, as he watched O'Neal hurry out the door.

The Hard Corps commander jogged across the parade field to the stockade, his Uzi held ready, barrel pointed toward the night sky above. The stockade was a simple structure, a big concrete block with a single door and no windows. It had been designed to hold prisoners only until the Hard Corps could decide what to do with them. But it was no crackerjack box. The sucker was built to keep people locked up. Somebody had managed to beat the system, and O'Neal wanted to know how.

When he approached the door, O'Neal was relieved to see it hadn't been tampered with. That meant that no one had broken into the stockade to help the prisoner escape. If the outside door had been jimmied or picked open, O'Neal would have to worry about enemies within the command area—either Vinh's men who had managed to reach the main base, Franklin Willis, or Trang Nih. But it appeared the escapee was flying solo, and he was still inside the stockade.

O'Neal stood clear of the heavy oak door and inserted the key. He unlocked the door and kicked it open, hard enough to slam the door into the wall—or into anyone who might be hiding behind the door to ambush him. He entered the guard station, Uzi ready for action. The room was bare, except for a small metal table with a radio, and a single chair. There was also a small bathroom behind the table. The door stood open and O'Neal peered inside at the sink and toilet. Nobody was hiding in there, unless it was a dwarf with an aqualung.

He turned toward the cellblock door. The controls to the electrical locking system didn't appear to have been tampered with. A signal light flashed, announcing what O'Neal already knew—that one of the cell doors had been forced. He moved to the thick metal door of the cellblock and peered through the dense, inch-thick glass. The narrow corridor along the cells was empty. A single barred door to a cell was open. O'Neal couldn't tell which cell it was and he didn't remember in which order he had put the prisoners there anyway.

But there were only four cells. Qui Nhung, the Laotian freedom fighter and Trang Nih's right hand man, had been locked in a cell by himself. The Cambodian

Psar Phumi had also been locked in a solitary cell. Trang Nih's other four fighters had been put in the remaining cells. That meant there was at least one prisoner, maybe two, out of a cell. O'Neal stood by the doorway as he put the key in the lock and turned it. He shoved on the handle and kicked the door open with the back of his heel, to avoid standing directly in the path of any weapon which might have been missed when they frisked the prisoners. Hell, there hadn't been time for a strip search. The prisoners could have smuggled wire garrotes, small knives, or razor blades or maybe a diminutive one-shot firearm. O'Neal had once searched a Vietcong spy in Saigon and found a tiny derringer jammed in the guy's asshole.

Neither bullet or blade plunged across the threshold —but a man's hurtling body dove from the cellblock into the merc. O'Neal swung his Uzi toward the shape, but a foot lashed out and kicked the subgun out of his hands.

Another kick caught O'Neal in ribs and knocked him into a corner. His assailant pushed with his hands and thrust out with his legs, jumping to his feet with a single motion. He turned to face O'Neal, hands poised like the talons of a bird of prey. Qui Nhung's stern features glared at the Hard Corps commander.

The Laotian feinted with his hands and snapped a kick at O'Neal's groin. The American shifted a leg and took the kick on his thigh muscle, then swung a left hook. Qui Nhung blocked with a forearm and thrust a fingertip stab for O'Neal's solar plexus. The merc parried with the heel of his right hand, hooking his bent elbow to the side of the Asian's jaw.

O'Neal followed with a backfist to Qui Nhung's skull and raised his left hand to deliver a karate chop. The Laotian suddenly lunged forward and drove both fists into the merc's torso, the powerful double punch driving O'Neal backward. Qui Nhung launched another high round-house kick at the American's head, and as O'Neal dodged the whirling foot, Qui Nhung continued to flow with the motion of his kick. When his foot touched the floor, he immediately lashed out with his other leg, driving a fast sidekick to O'Neal's chest.

The blow sent O'Neal staggering toward the guard table, and Qui Nhung charged, throwing another vicious sidekick at the merc. O'Neal side-stepped away, and the Asian's kick slammed into the field radio on the table, smashing it to the floor. O'Neal stepped behind his now off-balance opponent and slashed the side of his hand across Qui Nhung's kidney, following with a hammer-fist blow between the Asian's shoulder blades. As Qui Nhung sprawled across the table top, O'Neal jumped back and slammed a kick to the table, tipping it over on Qui Nhung, pinning him on the floor.

"Get up," O'Neal ordered, drawing his .45 Colt and snapping off the safety catch. "Do it slow and no more tricks, fella."

Qui Nhung followed instructions and rose from the floor, both hands raised to shoulder level. A small ribbon of blood trickled from the corner of his mouth.

"You fight well, O'Neal," he stated. "Perhaps we'll have a rematch when you're not carrying a gun."

"Right now I have a gun," O'Neal replied. "And I shoot just as well. How'd you manage to break out of your cell, Qui Nhung? Turn yourself into a snake and slither between the bars?"

"Where is Trang Nih?" the Laotian demanded. "I must see him."

"You feel like making a confession?" O'Neal inquired. "Talk to me first, fella."

"You think I'm a spy of Captain Vinh's?" Qui

Nhung snorted with contempt. "You're jumping to the wrong conclusions, O'Neal. I'm not the spy, but I think I know who is. He's still locked in his cell. Don't worry about him."

"Right now, I'm more worried about you," the merc replied. "You're the one who broke out of his cell and refuses to say how he did it."

"The buttons of my shirt contain a plastic explosive," Qui Nhung explained. "A variation of primacord was hidden in the elastic band of my trousers. The charge was small, but enough to blast the lock to my cell."

"Right out of a James Bond film, eh?" O'Neal mused. "You always carry stuff like that on you?"

"As a matter of fact," the Laotian replied. "I do. I was a prisoner of the Pathet Lao during the war. I managed to escape. Since then, I have always carried concealed materials to break out of chains—or prison cells —in case I was ever captured again."

"That's an interesting story, Qui Nhung," O'Neal said. "You want to see Trang Nih?"

"Very much," the Laotian urged. "I've been going mad, sitting in that cell, helpless while I listened to the war outside."

"Okay," the Hard Corps commander began as he stepped backward, his .45 still aimed at Qui Nhung. He scooped up his Uzi and tucked it under his arm. "I'll take you to him. But if you try to run or turn on me again, I'll splatter you like a bug on a windshield. Understand?"

"No problem," Qui Nhung assured him.

The Laotian didn't try to resist and O'Neal marched him outside. He found Trang Nih with Franklin Willis at a machine gun nest they had set up at the base. The Vietnamese freedom fighter was surprised to see Qui

Nhung being escorted at gunpoint by O'Neal.

"What's going on, Captain?" Trang Nih asked. "What are you doing with Qui Nhung?"

"He broke out of his cell," O'Neal explained. "Very clever and resourceful fellow we've got here. Did you know he carried plastic explosives and primacord concealed in his clothing?"

"I didn't know about that," Trang Nih admitted. "But Qui Nhung is an explosives expert. He often carries explosive plastic of different sorts."

"How about stuff to break out of cells and blast locks?" O'Neal asked.

"Oh, yes," Trang Nih confirmed. "He was formerly a prisoner of the Pathet Lao. Since then he has carried lock picks, hacksaw blades, and other items of that sort."

"Very resourceful," O'Neal mused. "You must be a clever guy, Qui Nhung. Too clever to be in the firing line when two men with shotguns broke into that condo in San Diego when Vinh planned to attack you guys there. Of course, Vinh could have attacked without warning you about it, but you'd have to be pretty stupid to continue to work for him after he proved he'd be willing to kill you in order to try to assassinate Trang Nih. I don't figure you're stupid, Qui Nhung."

"Does that mean you trust me now, O'Neal?" the Laotian asked. "Or do I have to go back to my cell?"

"I think we can trust you," O'Neal confirmed. "But the other five are staying in their cells."

"If you insist," Qui Nhung said. "But I'll tell you who the spy probably is."

"Who?" Willis asked with a frown.

"Psar Phumi," the Laotian answered. "I never really trusted him, and after that incident in San Diego, I was opposed to letting him participate in our group."

"I remember you wanted to get some scopolamine and give it to Psar Phumi," Trang Nih remarked.

"Scopolamine?" Willis asked, confused by the statement.

"A type of truth serum," O'Neal answered. "Psar Phumi is my number one choice among the suspects too. That bullet crease seemed suspicious to me. He wasn't at the condo because he and a couple of his men were allegedly ambushed by Vinh's people. His friends were killed, but Psar only received a superficial wound. Seems a little *too* lucky to be a coincidence."

"That's what I thought too," Qui Nhung agreed. "But Trang Nih thought we could trust Psar Phumi."

"I know," the Vietnamese freedom fighter sighed. "And my main reason for trusting him was simply because he was a Cambodian refugee. I didn't want to believe he could be a traitor."

"Motherfucker's probably a goddamn Communist," Willis growled. "You got any of that truth serum stuff around here?"

"No," O'Neal replied. "And nobody here is qualified to use it anyway. Scopolamine is a powerful drug. It can make a person's heart burst if it's not used right. We'll just have to keep Psar Phumi and the others locked up for now."

"The Cambodian is the spy, man," Willis insisted. "That bullet crease was self-inflicted. Hell, I knew guys in 'Nam who shot themselves in the foot to try to get out of the war. Wouldn't take any big deal to crease yourself with a bullet . . . especially when he knew if he ran either Vinh's people or Trang Nih's would catch up with his ass eventually."

"We still don't know for sure," O'Neal stated. "I'm not willing to let the other four go because we decided

Psar Phumi was guilty. One of them could be Vinh's inside man."

"Well, at least we got one more gun hand on our side," Willis commented. "Welcome aboard, Qui Nhung."

"Thanks," the Laotian replied. "Glad to be back in the game."

"I've got a feeling we'll need all the help we can get," O'Neal said grimly.

CHAPTER 20

CAPTAIN VINH DECIDED it was time to take the gloves off. He began deploying his forces in a horseshoe formation around the compound, ranging from the base of the cliffs on the southwest of the lake, and then continuing counterclockwise, to the north. Vinh directed his radioman to establish contact with the team leaders of his forces. The first was the commander of the group which had been driven off after the last skirmish with the Americans.

"That's right, Comrade Captain," the team leader said in a weary voice. "We've lost eighteen men, and two are badly wounded. Every time we get close to them, they rip us apart. Your intelligence reports must be incorrect. There have to be more than four Americans . . ."

"The accuracy of my intelligence reports is not your concern," Captain Vinh snapped. "We are preparing to attack the enemy base. The men you engaged in battle must not be allowed to return to their headquarters. Do not make the mistake of closing with them again. Use heavy weapons at a distance. If you can't finish them, at least keep them pinned down.''

"That might not be so easy, Comrade Captain . . .''

"I am not concerned with whether it is easy or not,'' Vinh said angrily. "Just do as you are told. I'm sending some reinforcements with mortars, machineguns, and rocket launchers. Don't worry about making noise. We'll kill the Americans and Trang Nih, then pull out before the police can arrive. The state patrolmen won't send anyone until they can put together a large number of troops. That will take time. If they are stupid enough to send only a car or two, we'll simply kill them when they arrive.''

"It isn't the police I'm worried about,'' the team leader remarked sourly. "But I will follow your orders, Comrade Captain.''

"Do so,'' Vinh commanded. Then he began contacting the others to coordinate the attack.

The landscape reminded Joe Fanelli of a primeval forest as he trailed behind Steve Caine and James Wentworth III, hauling the M-60 machine gun like a long steel suitcase. They had covered a hundred yards in their strategic withdrawal when the all too familiar *thunk thunk thunk* of multiple mortar fire shattered the forest quiet. The three combat veterans made no attempt to flee. They knew they were far safer if they dropped in place.

The exploding mortar shells formed three small mushroom clouds of smoke to the trio's immediate south, showering them with flying dirt. The Hard Corps mercs stayed down as the roar of the explosions echoed through the woods.

"So we broke their backs, huh?" Fanelli wisecracked to Wentworth. "Guess they're shooting at us from their wheelchairs now."

"Area fire for three men?" Caine mused. "That's a bit excessive."

"They're overreacting because we bloodied their noses," Wentworth replied.

"First we broke their backs," Fanelli muttered. "Now it's just bloodied noses. Next you'll decide we just offended their sensibilities."

The flat boom of three more mortar rounds hurtling into the air warned them to hug the earth. The next three explosions again came from their immediate south, and the slow cadence of a heavy machine gun started up from the north. The heavy rounds tore branches off of the towering sitka spruce above them, gouging the giant conifers.

"Those mortar rounds are well-spaced. They want to cut off our route to the south," Wentworth observed as he took the M-60 from Fanelli, and slapped the bipod into place. "They're certainly moving troops into position to outflank us. If they do, we're finished."

Steve Caine took a pair of field glasses from a case, and resumed the role of spotter. He soon located a heavy machine gun mounted on a jeep, which the enemy had driven off the road to get a better line on their position. Caine frowned. He didn't know the enemy had vehicles capable of traveling across the rugged terrain of the compound.

"Looks like a .50 caliber, mounted on a four-wheel drive," he reported. "I haven't caught sight of the mortar crews yet."

Wentworth brought the M-60 to bear on the enemy position, and walked a stream of 7.62mm rounds over the head of the vehicle. He moved the bullet-stream lower, blasting the jeep. Bullets popped the front tires, blew off the hood, and sent hot coolant spewing over the operators of the big gun.

Scalded by the hot liquid, the two Vietnamese hitmen bolted from the jeep. The third stayed and tried to pull the piece from its mount. He paid dearly for his efforts. The next three rounds caught him in the shoulder and neck. His arm has ripped from its socket, and his head toppled onto a shoulder, dangling by bloody threads of loose skin.

"We've got to change position," Wentworth directed. "Otherwise they'll be able to zero in on us—and they won't be satisfied just to pin us down."

"I'll bring the '60," Fanelli volunteered.

Wentworth's prediction proved accurate. As they scrambled from their position, more mortar rounds rained down on the forest. The pine needles which marked their last position were obliterated by an exploding mortar round.

"Shit," Fanelli rasped as he set up the M-60. "This business is getting more dinky dau by the minute, man."

The walkie-talkie on Wentworth's belt cranked to life.

"This is O'Neal," a familiar voice announced from the radio. "Come in. Over."

"Wentworth here," the Hard Corps XO replied. "Read you. Over."

"Return to home base most ricky-ticky," O'Neal instructed. "We've got big problems. According to what we can gather from motion detectors and microphones, the enemy has us ringed. Also, did you guys find Steve?"

"He found us, actually," Wentworth admitted. "But we're okay so far. But we've got a problem. The enemy has decided to avoid closing with us. Instead, they're maintaining a barrage of mortar fire to our south. They're also trying to zero in on us with another mortar. And they're pretty good at their job, Bill.''

"We need you back here at home base," O'Neal insisted.

"When we get back you'll be the first to know," an exasperated James Wentworth assured him and signed off.

The Hard Corps trio changed position again when they heard gears being shifted on a jeep advancing toward them. They had to keep the enemy from flanking them or they'd be trapped in a crossfire.

"Head west," Wentworth directed.

"Jesus," Fanelli muttered as he threw the trailing ammo belt for the M-60 over his shoulder. "I knew you'd find a way to make me play *Rambo*," he complained. "And I'm not even the one who's crazy about survival knives."

They reached a position which afforded the trio a firelane to the road. Three invaders suddenly approached in a jeep, another .50 caliber machine gun mounted to the vehicle. There was no time to set up the M-60. Fanelli quickly kneeled to establish a stable mount for the machine gun, and pulled the trigger.

He had his hands full trying to hold down the bucking weapon as bullets ripped up the road, slamming into the jeep. Wentworth and Caine swiftly brought their M-16's to play, blasting the occupants of the vehicle with twin streams of 5.56mm rounds.

Fanelli's M-60 slugs chewed into tires, causing the four-by-four to swing out of control while attempting to negotiate the next corner. A guy riding shotgun tried to bring his M-2 carbine to bear, but the driver suddenly released the wheel and threw up his arms, hit by multiple M-16 rounds. The guy with the M-2 was thrown from the vehicle just before it smacked into a tree. But the man at the big gun held on, bringing the weapon into action despite the crash landing.

"Split up!" Wentworth cried. "Give him multiple targets!"

"That's up to you guys," Fanelli grunted, remaining on the ground with the M-60.

Rounds from the two M-16s plowed into earth around the man behind the jeep, but then zeroed in on their target. The invader's body recoiled violently after each hit, until his nervous system no longer had the ability to respond. His corpse barely twitched from the last two bullets.

The machine gunner with the .50 had blasted half a dozen rounds at the Hard Corps team. The poorly-aimed, half inch slugs hit sporadically around Fanelli, kicking clouds of dust over the tough Italian from Jersey. Joe adjusted the aim of his M-60 by shifting his entire body, and managed to come on target first.

His 30 caliber rounds tore chunks of flesh from the machine gunner's body and lifted it up and away from the mounted .50 caliber. The man's body pitched over the side of the jeep before it slammed lifeless to the ground. Fanelli sighed with relief.

"Too much gun, Joe," Caine commented with infuriating calmness in his voice. "That jeep was our ticket outta here."

"Now you tell me," Fanelli growled. "All I ever get around here is complaints. I oughta quit and join the goddamn French Foreign Legion."

"You'd never get used to eating escargot," Wentworth commented. "Maybe the jeep isn't damaged that badly. Let's take a better look at it . . ."

He started to approach the vehicle when the whine of

a hurtling projectile alerted the mercs to more danger. They hit the ground an instant before another mortar round struck the jeep. The explosion seemed to engulf the trio, hammering their ears and shaking the ground under their bellies. When they looked up, the jeep was only a few chunks of metal on charred ground. Wentworth wiped dirt from his face as he rolled over to check on the others.

"You were saying, Lieutenant?" Fanelli asked dryly.

"Well," Wentworth said with a shrug. "It was a nice idea, but it's a little late now."

"We're not gonna get outta here if we stay bunched up together," Fanelli announced. "They'll keep up this hide-and-seek-bullshit until they pin us down and burn us, man. So haul ass, fellas. I'm gonna stay here and hold 'em off."

James Wentworth had been exposed to many situations in Vietnam when teamwork was more important than rank, but he had never gotten used to letting an NCO make decisions for him. He also didn't intend to let Fanelli sacrifice his life for the unit. The team was his responsibility. He was the commanding officer.

"I'll take the machine gun," he asserted.

"I've already got it, Jim," Fanelli replied. "You had it earlier. Now it's my turn."

"Let me have that weapon, Sergeant," Wentworth insisted. "That is a direct order, soldier."

"So court-martial me, Lieutenant," Fanelli shot back. "I haven't been court-martialed for a long time. But do it later, 'cause I'm stayin'."

"Look you guys," Caine interjected. "We've got to get out of here. There isn't time to argue, and I'm not going to carry one of you, so don't get any stupid ideas about knocking the other guy unconscious so you can be a hero."

"You intend to leave Joe here?" Wentworth demanded.

"The captain needs us at the base," Caine replied. "Now that our mission has changed. We should get back to help defend the lives and property there. More's at stake than our individual lives."

"He's right and you know it, Lieutenant," Fanelli said. "Go on. Get out of here before we all get wasted, man."

Wentworth placed a hand on Fanelli's shoulder.

"Good luck, Joe," he said gently.

"Next thing you'll be playing fuckin' violin music," Fanelli complained.

"Watch your ass, buddy," Caine said softly. "Don't get yourself killed if you can help it. Okay?"

"You do the same, pal," Fanelli urged.

Wentworth and Caine headed toward the base. The lieutenant removed his radio, canteen and empty weapon magazines. Caine followed his example.

"How's your time in the four-forty, Steve?" he asked.

"I'm no track star," Caine replied. "But the prospect of getting a bullet up my ass is enough to make me run like the wind."

The two men double-timed south and soon disappeared beyond the ground cover of the lodge-pole forest. Fanelli didn't watch them depart. He realized this would only contribute to his sense of loneliness and vulnerability. He took a position on top of a small rise, where the ground afforded him some cover. There was nothing else to do but wait.

He didn't have to wait long. Fanelli heard harsh words in Vietnamese drift from the forest. He couldn't make out what was being said, but it sounded like somebody wasn't too thrilled about following orders.

Three men soon appeared, advancing from the trees in a line. From the expressions on their faces, Fanelli figured they had been prodded forward at the point of a bayonet. He guessed Vinh was risking the lives of these men to try to "count the guns" of the Hard Corps. Vinh was one cold blooded son of a bitch, Fanelli decided.

He held his fire, aware he couldn't shoot without revealing his position. But he couldn't allow the trio to flank him either. He set down the bipod for the M-60 and drew an imaginary line from man to man.

"Here goes," he rasped through clenched teeth.

He opened fire. The second and third attackers located Fanelli when the first burst of 7.62mm tore the first man apart. The second man kneeled and returned fire, making himself a shorter but fatter target. The impact of the 7.62mm bullets smashed into his torso and catapulted him ten feet. The third man yelled something to his hidden comrades and tried to run. Fanelli's relentless fusillade took him in the lower spine. His broken back snapped in a death arch, as he slid forward on the pine needles.

Fanelli threw the remnants of the ammo belt over his shoulder and picked up the M-60 by its handle. He started to scramble to a new position when the *whoosh* of a rocket launcher echoed from the forest. The missile sliced through air, and the warhead exploded against a tree behind the merc. The fifty-foot tree creaked momentarily, then swayed forward.

It snapped at the trunk and fell. Fanelli tried to outrun the tumbling tree, but failed. It crashed into his position. The courageous Hard Corps pro fell felt the awful weight of the heavy branches. Then everything went black . . .

CHAPTER 21

JOSHUA ST. LAURENT sat behind his desk in his office at a CIA "observation post" in Ottawa, Canada. The place wasn't the posh setting moles always inhabit in fiction. The room was slightly larger than a closet. There were no windows, no wet bar, no imported booze on stacks of glass shelves, no secretary with big boobs and a tight skirt.

St. Laurent's office was a drab little dump in a cheap building the Company had rented because it was located where radio signals could be picked up from the Soviet embassy. It also offered the CIA clear reception of other radio wave-lengths. The case officer's agents in the field weren't cloak-and-dagger boys as much as electronic peeping toms who specialized in wire-taps, rifle microphones, light-density telescopes, and other Big Brother devices. Two men and a woman manned the radio receivers, television monitors, and computers in rooms twice the size of St. Laurent's puny little office.

Well, that was the spying game. They raked in intelligence on the Soviet, Czech, Bulgarian, and East German embassies for obvious reasons, but they also spied on friendly countries—including the British, French, Israeli and West German embassies.

It was a game St. Laurent had been playing for almost twenty years, though things were a lot easier back in the '60's. You could keep secrets back then—at least for a while—until the Freedom of Information Act made it impossible to keep crusading journalists out of Company files.

And now, if American intelligence wasn't completely shot to shit, St. Laurent thought, we'd know who the damn terrorists were before they left Libya, South Yemen or wherever. Then when they arrived in Beirut, or the Athens airport, we could nail them before they could do their dirty work. But the Company had had its claws clipped, its teeth filed down, and its allowance cut.

So St. Laurent envied the Hard Corps their freedom of government restrictions and red tape. Of course, although their profession was just barely legal and some of the actual assignments they took could be considered illegal as hell, they got the job done and they never betrayed the best interests of the United States.

He had first encountered the Hard Corps in Central America, where the CIA was involved in covert assistance to the anti-Communist contras in Nicaragua. The Company was trying to keep a low profile, but everybody knew they were training and arming guerrillas based in Honduras. Two years later, the stink about mining ports in Nicaragua and the so-called "terrorist manual" distributed to the Contras by the CIA made it clear how involved the Company really was. But in 1982, the CIA was still keeping a lid on its activities.

Then along came the Hard Corps. They had been hired to rescue some counterrevolutionary leaders from a political prison in Managua. St. Laurent didn't learn about the mercenaries until they had already managed to sneak into Nicaragua, but damn it, the Company couldn't afford a scandal caused by a group of merc cowboys. If the four American vets got caught by the Sandinistas, Ortega would immediately claim the CIA had sent in the Hard Corps. The Company, the President and U.S. policies in Central America would get another black eye from such an incident.

The CIA, like most intel outfits, is better at sneaking-and-peeking than taking direct action, so they managed to locate the mercs and even photographed them with a zoom lens. Computer checks of military records confirmed they were ex-Green Berets with extensive combat experience in Vietnam. They even had a nickname—the Hard Corps. Two had been officers—one had come up through the ranks, and the other was a West Point graduate. The other two had been NCO's. One of them had a history of alcoholism, and the other was still officially listed as MIA. They all sounded pretty weird to St. Laurent. The Hard Corps had to be crazy to think they could just slip into the capital of Nicaragua, rescue political prisoners from a maximum security prison, and get away with it. The four yahoos had to be stopped. But how?

St. Laurent was still trying to figure out what to do when the mercs made their move. Nobody knew the Hard Corps had struck until the next morning, when the commandant learned several guards were not at their posts. A couple others were at their guard watch, but they were dead as old shit, propped up on wooden braces. Apparently the Hard Corps had killed the guards with silenced weapons, knives, or whatever. Then they managed to shut off the alarms, locate the prisoners, and free them. The mercenaries and the fugitives slipped away soundlessly.

The former prisoners later showed up in Honduras, and the Hard Corps seemed to vanish. The Sandinistas were too embarrassed to make the incident public. The Company uttered a secret sigh of relief, and St. Laurent secretly saluted the mercenaries on a job well done.

A few months later, after St. Laurent began his new assignment as case officer in Ottawa, he was contacted by the Director concerning the Hard Corps. The mercenaries had just purchased 500 acres of land in Washington state, land that used to belong to some marijuana czar who needed cash in a hurry. The four lunatics were setting up some sort of base. Since St. Laurent was familiar with their style in Central America, the Director wanted him to contact the mercs. The CIA had found mercenaries to be useful in the past and the Hard Corps sounded as if they might have potential for future operations.

St. Laurent wanted to get a handle on the mercs. There was nothing illegal about purchasing land and establishing a paramilitary base, as long as laws concerning firearms, explosives, and building regulations were obeyed. St. Laurent was certain the Hard Corps wasn't following all the state and federal regs about the weapons and explosives. If they could afford to buy such a large amount of land and stock it with some pretty impressive hardware, the mercs were earning a lot of cash from their trade. And since most of their income was illegal, they sure wouldn't declare it on their tax forms.

St. Laurent decided to look into these matters before contacting the Hard Corps.

A couple of months later, the CIA officer met with William O'Neal, the unit commander of the Hard Corps. He was pretty square with O'Neal. St. Laurent told him what the Company knew about their activities. He also made it very clear that the mercenaries could be in big trouble with the IRS, HUD, the World Court, and practically everybody else in the world if the CIA moved against them. The Company could also convince the Army to press charges against Caine, since the guy had technically gone AWOL in Vietnam.

"Sure," O'Neal said with a grin. "But the CIA wants to make a deal or you wouldn't be here. So make your pitch, fella."

"We'll let you run your business as usual," St. Laurent stated. "But you'll share any information with us which concerns national security. We'll even share information with you in return. Of course, Uncle Sam will expect you to do an occasional favor for this sort of cooperation. You scratch my back, I'll scratch yours."

"Okay," O'Neal decided. "I think we can live with that. But understand something. If the CIA gets too chickenshit with us, we can always strike base and set up somewhere else. Maybe Texas or Alaska. Maybe outside the U.S. Don't think you can just pull the strings and make us jump, Old Saintly."

The relationship between the Hard Corps and St. Laurent had been one of mutual cooperation . . . more or less. The mercs shared information, but it usually concerned the results of missions they had already accomplished. But the news had always been good news, so "Old Saintly" couldn't complain too much. The Hard Corps were really doing a lot of good for the

United States. The only people they hurt were enemies of the U.S.—or lowlife scum who were enemies of civilized people everywhere.

Unfortunately, St. Laurent had fucked up by sending Trang Nih—a man with an enormous price on his head —to the compound. He realized that now, although he had thought at the time that he was using the best procedure to maintain security. Instead, he had put the merchandise in jeopardy, and they were fighting for their lives. He had helped get them into trouble and he felt obliged to try to get them out of it.

Lieutenant Colonel Brigger opened the door and entered without knocking. The tall, whip-thin Army officer had pulled on his uniform and rain coat, but his eyes were still blurry. Brigger was obviously unhappy about St. Laurent's phone call, which had roused him from his bed an hour before.

"All right, Josh," Brigger announced. "I'm here. Now what the hell is this emergency that couldn't wait until morning?"

St. Laurent explained the situation as best he could, without giving any details about the Hard Corps or their compound. Lt. Col. Brigger was with United States Army Intelligence. He didn't expect St. Laurent to tell him more than he needed to know.

"So some mercenary hired guns are in a shitload of trouble," Brigger remarked. "What do you expect me to do about it?"

"Is it possible for you people to send in reinforcements?" the CIA officer inquired. "Maybe some Special Forces or Rangers."

"Without authorization or even an explanation?" Brigger shook his head. "No way, Josh. I'd have to some sort of justification for something like this. Even then, it would take hours to put the gears in motion . . .

278

even if I could swing it. That would be too late to do your merc pals any good. Besides, we couldn't send a battalion into the Washington forest and keep it from the press. What do we tell the media? The U.S. Army helps protect mercenaries? That'd be a great story, huh?''

"You're right," St. Laurent admitted. "The mercs are on their own."

"That won't save you from media problems," the colonel warned. "From what you tell me, they've got a war going on down there. Somebody is bound to report all the shooting."

"Yeah," St. Laurent agreed. "Well, if the mercs survive, we'll formulate a story for the press that the Army Corps of Engineers was getting rid of some old explosives and ammunition and had a little accident. Lots of noise, but nobody hurt. Of course, the area will have to be roped off and restricted until we can be sure all the explosives are disposed of. The area is private property anyway, so we shouldn't have too much trouble with rubber-necking trespassers there."

"Why rope off the area?" Brigger asked.

"To give us time to haul out the bodies," St. Laurent answered. "And to take care of other evidence that needs to be disposed of."

"I guess that cover story will work," the colonel muttered. "Not the best publicity for the Army, but I guess we can handle it."

"Maybe we can make it the Marines instead," the CIA man suggested with a shrug.

"What if the mercs get killed?" Brigger asked.

"Then the Company will contact the DEA and we'll come up with a story that the compound was the center of pot-growing hoodlums," St. Laurent sighed. "Not too hard to believe, since the previous owners were harvesting grass and selling it. We can say they were processing cocaine, too. Lots of ether tanks would have exploded during a shootout with the DEA. Yeah. The names of the mercs might be released, but we'll try to repress that. I don't want four brave men to be publicly depicted as crooks and dope pushers."

"They're Vietnam veterans, right?" Colonel Brigger said bitterly. "Just what we need. More shitty press for the men who risked their ass for their country. Christ, I think Vietnam vets'll always be getting the shit end of the stick."

"Then let's just hope the good guys win," St. Laurent told him. But he knew that far too often, they don't.

CHAPTER 22

THE HARD CORPS had been holding off Captain Vinh's assault force, driving the invaders back again and again. But Vinh was no longer sending individual squads to tangle with the mercenaries. The North Vietnamese commander had decided to use his greatest advantage against the Hard Corps . . . superior numbers.

His horseshoe formation was slowly closing around the heart of the compound. Vinh wasn't taking any chances. His mortar gunners fired shells at the base as the invading force advanced. Mortar rounds showered down on the buildings surrounding the parade field. Explosions roared throughout the compound.

A shell struck the head shed, blasting a wall from the building. O'Neal and Trang Nih were outside, setting up sandbags knocked over from a machine gun nest. But John McShayne was still inside. O'Neal watched with horror as half the roof fell in.

"Top!" he cried, as he dashed toward the crumbling building.

A familiar, chunky figure emerged from the cloud of plaster dust which rolled from the wreckage. McShayne carried his M-14 in one hand as he waved at the dust with the other. O'Neal sighed with relief.

"I'm comin', damn it," McShayne growled. The grizzled veteran sergeant regarded having a roof cave in on him as nothing more than an inconvenience. He took it all in stride.

"Are you all right?" O'Neal asked, raising his voice to be heard above the boom of exploding mortars.

"Yeah," McShayne answered, shaking dust from his hair. "But I think the computers are shot to hell."

"If you're okay, help me fire some mortars back at these bastards," O'Neal said with mock gruffness.

"Why not?' McShayne snorted. "I gotta do everything else around here, don't I? By the way, I noticed the cameras and detectors are virtually all out now."

"I think we've got a pretty good idea where the enemy is anyway," O'Neal muttered. "About to blow our asses in the weeds. Help me with the mortars."

"Someone is coming," Trang Nih said tensely, swinging his M-16 toward the two shapes approaching them.

"Hold your fire!" O'Neal instructed when he recognized the pair. "That's Wentworth and Caine!"

The Hard Corps XO and Sergeant Caine came to a weary halt. Both men were coated with dust. Wentworth carried a long samurai sword, a *katana,* the traditional primary weapon of the warriors of Japan. Wentworth slid the long sword into his belt.

"What took you guys so long, for crissake?" O'Neal demanded. "And where's Fanelli?"

"Joe stayed behind to hold them off so we could escape," Wentworth answered grimly. "I ordered him to give me the M-60, but he refused."

O'Neal didn't reply. There was nothing to say. They all knew Fanelli—his strengths, his weaknesses.

"Help Top with the mortars," O'Neal declared. "We've got to start throwing more firepower at these bastards."

"Yeah," Wentworth said bitterly. "A motor struck my hootch. Blasted half of it apart. My imported china tea set was shattered. I don't think a single cup survived. My VCR was smashed, and it looked like several of my best tapes were ruined. My copy of *Yojimbo* had better be intact."

"Maybe you can sue 'em later," O'Neal said with annoyance. "You want to move your ass, Lieutenant?"

"Of course," Wentworth replied stiffly. "At least I managed to salvage my *katana*. The sword is the soul of a samurai, you know."

"Well, get your *bushido* butt in gear," O'Neal snapped. "Those mortars aren't going to fire themselves."

"I'll help you, Lieutenant," Caine told Wentworth, as they headed toward the mortars set up by McShayne. "I know how you feel, sir. My hootch was hit too, but I did manage to retrieve a survival knife from the wreckage."

He patted the camouflage-print handle of the big knife on his hip. Wentworth glanced at the survival knife and sighed.

"How many of those things do you own?" he asked.

"A couple dozen," Caine said with a shrug.

"How can you compare that to a one-of-a-kind genuine *katana?*" Wentworth sniped, offended by the very notion.

"They both have blades," Caine answered simply as

he knelt by the first mortar. He frowned when he counted the number of shells in the ammo case by the mortars. "Eight rounds? Is that all we've got, Lieutenant?"

"That's what I came up with on the inventory," Wentworth replied. "And we only have three mortars. Sorry, but we didn't really plan to fight a war here."

"Two of these shells have white tape on them," Caine sighed. "They're either marked incorrectly or these are just smoke-filled warheads."

"We use them for training," Wentworth replied. "Remember?"

"They're shooting heavy explosive rounds at us and we're going to fire back with smoke bombs?" Caine chuckled with macabre amusement. "Well, maybe the enemy will start laughing real hard and we'll be able to sneak up behind them while they're still hysterical."

"The Captain and I discussed this earlier," McShayne declared. "We'll fire the smoke for effect to disorient the enemy and reduce their visibility, then we'll rake the area with M-60 fire. Try to zero in on the enemy and hit 'em with the live mortar rounds."

"Pretty iffy tactics," Wentworth said with a frown. "But I guess we don't have a hell of a lot of choice."

"That's right, Lieutenant," McShayne agreed. "No fuckin' choice at all, sir."

Caine, Wentworth, and McShayne inserted the smoke rounds in the stubby muzzles and fired two mortars. They aimed at the general area where the last enemy rounds had come from. Startled cries echoed from the forest as the shells hit. Billows of dense white smoke rose from the trees to the north and the west.

The enemy opened fire with automatic weapons, but no mortars. Apparently Captain Vinh hadn't been prepared for an extended mortar battle either. O'Neal and Trang Nih trained their M-60 on the muzzle flashes of weapons to the south while Qui Nhung and Franklin Willis fired the machine gun at the invaders to the east.

Screams of pain announced that some of the random shots had struck targets among the trees. Suddenly, a large projectile streaked across the compound toward the Hard Corps. A long tail marked the path of the hurtling missile, as it cut through the darkness past Willis and Qui Nhung. The startled pair dropped to the ground behind the sandbag shelter of their machine gun nest.

However, the rocket had missed them, connected with the stockade to the east, and then exploded. Concrete burst from the sturdy structure. Trang Nih yelled something, but his voice was drowned by the chatter of the M-60 machine gun O'Neal fired in the direction of the opponent with the rocket launcher.

John McShayne fired a mortar in the same direction. The exploding shell uprooted two small pines and launched the damaged trees into the sky—along with assorted human parts. Wentworth and Caine launched their mortars as well, sending explosive messengers north and south.

Dust rose from the woods where the shells had torn up earth, trees, and enemy Vietnamese. Captain Vinh's assault force ceased firing. The Hard Corps did likewise. But the silence didn't last long.

Suddenly, a dozen invaders attacked, firing automatic rifles at the Hard Corps. They were spread out, forming a circle around the base. Qui Nhung turned his M-60 toward a pair of attackers who closed in from the damaged stockade, and sprayed the pair with 7.62mm slugs. As they crumbled and fell, two more figures emerged from the shattered wall of the jail. Qui Nhung was too far away to be certain who they were, but he thought the shorter of the pair might be Psar Phumi.

The harsh whistle of a flying projectile was the only warning Qui Nhung and Franklin Willis received before the 40mm grenade shell impacted with the ground near their machine gun nest. The blooper round blasted heavy clumps of earth, and spewed shrapnel at the two warriors. The explosion also sent the M-60 hurtling from their bunker.

Blood oozing from shrapnel wounds, the stunned and injured pair were unable to respond when a lone Vietnamese assassin approached and opened fire with a CAR-15 carbine. A three round burst ripped into Willis's chest. The black man's body twitched from the force of bullets that slammed into flesh, pulverized bone and destroyed vital organs.

The gunman turned his weapon toward Qui Nhung, but Steve Caine had spotted the invader. He aimed his M-16 and fired from the hip, a trio of 5.56mm slugs ripping open the guy's face from the upper lip to the bridge of his nose. As the Vietnamese triggerman tumbled backward, and a faint muscle reflex triggered his CAR, the carbine spat a single useless round into the night sky before it fell across the lifeless chest of its dead owner.

John McShayne nailed one invader in the center of the chest with a heavy slug from his M-14, which was all he needed to send the man tumbling to the ground and sliding into the next world. William O'Neal fired a volley of M-60 rounds at a trio of opponents closing in from the north. One man was slammed into death by three 7.62mm missiles. Another had his weapon torn from his grasp and lost two fingers in the process. He retreated with the third man, who was lucky enough to escape unscathed.

James Wentworth and Trang Nih also fired at the assault team, using M-16's, each man claiming the life

286

of an invader before the remnants of the attack squad withdrew. McShayne and Caine checked on Qui Nhung and Franklin Willis. The Laotian was hurt, but alive. The same could not be said for the black chopper pilot.

"Hold your fire!" O'Neal told his men. "Since nobody is presenting a target, we can't afford to waste ammunition."

"We're all getting a bit low on ammo," Wentworth agreed.

"Yeah," Caine said dryly, "It looks like the goddamn Alamo all over again."

CHAPTER 23

AN ENEMY JEEP and a one ton four-by-four rolled slowly by the fallen tree. After the trucks were well past, a dirt-covered hand slowly pushed away a large fern that had been displaced during the mortar explosions.

Joe Fanelli slowly crawled from under the branches of the spruce. He had recovered consciousness under the tree and remained there during the shelling. Fanelli's body had been well camouflaged by the dense foliage of the branches and the cover had also protected him from falling shrapnel and loose rocks hurled by exploding mortar rounds.

The M-60 machine gun was gone, confiscated by the enemy, but Fanelli still had his .45 Colt auto and .38 backup piece. He also had a single block of C-4 plastic explosive, and a tiny styrofoam cup containing the detonators. He did not have his assault rifle or even the NATO pushbutton knife, which was still stuck in the eye socket of a dead invader.

"Everybody's left town," Fanelli whispered to the

forest around him. "Let's see where they got to."

He moved toward the base, and Fanelli discovered he was actually behind the enemy forces. Captain Vinh's private army had the place surrounded, but the Vietnamese hitman's unit had suffered plenty of casualties. A lone medic was frantically trying to tend to half a dozen wounded men. Fanelli crept behind bushes as he slowly headed toward the clearing, where a burly figure with a commanding attitude and hard golden eyes addressed a group of men. The Hard Corps NCO didn't speak Vietnamese fluently, but he had a good working knowledge of the language.

"Ban Ban," Captain Vinh called out. "Bring me those two Americans. It's time they earned their keep."

"Thua co, Comrade Captain," Ban Ban responded. He took two men and headed toward the jeep and four-by-four parked a hundred yards from the group. He soon returned, pushing the reluctant Jacque and Slim ahead of him.

"Easy on the threads, man," the tall American protested, as Ban Ban shoved him forward.

"Careful, Slim," Jacque cautioned, glancing around at the hard faced Asians. "We ain't outta the woods yet."

"Yeah," Slim smiled. "I can smell the fuckin' evergreens."

"There you are," Vinh smiled, switching easily to English. "How nice of you to grant my request."

"What request?" Jacque asked, pretty sure he wouldn't like the answer. "We were just hired on to drive a truck, sir . . ."

"But you have the opportunity to play a much more important role in my mission," Vinh chided. "The amount of your compensation is, of course, adjustable. Upward or downward."

Jacque greedily estimated in his head how much more heroin they might receive if they played their cards right. He realized the risk would be greater, but he also felt a need for more dope. Jacque and Slim had already shot up half of the horse they had been given to secure the truck; the monkeys on their backs would soon gobble up the rest.

One of Vinh's men handed the two junkies two sets of olive drab fatigue uniforms. Jacque glanced down at the screaming eagle insignia on a shoulder patch. He wasn't sure, but he thought it was some sort of Army Airborne emblem.

"Listen carefully," Vinh demanded. "You will drive this truck," he indicated the one ton four-by-four. "That's one part of your job we can agree on, yes?"

"I meant like an eighteen wheeler," Jacque said weakly.

"You will drive back in the direction from which you came," Vinh continued.

"Away from the fighting?" Jacque said hopefully.

"Then you will circle around to the front gate of the mercenaries' base," Vinh added. "You will be dressed in those uniforms. The enemy will stop you and you will claim to be members of a special rescue team of American paratroopers sent by 'Old Saintly'. Remember that. It is important."

"They won't believe that bullshit for a second," Slim laughed with derision at the plan. "They'll know you're up to somethin'. Those fuckers will shoot our asses off before we get a chance to open our mouths."

"Indeed," Vinh smiled thinly. "Then I think you'd do better to keep your mouth shut."

Ban Ban took the captain's cue and rammed the barrel of his MAC-10 machinepistol into Slim's kidney. The tall junkie groaned and started to sink to his knees.

Ban Ban jammed the muzzle of his weapon under the guy's jaw.

"Stand at attention in front of Captain Vinh," he ordered.

"Jesus," Slim rasped as he straightened his body.

"The mercenaries will believe you were sent by the one they call 'Saintly'—after they've witnessed the special exhibition of firepower I have arranged to accompany your arrival and lend credence to your story," Vinh promised.

He showed the dopers a small black box. "This device is a remote control detonator," Vinh explained. "See the switch in the center? It can be used to explode a bomb which will be placed in the back of the truck."

"A bomb?" Jacque asked.

"It can be detonated by activating the switch on the box," Vinh told him, handing the contraption to Jacque. "There will also be a powerful radio microphone planted in the jeep so we can hear what happens. After you're safely inside, and the enemy drops their guard, we'll make our big advance forward. Then you'll dive for cover and detonate the bomb."

In fact, Vinh had no intention of leaving this up to a pair of dimwitted drug addicts. The black box was a dummy, much like the two men who would carry it. Vinh knew if the American mercs got their hands on Slim and Jacque, they would wring out all that the two idiots knew about Vinh's team. Although what they knew was minimal, Jacque and Slim did know enough about the invaders to reveal the fact Vinh's unit had lost two-thirds of its personnel and that their situation was almost as desperate as that of the Hard Corps and Trang Nih.

The two junkies were obviously too stupid to convince the ultra-professional mercs, but that wouldn't be necessary, anyway. Vinh had the real control switch to the truck bomb, which could be used manually or be activated on a timer what would start a lethal countdown as soon as the truck was admitted into the base area.

The explosion would throw burning white phosphorous over a thirty meter radius, and would certainly kill some of the defenders and dispose of Jacque and Slim as well, who were totally expendable, anyway. The resulting death, destruction, and confusion within the heart of the compound would assure Vinh of victory when he launched his final raid on the installation.

Still hidden behind the bushes, Fanelli took in as much of the conversation as he could. Then he retreated into the forest, staying under cover to consider his best choice of action.

Fanelli had several options. He could sit tight and look for a chance to help during the upcoming battle or make a dash for the home base, which was now guarded from within and without. He might get shot by his own side, as well as presenting a target to the enemy.

They're trying to pull a Trojan Horse routine, he realized, comparing Vinh's plan to the famous Greek tale.

He decided his best course of action lay in making sure that nobody in the Hard Corps base would be wiped out by the explosion. He stripped off his shirt and ripped off a strip of olive fabric to make a head band. One benefit of his Italian bloodline was his olive complexion and glossy black hair. In the dark, he could pass for an Asian, if nobody got a real good look at him. He removed a field dressing from his first aid kit, bound the bandage around his head, and covered one eye. He then found a brim over the other which, hopefully, would cast a shadow over it and conceal the Caucasian cast of his eye.

Fanelli stealthfully approached Vinh's camp again. Several of the enemy were walking to and fro, hauling guns and ammunition for the final assault. He took a deep breath and stepped from the bush, fumbling with his fly as if he had finished taking a leak.

"Ong duong lam gi do?" one of the Vietnamese snapped.

Fanelli recognized the expression. The guy was asking; "What are you doing?" The Hard Corps merc felt his stomach knot as he tried to think of a logical reply. He realized his accent would give him away if he spoke more than a couple sentences. However, much to Fanelli's relief, Ban Ban wasn't talking to him, but to somebody else.

The merc didn't press his luck. He gathered up a crate full of ammunition, which was less than half-full. He faked a limp and hobbled closer to the one-ton truck containing the bomb. An enemy soldier said something to him, but Fanelli's back was turned, so the soldier didn't see his face. Fanelli didn't know what sort of response to make.

"Toi rat an han," the Vietnamese said, noticing Fanelli's wounds.

"Tot toi," Fanelli replied, mumbling to the guy that it was okay.

The Vietnamese thought little of it, and headed back to his group of his comrades. Temporarily alone, Fanelli put the crate in the bushes and moved to the truck. He lifted the edge of the tarp and climbed in, tucking the corner of the heavy cover into place. There was nothing else to do but wait—and pray he lived long enough to kill the "Vietnamese Horse."

CHAPTER 24

"QUI NHUNG'S BEEN hurt pretty bad," John McShayne told James Wentworth as the XO joined him in the mess hall galley, which had been converted into a battlefield dispensary. The choice of location had not been random. A section of the wall was hinged like an old Murphy bed. When it folded down, it was an operating table complete with side drains and surgical instruments in stainless steel trays. These were covered by sterilized linens and sealed with striped autoclave tape.

"Hell, Top," Wentworth sighed, glancing down at the torn, bloodied mess of ravaged flesh and crushed bone which had been Qui Nhung's left arm. "My training doesn't go much further than basic field medicine, unless you count the assistance I gave Doc Adams when he had to operate on some livestock."

"Any experience is better than none, sir," McShayne replied. "I'm afraid we're gonna have to amputate that arm."

"Yeah," Wentworth agreed grimly. "We'll have to do this as quick and as clean as possible. You know, before general anesthesia came along, surgeons were judged by their speed on the operating table. A good surgeon could take off a man's leg in less than two minutes . . ."

"You sure know a lot of interesting stuff, sir," the Top Kick said, a bit more sharply than he meant to. "Maybe you could tell me about it later. Now, I've already given Qui Nhung atropine and an additional inducing agent, hydromorphone, to help ease the pain, as well as prepare him for the main anesthetic."

"Just tell me what to do, Top," Wentworth declared.

"You'll be in charge of pumping the air bag. The fuckers cut off our power, so we'll have to use the diesel backup generators to supply enough light. Can't risk an overload by using power on the pump, so we're stuck with manual respiration. Situate yourself so you can hand me instruments when I call for them."

Wentworth set the pacer function on his wristwatch to the rate of breathing given to him by McShayne. The continuous beat from the crystal in the watch would make his job that much easier. They scrubbed down and prepared for the grisly task of amputating Qui Nhung's arm.

Outside, William O'Neal and Steve Caine were engaged in damage assessment to determine how to best continue the defense of the compound. All of the buildings had received some damage. Two storage houses were totally collapsed. A year's supply of freeze-dried foods was buried under the rubble as well as a cache of ammunition.

"It's not as bad as it looks," Caine commented.

"Whatever isn't ruined already should be okay until we get a chance to dig it out."

"If we're still alive," O'Neal muttered. "Trang Nih will alert us if he sees anything coming from the bush. Let's check out the stockade. We're responsible for the safety of those men—and we don't know for sure which one is the traitor."

As they approached the stockade, they saw five bodies sprawled on the ground, three of them slain enemy troops clad in camies. The other two had been members of Trang Nih's team, easily recognizable with their white shirts and trousers. All five men had been shot to death.

"Holy shit," O'Neal rasped, examining the stockade. "The shell took out an entire wall."

Caine stepped through the gap into the building, his M-16 held ready in case any opponents were lurking inside. O'Neal waited outside. He didn't have any time for daydreaming. Caine reappeared seconds later.

"Any survivors?" O'Neal asked, although Caine's expression seemed even more grim than usual.

"The other two bodyguards never ever got out of their cell," Caine answered. "They had a different wall to their backs and it's still intact. They were shot to death in their cells. Poor bastards never had a chance, sir."

"But Psar Phumi isn't among the dead," O'Neal said, his voice as cold and hard and arctic steel.

"The enemy might have taken him prisoner," Caine ventured.

"I doubt it," O'Neal replied. "Why would they kill the bodyguards in their cells and keep Psar alive? That little fucker is the traitor, goddamn it. I suspected that son of a bitch from the beginning. If I'd segregated him from the other prisoners, they might be alive now."

"You couldn't be sure about Psar, sir," Caine said. "You did what you had to, Captain."

"Doesn't make me feel any better about the four freedom fighters Psar murdered," O'Neal said, glancing down at the two dead bodyguards. Apparently, Psar had taken a weapon from a slain invader and shot the first pair in the back. Then he slipped back into the stockade to kill the other two men in their cell. "But I know what will make me feel a helluva lot better," O'Neal said grimly.

"Psar might still be on base," Caine suggested.

"I've got an idea where he might be," O'Neal commented. "He'll either try to kill Trang Nih or contact Vinh. You find Trang Nih and stay with him. If you see Psar, kill the son of a bitch on sight. I sure plan to, when I find him."

Caine headed back toward the mess hall. O'Neal decided to check the most obvious areas first. He figured Psar might head for the nearest radio transmitter. That meant he'd be at the observation and flight direction tower at the helipad. It contained a radio.

The merc leader approached the pad from the bush, noting that the two Hard Corps choppers hadn't been damaged by mortar fire. Perhaps the enemy had spared the gunships in case they needed the copters for their own escape from the forest.

O'Neal reached the tower by using the backside of the ladder instead of the stairway, to eliminate the risk of being spotted by the treacherous Cambodian. When he reached the top, O'Neal swung himself onto the stairs and drew his .45 pistol.

He heard Psar Phumi's voice from the room above. The Cambodian was speaking Vietnamese over the radio, reporting the Hard Corps's position to Captain

Vinh. O'Neal understood every word the bastard said. He wanted to strangle Psar with his bare hands, but he warned himself not to get careless.

O'Neal tried the door. It was locked. He aimed the .45 at the knob and opened fire. A big 185 grain hollow point smashed the lock. O'Neal kicked the door open and darted clear, just in time to avoid a stream of 9mm rounds from the Uzi that Psar Phumi had taken from a dead invader.

O'Neal heard and felt the sound and vibrations of a heavy object striking the floor in the observation room. He guessed Psar had turned over the table inside. It was solid hardwood—good cover.

He reached around the top of the doorway and shot downward, the heavy .45 slugs nudging the thick slab of solid hardwood back a fraction of an inch, without penetrating it. Anticipating another salvo of 9mm bullets, O'Neal timed his next shots accordingly. *Hit 'em high, then hit 'em low,* he thought as he knelt by the doorway and waited for the deadly hail of Uzi slugs to cease.

Then William O'Neal poked his head around the bottom of the doorjamb and commenced return fire. A carefully aimed .45 round smashed into the forehead of Psar Phumi before the Cambodian scum could duck behind the table for cover. The bullet took off the top of his skull and splashed his brains against the upper wall.

O'Neal strode to the radio and picked up the microphone.

"Better cancel your plans, Vinh," he declared, "and you'd better break out a body bag for Psar Phumi. He's history, man. And don't forget to keep another one in reserve for yourself, asshole."

He switched off the radio, spat in what was left of Psar Phumi's face, and headed down the stairs.

• • •

Captain Vinh Chi Lam cursed under his breath. His commo officer pulled off his headset and shook his head. The entire campaign seemed to be dogged by disaster.

"Psar was just a Cambodian," Vinh said with a shrug. "It hardly matters that he's dead. That incompetent wasn't doing me much good anyway. At least he managed to disable the helicopter and kill all the bodyguards—except Qui Nhung. In the end, that damned Laotian filth is as big a traitor as Trang Nih. I will piss on their corpses."

"They're not dead yet, Comrade Captain," the commo officer remarked dryly. He had seen enough killing, enough of his fellow soldiers hauled on stretchers, their bodies torn by bullets and shrapnel. He wanted to get away from the slaughter and return to his wife and children in Hanoi.

"You doubt my ability to command?" Vinh demanded. "Perhaps you plan to make a formal complaint to Colonel Ngo when we return to Vietnam."

"I worry that the morale of our men is being destroyed by this mission," the officer answered. "The men are beginning to whisper that these four Americans must be supernatural beings. Demons or spirits . . ."

"Superstitious peasants," Vinh snapped. "They're supposed to be professional soldiers, not cowards who fear the darkness, like ignorant children."

"Their hands shake in battle," the commo man stated. "Yet they are veteran soldiers. This war is unlike the battles we fought in our own country. The Americans are not shackled by their politicians here. They're better trained than our people."

"I could have you shot for treason, Comrade," Vinh said angrily. "At the point of victory, you dare speak of defeat."

"You won't shoot me because we can't spare the ammunition," the commo officer said with a shrug. "Yet you plan to waste valuable ammo and explosives in an attempt to trick the Americans. I wish no disrespect, Comrade Captain, but I believe this would be a mistake. What you propose is an act of desperation, and the men recognize this . . ."

Vinh's hand suddenly struck, the hard edge hitting the lieutenant under the solar plexus. The commo officer doubled up from the blow and Vinh slammed a knee into his face. The lieutenant fell, blood oozing from a broken nose.

"When this is over I intend to have you court-martialed, Lieutenant," Vinh hissed. He glanced about, as Ban Ban and several other soldiers approached. "Sergeant Ban Ban, you will take the lieutenant's weapon."

"Yes, Comrade Captain," Ban Ban replied. He knelt beside the fallen officer and removed the man's sidearm.

"The lieutenant is a disgrace and a coward," Vinh announced. "He is hereby stripped of rank, and will later face charges of treason and disrespect to a superior officer. Unfortunately, we cannot spare guards, so he cannot officially be placed under arrest at this time. Instead, we will take the lieutenant into combat and put him in the front lines . . . unarmed."

"May I make a suggestion?" Ban Ban asked, unable to repress a smile. "Perhaps we could give him an unloaded weapon instead?"

"Tot!" Vinh smiled in response. "That's an excellent suggestion, Ban Ban. Perhaps the Americans will execute this coward for us."

The commo lieutenant started to reply but realized it was hopeless. Vinh was using him as a whipping boy and there was nothing he could do about it. Vinh ordered Jacque and Slim to step forward. The junkies had already donned the Army Airborne uniforms which fit poorly.

"It is time for us to carry out my plan," Vinh declared. "You two get in the truck and follow the route I gave you. Don't even think about escape. We'll be able to see you regardless of which direction to head. Unless you think you can outrace our bullets, I suggest you simply follow orders."

"Yes, sir," Jacque assured him. Slim kept his mouth shut, which was probably the most intelligent thing he had done for a long time.

The pair climbed into the truck. Fanelli, still hidden beneath the tarp, held his breath as he listened to the treacherous pair of American burnouts whisper to one another.

"I got a real bad feelin' about this," Jacque muttered as he started the engine.

"Let's check out that bomb in the back," Slim suggested. "I want to know what I'm carrying."

Fanelli stiffened and eased off the safety catch to his .45 ACP. He felt the vehicle rock slightly as Slim jumped onto the ground. The tarp moved. The tall junkie was about to remove the cover.

"Get back in that truck!" Vinh shouted. "If you two can't follow orders, I shall consider penalizing you part of your fee. And leave the bomb alone. If you don't know what you're doing with explosives, you might damage the detonating device. If you want to blow yourselves up, do it after this mission is completed!"

"Fuckin' gook asshole," Slim whispered, as he climbed into the vehicle beside his partner. "I'd like to kick that fish-faced fucker's ass . . ."

"Don't try it," Jacque warned. "He'd have your

balls in his teeth. Let's just do this and hope we can get outta here alive."

They drove the truck up the logging road to the north and turned onto the highway beyond the compound. Automatic fire and exploding grenades began to thunder from the forest. Jacque considered bolting from the area, but decided he'd better play it straight with Vinh. The Vietnamese killer was nobody to mess with.

"They're starting a mock battle to try to trick those mercenaries," Jacque commented.

"Think it'll work?" Slim inquired.

"I don't know," Jacque said with a shrug. "Nothin' else has. Those guys in the base are mighty bad dudes."

"So are these gooks," Slim commented. "Sure hope that smack is top quality, after all the shit we've gone through to get it."

"I just hope we live to enjoy it," Jacque added.

The truck moved toward the front gate to the Hard Corps compound. The vehicle rolled across the smashed gate and headed for the main base, as the last of the gunshots from Vinh's mock battle echoed into the night. They approached the ruins of the headshed. O'Neal and Caine suddenly materialized in front of the truck, rifles pointed at the startled junkies. Jacque brought the four-by-four to an abrupt halt.

"We're an advance party from the 82nd Airborne," Slim called out.

"Saintly sends greetings," Jacque added nervously.

"Airborne, my ass," Caine muttered, loud enough for O'Neal to hear.

"Get out of the truck," O'Neal instructed. "Real slow and with your hands up."

Suddenly, a hand pushed the tarpaulin from the back of the truck. Fanelli held the .45 Colt in one fist and his

.38 snubnose in the other. He fired the autoloader less than a foot from the back of Jacque's head. The big 230 grain solid-ball projectile smashed into the junkie's skull, splattering his junk-soaked brains across the windshield.

"Holy Fuck!" Slim exclaimed, as he turned his head.

Fanelli's .38 barked twice. Bullets shattered Slim's face and punched gory exit wounds at the base of his skull and the top of his neck. The tall man's corpse toppled sideways and landed on Jacque's corpse. Fanelli glanced up to find himself staring into the muzzles of O'Neal and Caine's M-16's.

"I'll be a son of a bitch!" O'Neal exclaimed when he saw Fanelli. "We thought you were gone, Joe."

"There's a bomb in this rig," Fanelli told his teammates. "Those two jackoffs had a remote detonator, so I had to waste 'em."

He tossed back the tarp and knelt by the bomb in the back of the truck. It was a military shell, converted into a bomb. The nose cap had been removed, and three wires led to a small black box with a brush metal finish, sporting a short antenna and a blinking red light. A metal alarm clock, secured by tape to the bomb casing.

"We were afraid you were dead," Caine stated.

"We all might be if I can't disarm this thing," Fanelli replied. "Vinh gave them a detonator, but I don't think he'd trust 'em to use it. He also claimed he had a radio mike in the truck, but I haven't found it. I think that was a bullshit story to try to convince those two idiots they'd be covered while they were in here."

"I hope you're right about the mike," O'Neal commented. "Otherwise, Vinh would know his plan failed and he'd detonate the bomb."

"He would have done it by now," Fanelli replied, searching through his pockets for a small leather packet.

He unzipped it as he spoke. "Those two guys were really dumb not to realize Vinh planned to sacrifice them."

He examined the wiring, as he removed a small pair of wire cutters from his kit. Fanelli cut the wires to the detonator and tossed the radio-operated device to Caine.

"Take the batteries out of that thing," he instructed. "Just in case. I think I did this right . . ."

"You *think?*" Caine replied with a sigh.

Fanelli clipped the alarm clock wire next and used a screwdriver to loosen the bolts within the shell detonator. He smiled as he removed the small red metal tube. The Italian tough guy pitched the detonator away from the truck.

"That's it, fellas," he announced. "You can applaud now. I just saved the day."

"Qui Nhung made it through surgery," Wentworth began as he approached from the mess hall. "But he's in no condition to . . . my God, it's Fanelli!"

"Hey, I'm okay," Fanelli grinned. "But there's no need to fall down and worship me, Lieutenant."

"Up yours, fella," Wentworth growled.

"Got some good news," Fanelli said, jumping down from the truck. "Vinh has lots of casualties. He's lost most of his men already—and what's left is low on morale. They're not too thrilled with how this has been going. They're already low on ammo and their situation is even shittier since Vinh ordered his men to burn up ammo and set off some explosions to try to make you guys fall for that fake battle shit."

"His side isn't the only one with problems," O'Neal stated. "We're low on ammo too. Willis was killed, Trang Nih is still alive and well, but his bodyguards are dead, and Qui Nhung isn't going to be able to fight for a while."

"We had to amputate his left arm at the elbow," Wentworth said. "That leaves six of us against however many men Vinh has left. Any estimate, Joe?"

"I didn't see all his forces," Fanelli answered. "But he's gotta have more than twenty guys left."

"It'll be dawn in about three hours," O'Neal announced, consulting his wristwatch. "Vinh will either hit us immediately, like he always does—following up a failed hit with another hit, hoping to hit his opponents when they're off-balance. Or he'll strike just before dawn."

"Why do you say that?" Wentworth asked.

"Because that's what I'd do in his place," O'Neal answered. "The best time to attack a fortress is in twilight, just before nightfall or just before dawn. Shadows from the movement of the sun and the gradual change in the color of the sky make movement more difficult to detect. Sentries tend to get careless then, too."

"True," Caine confirmed. "In the daylight men can see better and at night they feel more vulnerable so they're more alert. The few minutes between these two are when they are most vulnerable."

"Vinh hasn't attacked yet," Fanelli remarked. "How much longer do you think it'll be before we can figure he'll hit before dawn?"

"We can't afford to get careless—period," O'Neal warned. "Even if he doesn't launch an all-out attack, Vinh will probably have snipers posted. The VC were always fond of sniping. They'll try to pick us off or at least keep us off-balance. Prevent us from forming solid defenses . . ."

"Captain O'Neal," Trang Nih called as he approached from the messhall. "This has gone too far. I can not allow any more death and destruction to take place in your camp which I might be able to prevent."

"You're not going to surrender to Vinh," O'Neal told him.

"It's me he wants," Trang Nih insisted. "I can't permit this to continue, Captain. You have already sacrificed too much for my sake . . ."

"Trang Nih," O'Neal began. "You came to us for help to fight for freedom of your people, and the people of Southeast Asia. Freedom fighters in Vietnam, Laos, and Cambodia look to you as their leader. That's why the Communists have gone to so much trouble to try to kill you, and that's why we're not about to let them take you without a fight."

"You have already given them a fight," Trang Nih stated.

"Fighting is what we do for a living," Fanelli said with a shrug. "Nobody forced us to do it."

"I realize that," Trang Nih said. "But others will take my place if I die. It is not right that all of you should risk your lives for my sake."

"It's not that easy," O'Neal said. "You matter as an individual, Nih. Sure we're mercenaries, but give us a little credit for caring about something other than just money."

"I was already aware of that," Trang Nih smiled. "Thank you, my friends."

He groaned suddenly, his features contorted in pain, as a rifle roared from the forest. Trang Nih clutched at a crimson smear on the right side of his chest as he started to fall. Fanelli caught him, as the others opened fire in the general direction of the sniper.

"Goddamn it," O'Neal hissed bitterly. "Goddamn it!"

CHAPTER 25

THEY CARRIED TRANG NIH to the mess hall. John McShayne had just lit a cigarette when the four mercs entered, carrying the wounded freedom fighter. McShayne tossed the cigarette on the floor, and quickly turned to the operating table.

"Jesus Christ," Top barked. "Put him over there!"

"Sniper shot him," Fanelli explained, as he and Caine placed Trang Nih on the table. "I don't know how bad it is."

"He's been hit in the chest," McShayne said grimly. "That ain't good. Lieutenant, you want to scrub up and give me a hand?"

"You got it," Wentworth answered. He was already washing his hands. "You ever take a bullet out of a man's chest before, Top?"

"Once in Korea and twice in 'Nam," the senior veteran replied. "One of 'em lived, and the other two died on the table. Kinda hoped I'd never have to do it again.''

"Top,'' O'Neal said. "We can't all stay here. If we're boxed inside the messhall, the enemy could take us out with a single grenade . . .''

"Go,'' McShayne said impatiently, as he examined Trang Nih's wound. The Vietnamese had gone into shock. "I don't want you throwing up on my floor, anyway. Before you go, prop his feet up. His heart's still beating, but it won't be if he stays in shock much longer.''

Caine jammed two pillows under Trang's feet. Then he followed O'Neal and Fanelli to the door. The Hard Corps commander handed his M-16 to Fanelli and drew his Colt pistol. Caine already held his rifle ready for action.

"Okay,'' O'Neal began. "Cover me.''

He opened the door and darted outside, hitting the ground in a fast shoulder roll. A sniper's weapon cracked. The bullet missed O'Neal's hurtling form and struck the mess hall wall. Caine heard the slug impact into the solid surface. He barely flinched as he raised the stock of the M-16 to his shoulder and aimed at the muzzle flash of the sniper's weapon.

Caine fired a three-round burst at the enemy, then rushed outside. The sniper didn't fire; he was either dead or staying down. Fanelli followed Caine, as another sniper's weapon erupted from a different position. The tough Italian from Jersey hit the dirt, as the bullet ricocheted behind him.

Fanelli scrambled to the cover of the head shed. O'Neal waited for him there. The Hard Corps commander held an Uzi submachine gun. He handed Fanelli an M-16 magazine.

"You may as well use the ammo," O'Neal told him.

"That Uzi won't do much good against a sniper," Fanelli stated, accepting the 30 round mag for the M-16.

"Yeah," O'Neal agreed. "But we're low on ammo. I've got two full mags for the Uzi. Just have to hold my fire until the enemy comes within range."

"Where's Steve?" Fanelli inquired.

"He slipped into the shadows somewhere," O'Neal replied. "Caine will probably handle the situation better if we just let him do it his way. Just be careful you don't shoot him by accident."

"You still think Vinh will make his big push just before dawn?" Fanelli asked.

"Yeah," O'Neal confirmed. "But we're not going to get any sleep between now and then, Joe."

"Sure wish we'd had time for supper," Fanelli sighed. "I'm getting hungry. Tell you the truth, Captain. For the first time in five years, I really want a drink."

"That makes two of us," O'Neal admitted. "But you can't drink, Joe. You know that. You start boozing again and you're no good to anyone . . . including yourself."

"I know," Fanelli sighed. "Sometimes it's a pain in the ass to be a drunk who don't drink no more."

"You know," O'Neal began. "We're all proud of you for the way you beat the bottle, Joe. I don't know if I ever told you that before. Seems like we never tell people what we feel until it's too late."

"It's not too late, sir," Fanelli grinned. "Thanks."

It was the first time he had ever called anyone "sir."

William O'Neal's prediction about when the enemy would strike was right on the money. Captain Vinh's assault force attacked when the sky was just beginning to change color, gradually shifting from darkness to dawn. They advanced from all sides. Of one hundred twenty-four men, Vinh only had thirty-one left who were fit for combat. Only the seriously wounded, unable to walk or carry a weapon, remained behind. The North Vietnamese strike force had also lost every vehicle brought for the mission, except one jeep and the stolen eighteen-wheeler still parked by the highway.

Many of Vinh's men wanted to retreat, but Vinh couldn't go back until Trang Nih was dead. His reputation, career—his very life—depended on the outcome of this mission. Hanoi had given him unlimited funds and plenty of manpower to accomplish the assignment. They expected results.

Even if he succeeded, he would not receive the double promotion from senior captain to lieutenant colonel which he had been promised. He had lost too many men during the mission. Vinh might get promoted to major, but it would be a long time before he'd see colonel. If he failed, there would be a firing squad waiting for him in Hanoi. Vinh had no choice. His very survival depended on the success of his mission.

Captain Vinh personally led the final assault force. He was no coward, and it was important, at this point, for his men to see him on the fields of fire. Besides, he had nothing to lose. If he failed, he would die, and it made little difference if the Hard Corps or the Vietnamese government killed him.

Ban Ban commanded a ten man team, which advanced from the north. He shoved the commo officer who had fallen from Vinh's favor, pushing the poor bastard into the open. As soon as Fanelli saw him carrying his empty rifle, Fanelli aimed his M-16 and opened fire. At least the Commo man died swiftly, one of Fanelli's 5.56mm rounds catching him right between the eyes.

Ban Ban was delighted. He had used the cowardly officer to flush out the enemy. The Vietnamese killer pointed his favorite weapon in Fanelli's direction and squeezed the trigger.

The M-79 grenade launcher had had a special place in Ban Ban's heart ever since he had taken one from the body of a slain American soldier when he was a child. He loved the blooper. It was a wonderful weapon for killing Americans.

"Shit," Fanelli rasped, recognizing the short, thick barrel of the M-79 an instant before Ban Ban fired the weapon.

He ducked behind the head shed and covered his cranium with an arm. The 40mm shell crashed to earth near the building, but far enough for the explosion to shower Fanelli with flying dirt without harming him.

Other invaders took note of Fanelli's position and opened fire. Fanelli stayed down as bullets burned air above him and hammered into the walls of the head shed. He held onto the M-16 with one hand as the other crept toward a black tube attached to a long wire. His fingers touched the device, but he didn't press the plunger.

Not yet, he thought as he clenched his teeth and waited for the hail of flying projectiles to subside.

O'Neal had positioned himself near the mess hall. He noticed that three or four muzzle flashes of enemy weapons were within range of his Uzi, and the Hard Corps commander raked the area with 9mm rounds. Two voices screamed and one body tumbled into view, its chest riddled with fresh wounds.

Two of the men in Ban Ban's group turned their weapons toward O'Neal's position and prepared to open fire. High velocity slugs slammed into the spine of one gunman, and he quickly fell to earth. His comrade heard the report of the M-16 and turned as Steve Caine shot him in the chest with a three-round burst.

"One of them is attacking us from the rear!" Ban Ban shouted, slinging the M-79 over his left shoulder in order to use the MAC-10 machinepistol, which hung from a strap on his right shoulder.

"How did he get behind us?" a frightened and unnerved man in the sergeant's group wondered aloud. "We saw no one. We heard no one . . ."

"Shut up!" Ban Ban snapped. "Just find the *que lam* and kill him!"

Four invaders under Ban Ban's command set out to accomplish this task, moving toward the dense foliage where Caine had launched his attack. The area was filled with heavy brush and pine trees, which offered the Hard Corps merc plenty of camouflage, but it also gave the enemy lots of good cover as well.

They advanced carefully, moving from tree to tree, as Caine watched them from a wall of ferns while he lay on his belly. In his right fist he held an improvised spear with the straight branch shaft jammed into the hollow handle of his survival knife. In his left, he held the end of a ten foot fishing line, taken from the contents of his knife handle, the other end tied to the trigger of his M-16, which was braced at a Y shaped branch and weighted in place with rocks. Caine also carried the wire saw from his knife kit, with two sticks in the rings for a firm grip.

Caine waited for his opponents to move into position. At last, one adventurous VC stepped directly in front of the hidden M-16, and Caine pulled the line which yanked the trigger. The rifle snarled, firing a long burst upward into the belly of the unlucky Asian.

The other three opponents started shooting at the M-16. Caine crept closer to the invaders while they were busy firing at where they thought he was hidden. Ceasing fire, the two enemies slowly advanced, while the third stayed behind the thick trunk of a spruce tree to cover them. Unfortunately, he didn't hear Caine slip up behind him. The silent merc suddenly swung the wire saw around the guy's neck, stamping a boot into the back of the man's knee to throw him off-balance as he pulled the handles of the saw. The wire cut into flesh and severed the carotids. Caine throttled him for two more seconds after the body had stopped moving, just to be certain he was dead.

The other two opponents pushed through the bush, found the rigged M-16, and their astonishment immediately turned to terror, as one Vietnamese felt the sharp steel catching him between the shoulder blades, severing his spine. He fell on his face, Caine's spear jutting from his back.

Terrified, the last enemy whirled and hastily opened fire, not realizing he had shot one of his own comrades until he saw the man's body convulse and stagger before it fell. Confused and panic-stricken, the gunman bolted for safety. He ran past the tree trunk where Steve Caine was hidden, and the merc let him pass before shooting him in the back of the head.

The sounds of gunfire and explosions alerted Wentworth and McShayne that the invaders had finally struck. Wentworth and McShayne were still in the mess hall/operating room, with Trang Nih stretched out on the table. McShayne had removed the bullet from Trang's chest and clamped together a damaged artery. He sewed the patient up and treated the wound for infection, but there was still a lot of internal bleeding.

"You'd better get out there, sir," Top told Wentworth. "Sounds like they need you. I'll stay with Trang Nih and Qui Nhung."

"Okay," Wentworth agreed as he grabbed his FAL rifle. "What are Trang's chances?"

"50-50," McShayne answered. "But if we don't get him to a hospital within an hour, we might as well take him to the morgue instead."

"Take care of yourself, Top," Wentworth urged, moving to the door.

The remaining enemy were exchanging fire with Fanelli and O'Neal. Several gunmen fired at the two defenders, trying to keep them pinned down while other invaders rushed into the heart of the base. Wentworth saw half a dozen opponents dash toward the mess. He opened the door and sprayed the attackers with a dose of full-auto rounds.

Two men were cut down where they stood, 7.62mm slugs drilling through their chests. Others ran for cover. Wentworth nailed another opponent in the rib cage before he could reach his destination. A third invader ducked behind the ruins of a storage house, but failed to draw in his leg before Wentworth exploded the guy's kneecap with an FAL round. The man tumbled into view and Wentworth finished him off with a shot in the upper torso.

With the FAL in his fists, a .45 Colt on his hip and the *katana* samurai sword in his belt, Wentworth charged outside. He fired another salvo at the invaders and darted to the rear of the building. Another gunman tried to shoot him in the back, but O'Neal covered his XO's progress and blasted the would-be assassin with a trio of Uzi slugs.

"How are we doing?" Wentworth inquired as he joined O'Neal.

"I don't have a definite body count for you," O'Neal answered, shoving a fresh mag into his Uzi. "But I figure we've taken out about ten so far. Maybe more. Hard to tell how Caine's doing. He's somewhere in the dense forest, so don't spray any rounds in that direction."

"I've only got one more mag for this FAL," Wentworth stated. "How's your ammo holding out?"

"Last mag for the Uzi too," the commander answered. "I just hope the enemy is as low on ammo as we are."

Wentworth switched his FAL to semi-auto to conserve ammo. He chose targets with care, picking off his opponents in sniper style, unless they charged directly into the compound. In the forest to the north, Caine confiscated weapons from slain opponents and also picked off targets. As good a marksman as the Hard Corps XO was, Caine was gradually whittling down the number of opponents as he played hide-and-seek, using his superior Katu camouflage techniques to avoid detection.

Frustrated by his inability to take out Caine, Ban Ban was now left with only one man of his original command. He led the lone trooper to the west where they joined up with another group that had only six men left. Ban Ban contacted Vinh by radio, and asked what action to take.

"The Americans are running low on ammunition," Vinh replied, well aware that the same applied to his own forces. Some of the men had drawn machetes and hatchets, because they had no ammo left. "We'll pin them down and your group will rush them. Understand?"

"I understand, Comrade Captain," Ban Ban confirmed, still blindly loyal to the man who had used him as a pawn since the days when he was a child warrior in Vietnam.

Vinh's forces, concentrated in the east and north, fired a heavy salvo of rounds at the Hard Corps defenders. Then Ban Ban led the charge from the west. Fanelli saw eight opponents advance from the west, and finally reached for the black tube.

"Just a little bit closer," he whispered, watching the attackers.

They obliged, and Fanelli hit the plunger. Ban Ban and his men failed to notice the wires which extended behind a small bush, and were attached to the green-gray Claymore mine hidden behind the shrub. The Claymore exploded, blasting a tidal wave of shrapnel into the attackers.

Ban Ban was literally torn to pieces by the blast. Five other invaders were also killed, and the remaining two were severely injured. Vinh cursed helplessly and ordered his men to keep fighting.

After both sides soon exhausted the last of their rifle ammunition, Vinh ordered his forces to close in. With only eight men left, the Vietnamese assassin plunged into the heart of the compound. Close quarters weapons were drawn—pistols, knives, machetes, and hatchets. A couple of Vietnamese fixed bayonets to the barrels of their now empty rifles.

O'Neal, Wentworth and Fanelli unsheathed their pistols and exchanged shots with the invaders. Most of Vinh's men were not armed with pistols, so they were reluctant to get too close until the Hard Corps ran out of ammo all together.

One Vietnamese trooper, armed with a hatchet, saw Fanelli's Colt had fired its last round. The slide locked back into open position, exposing the empty chamber. The invader saw this as an opportunity to attack and charged for Fanelli, hoping to strike him down before the merc could reload his pistol.

Fanelli saw the Vietnamese attack, hatchet raised overhead. The Hard Corps pro quickly drew his snubnose .38 from the holster at the small of his back. He pumped three rounds into the chest of his attacker. The man dropped his hatchet and fell to his knees, the expression on his face suggesting he believed he had just made the dumbest mistake of his life. It was certainly his last.

Captain Vinh and two of his men dashed to the door of the mess hall. O'Neal saw them and fired two shots into the scum at the rear. The man's body was pitched backward into an awkward cartwheel by the force of the big .45 slugs. O'Neal's pistol locked back on empty, but he pursued the invaders, reaching for a spare mag as he ran.

A cold shiver traveled up his spine when he felt the empty ammo pouch.

Wentworth started to follow O'Neal, but two invaders suddenly blocked his path. One man held a CAR-15 with a fixed bayonet, and the other wielded a machete. Wentworth's .45 was also empty, so he drew the only weapon he had left—the long flawless steel blade of the *katana* flashed in the morning sunlight, as he drew the sword from its scabbard.

The man with the machete attacked, hoping to close in fast enough to neutralize Wentworth's blade. The Hard Corps XO blocked the jungle knife with a powerful stroke from the *katana*. He then pivoted sharply, spun around before his opponent could swing the machete, and delivered a diagonal cut. The sword sliced the man from collar bone to sternum. Blood gushed from the deep wounds as the invader fell forward.

With a battle cry, the attacker with the CAR lunged, his bayonet aimed at Wentworth's belly. The mercenary swordsman sidestepped from the path of the bayonet and struck out with the sword. Sharp steel cut through the stalk of the aggressor's neck. The man's head hit the ground and had tumbled six feet before his decapitated corpse fell.

McShayne saw the door to the messhall burst open. He grabbed his .44 Magnum and aimed the big revolver at the Vietnamese flunky who charged through the doorway. He squeezed the trigger, and the high velocity 210 grain bullet smashed through the chest of the invader, kicking his body back across the threshold.

Captain Vinh fired from the edge of the doorway, triggering his 9mm Beretta twice. One bullet hissed above McShayne's head and punched a hole in the wall behind him. The other hit the veteran soldier in the right ribcage, knocking McShayne backward with the impact. His head struck the wall and he slid to the floor in a dazed heap.

"Trang Nih," Vinh declared with a cold smile when he recognized the figure on the operating table. He aimed his pistol at the helpless freedom fighter.

O'Neal appeared and charged across the threshold, pouncing on Vinh like an angry puma. He hammered the butt of his empty .45 across Vinh's wrist, striking the Beretta from the man's grasp. The Vietnamese killer quickly reacted with an elbow smash to O'Neal's chest.

O'Neal staggered backward from the blow, and Vinh whipped a backfist to the center of O'Neal's face. Pain

320

shot through the American's skull as cartilage cracked in the bridge of his nose. Vinh's boot lashed out and adroitly kicked the empty pistol from O'Neal's hand.

Vinh then slashed a karate chop at O'Neal's neck, but the stroke missed its mark and struck O'Neal on the side of the face, propelling the Hard Corps commander into a wall. Vinh chuckled, amused by how easy it was to kick the shit out of this American. *Take away their weapons and their money,* he thought, *and Americans are nothing.*

He threw a kick aimed at O'Neal's solar plexus, but O'Neal crossed his wrists and blocked the kick with the X shape of his arms, then pushed to the right and spun the startled Vinh around. O'Neal quickly kicked his opponent in the kidney and followed with a stomp to the back of his knee. Vinh's leg buckled and he fell to his knees.

But Vinh was well-trained. He immediately threw himself to the side to get leverage for kicking at his opponent, and lashed out with a boot. But since O'Neal had already stepped forward, he was able to dodge Vinh's kick and swung his own, slamming a boot heel hard into Vinh's face.

The Asian's head bounced back from the kick, and O'Neal quickly bent a knee and thrust it under Vinh's chin, with all his weight behind it. The blow landed in the assassin's throat, crushing his windpipe. As Vinh's body thrashed about wildly, as he choked to death on his own blood, the Hard Corps commander stared into Captain Vinh's golden eyes, watching the last trace of life vanish from them.

"Bill!" Wentworth called out as he entered the mess hall. "You all right?"

"Yeah," O'Neal said, wiping blood from his nostrils. He winced from the pain of his broken nose. "But check out Top! Bastard shot him!"

Wentworth hurried to McShayne, but the rugged old soldier was already starting to rise. A crimson stain marked his shirt where the bullet had struck. Wentworth insisted McShayne stay put.

"How we doin' out there?" McShayne asked, breathing hard.

"I think it's over," Wentworth replied, listening for the sounds of gunshots or screams, hearing none.

"Hey!" Fanelli called out cheerfully as he appeared in the doorway. "We won, man! Caine is okay. He says they're all dead ones . . . Shit! What happened to Top?"

"I spilled catsup on my shirt, you asshole," McShayne muttered sourly. "It isn't much. A little crease. Trang Nih is still in worse shape than I am."

"Did you get the bullet out?" O'Neal asked, moving to the operating table. He gazed down at the wounded Vietnamese freedom fighter. Trang Nih was still breathing.

"Yeah," McShayne confirmed. "The slug missed the heart and lungs. The guy was lucky."

"He seems awful pale and weak," Fanelli remarked, joining O'Neal at the table. "You sure he'll be okay?"

"He needs a blood transfusion," McShayne answered. "The card in Trang Nih's wallet says he's type O positive."

"That's my blood type," O'Neal announced as he rolled up his sleeve. "Let's do it."

EPILOGUE

THE HARD CORPS contacted St. Laurent via the radio at the observation tower. The CIA case officer arrived with a medical team in two Bell UH-1 choppers several hours later. St. Laurent sheepishly approached O'Neal at the helipad.

"I wouldn't blame you if you knocked me on my ass, Bill," he said wearily.

"Maybe I would, if I wasn't so fuckin' tired," O'Neal replied with a sigh. "Don't ever do anything like this again, Saintly. No more surprise visitors. Understand?"

"Understood," the CIA man assured him.

Fanelli, Caine, and four medics carried McShayne, Trang Nih and Qui Nhung to the helicopters. McShayne complained that he didn't need a stretcher, but they carried him on one anyway.

"And my mess hall had better be cleaned up by the

time I get back," McShayne growled as they slid him into the cabin of the chopper.

"Don't worry about it, Top," Fanelli said with a grin. "Have we ever let you down?"

"Don't be cute, soldier," McShayne muttered.

The medics were about to load Trang Nih into the chopper, but the Vietnamese urged them to wait for a moment. He called out to William O'Neal. The Hard Corps commander approached.

"I'm sorry about the damage to your base, Captain," Trang Nih told him.

"That's okay," O'Neal said with a smile. He tilted his head toward St. Laurent. "My insurance man is here."

"If I laugh it will hurt," Trang Nih stated. "You saved my life . . ."

"That's what soldiers do for each other," O'Neal replied.

"Thank you for everything, Captain," Trang Nih said, his voice choked with emotion. "I was told your blood was used for my transfusion . . ."

"That's right," O'Neal confirmed. "And you'd better take good care of it. Now get out of here and make sure my first sergeant behaves himself in the hospital."

Trang Nih chuckled and groaned.

"I knew it would hurt if I laughed," he said through clenched teeth, but a smile remained on his lips.

O'Neal watched as Trang Nih and Qui Nhung were placed in the 'copters. St. Laurent turned to the Hard Corps commander.

"Is there anything we can do for you?" he asked.

"We'll need help covering this up," O'Neal began. "But I figure you're already working on that."

"Oh, yeah," St. Laurent assured him. "If the government can't manage a cover up from time to time, what good is it?"

"Spoken like a true Company man," O'Neal said dryly. "We could use some help cleaning up this mess, too. And you might also see about throwing some business our way, if you hear of anything."

"As mercenaries?" St. Laurent inquired.

"Naturally," the Hard Corps commander replied. "That's the name of the game, isn't it?"

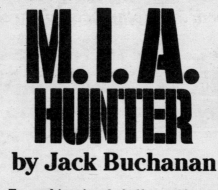